RICHARD BEGAN SEARCHING THE CELLAR ONCE MORE.

"I'm looking for more candles. We may as well try to keep as warm as we can."

Elizabeth watched in some amusement as he began to light them. "I feel like a sacrificial lamb placed at the altar," she quipped, seeing the semicircle of light.

There wasn't so much as a ghost of a smile around Richard's mouth, however, and the expression in his eyes was faintly disturbing. "That, my dear girl, is precisely what you shall be if we're not rescued soon."

Anne Ashley was born and educated in Leicester, U.K. She resided for a time in Scotland, but now lives in the West Country with two cats, her two sons and a husband who has a wonderful and very necessary sense of humor. When not pounding away at the keys of her typewriter, she likes to relax in her garden, which she has opened to the public on more than one occasion in aid of the village church funds.

LADY KNIGHTLEY'S SECRET
ANNE ASHLEY

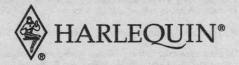

TORONTO • NEW YORK • LONDON
AMSTERDAM • PARIS • SYDNEY • HAMBURG
STOCKHOLM • ATHENS • TOKYO • MILAN • MADRID
PRAGUE • WARSAW • BUDAPEST • AUCKLAND

ISBN 0-373-51168-X

LADY KNIGHTLEY'S SECRET

First North American Publication 2001.

Copyright © 1999 by Anne Ashley.

All rights reserved. Except for use in any review, the reproduction or
utilization of this work in whole or in part in any form by any electronic,
mechanical or other means, now known or hereafter invented, including
xerography, photocopying and recording, or in any information storage
or retrieval system, is forbidden without the written permission of the
publisher, Harlequin Enterprises Limited, 225 Duncan Mill Road,
Don Mills, Ontario, Canada M3B 3K9.

All characters in this book have no existence outside the imagination of
the author and have no relation whatsoever to anyone bearing the same
name or names. They are not even distantly inspired by any individual
known or unknown to the author, and all incidents are pure invention.

This edition published by arrangement with Harlequin Books S.A.

® and TM are trademarks of the publisher. Trademarks indicated with
® are registered in the United States Patent and Trademark Office, the
Canadian Trade Marks Office and in other countries.

Visit us at www.eHarlequin.com

Printed in U.S.A.

Chapter One

1815

Sir Richard Knightley woke with a violent start. He was sweating profusely and his every muscle seemed suddenly to have grown taut. What in the world had woken him? he wondered. Cannon fire? No, it couldn't have been. Just a bad dream—that was all: nothing more than vivid memory; a deep-seated fear. It was over… Surely it must be over? He just couldn't go through it again, not that carnage! He detected the distant rumble once more and released his breath in a deep sigh of relief. Thunder…only thunder.

Trying to ignore the throbbing ache in his shoulder, and the sudden darting pain in his left leg, he eased himself into a sitting position. His night-shirt, damp with perspiration, clung to him like a second skin. Ye gods, wasn't it oppressive tonight! he thought, pulling the offending garment over his head and tossing it aside in disgust.

Perhaps this storm might clear the air. Mary had warned him earlier that there was one brewing. He could quite easily discern those claps of thunder getting steadily louder, even if he was oblivious to the flashes of lightning.

Instinctively he raised a hand to touch the bandage over

his eyes. The sabre gash in his right shoulder had been excruciating, and so too had the lead ball which had torn through the flesh in his thigh, but it had been the damage to his eyes when that pistol had been discharged which had caused him most concern. To be deprived of one's sight didn't bear dwelling on. To be led about by the hand for the rest of one's life...

A further clap of thunder, which seemed to shake the house to its very foundations, broke into his depressing thoughts and brought him back to the present by reminding him of how oppressive it was in the room. Had Mary inadvertently closed the window when she had paid that last visit before retiring for the night? He turned his head in the direction in which he knew the window to be, and after a moment's indecision decided to make the attempt.

Wincing slightly as he moved his injured leg, he swung his feet to the floor, and then reached out a hand to the wall. Mary had not delayed in encouraging him to exercise his muscles by taking a gentle turn about the bedchamber twice a day. He quickly discovered, however, that it was one thing having that blessed girl to guide him, and quite another trying to feel his way about a room he had never yet seen, a room where every object was a potential danger to a man who had been as good as blind for the past month.

'Oh, confound it!' he muttered as his elbow made contact with something, sending it crashing to the floor. What the devil had he broken? he wondered before his toes came into contact with a wet patch on the floor. It must have been the pitcher.

'Don't you be taking another step, sir!' came a gently warning voice, spiced with an unmistakable West Country accent, 'otherwise you'll be a-stepping on broken porcelain.'

'Oh, I'm sorry, Mary. I hope it wasn't valuable.'

He discerned the slight click as she closed the door, and

then heard that soft footfall of hers as she came across the chamber towards him.

'As you know, sir, this don't be our 'ouse, so whether it be valuable or no I can't rightly say, but it's of no matter, anyhow. What be you a-doing out of bed? 'Ave you need of the chamber-pot?'

He couldn't prevent a smile at this rather base enquiry. But then, he reminded himself, anyone less matter-of-fact, less practical would hardly have coped so admirably in nursing the six British casualties brought into this house.

Not that he retained any memory whatsoever of the journey back to Brussels in that lumbering cart filled with the dead and wounded. It had been Sergeant Hawker who had informed him that it had been Mary herself who had agreed to the army surgeon's request to offer sanctuary to the injured men, and it had been she who had insisted that three of those six must be men from the lower ranks. There would be no discrimination under her roof, no preferential treatment to those higher born.

Richard couldn't recall being carried up to this room, nor had he any memory of those first few days after the surgeon had tended the deep gash in his shoulder and had removed the piece of lead shot from his thigh. The last thing he could remember was having his mount shot from under him and seeing a blinding flash whilst he lay, momentarily stunned, on the scorched, bloodstained ground; though who had discharged the firearm, a fellow soldier or the enemy, he had no notion. Then, as he had made to rise, his vision blurred, his eyes smarting, he had been felled again by a French cavalryman wielding a sabre. The next thing he remembered was someone gently raising his head and coaxing him to take a little water.

That, of course, had been Mary, several days after he had been carried into this house. Since then she had administered to his every bodily need, had nursed him back to health and had forced him to come to terms with his brother's tragic death.

'No, my darling girl, I don't have need of that particular receptacle at the moment. But I do require the window opened before I expire from the heat.'

'It is open, but I'll open it a little more, once I've got you safely back into bed.'

He felt the warm touch of gentle fingers on his wrist before a slender arm encircled his back. He was instantly aware of soft curves pressed against his side, and was both astounded and faintly embarrassed by his body's immediate reaction. He recalled that it had been some weeks since he had assuaged his needs in that particular direction, and was aware in those moments before returning to his bed that he was far stronger than he had realised.

Praying she hadn't noticed his arousal, he didn't waste a second in pulling the covers up to his chest. He heard the grating of the sash window as it was raised higher, and then felt a blessed waft of fresh air. 'That's better!' he remarked with genuine relief before he detected a faint chink as Mary busied herself with picking up the fragments of porcelain.

'I suppose it never occurred to you to throw the bedcovers off?' she chided, placing the broken pieces in the bowl. 'There! That's cleared that up. Now, let's have no more middle-of-the-night wanderings!'

He couldn't forbear a smile at the scolding tone; he had grown quite accustomed to it by now. He heard her light tread once more and arrested her progress to the door by asking her to stay for a while.

He felt the bed go down slightly under her light weight, and instinctively sought one of those infinitely capable hands. 'I'm a selfish devil, because you must be tired, but just sit with me for a while.'

He couldn't see the smile which played around the exquisitely formed lips, but couldn't mistake the gentle understanding as she said, 'I know you must be concerned about tomorrow, Richard, but everything will be all right... I know it will.'

He brushed his thumb back and forth over the soft skin, easily detecting the small bones beneath. How often during these past weeks had he held these tapering fingers for comfort and support? He would know these caring hands anywhere. He had not infrequently marvelled at the fact that such a slender creature could be so strong, manoeuvring his six-foot frame in those first early days when he had been too helpless to do anything for himself. He had learned from Sergeant Hawker, the old rogue, that she was a very pretty young woman; knew too, from Mary herself, that her long hair was the colour of sun-ripened corn and that her eyes were blue. Such a delicious combination! But he had never looked upon what Hawker considered the sweetest smile in Christendom... Would he ever be privileged to see it?

'I wish I had your confidence, Mary.'

Her soft laughter had a teasing quality. 'You will see,' she assured him again. 'Call it the gypsy in me that knows.'

He was still far from certain, but knew he was probably being too pessimistic; behaving like a spoilt child, as Mary had told him in no uncertain terms on more than one occasion during these past weeks. Darling little scold! His sight hadn't been permanently damaged—the doctor had assured him of that. His eyes had been inflamed, certainly, and everything had been just a blur, but the condition was only temporary. His eyes had needed only resting and nature would effect its own cure. Tomorrow, when the bandages were removed, he would see again. He must believe that! Surely life wouldn't heap the torment of blindness upon him on top of everything else?

He found himself experiencing that same gnawing ache

of grief, infinitely more painful than any one of the several wounds he had sustained during his years in the army. It had been just over two weeks since Mary had read that letter informing him of his brother's tragic death. He still found it difficult to accept that, when he did eventually return to England, Charles wouldn't be standing outside the ancestral home waiting to greet him, as he had done so many times in the past; that dear Margaret wouldn't be there either, nor little Jonathan. A racing curricle, driven at breakneck speed, had forced his brother's carriage off the road and it had tumbled down a ravine. Because of some mindless fop's attempts to win a wager, Charles and his wife, and their nine-year-old son, now lay six feet beneath the earth.

Learning about the tragedy so soon after seeing so many comrades fall at Waterloo had been almost too much for him to bear. He had come perilously close to losing the will to live; might well have not survived his injuries; might never have attempted to come to terms with his tragic loss if it hadn't been for Mary.

Mostly gently coaxing, but occasionally rounding on him like a spitting virago, Mary had somehow managed to transfuse a small part of that indomitable spirit of hers into him, lifting him from the nadir of despair, and instilling in him a determination to face up to the responsibilities which had been placed upon him by his brother's untimely death. It would take a long time before he got over his loss; perhaps he never would, fully; but, for the sake of the baby niece he had never yet seen, he must face the future.

Charles and Margaret had considered their baby daughter too young to make that long journey to Derbyshire to stay with their friends, and had left her in the care of a close relative residing in London. Thankfully, Juliet was too young to understand the tragedy which had struck. Now it was up to him to ensure that her life was as carefree and happy as possible by taking the place of the father she would never remember.

He automatically reached out for his sweet preserver with his other hand and, pulling her down against his chest, ran his fingers through that long mane of silky hair which always smelt so deliciously of lavender-and-rose water. 'What would I have done without you, you darling girl!'

Without conscious thought he removed his hand from her hair to run an exploratory trail down her cheek, brushing gently against the outline of her jaw before taking a hold of the softly rounded chin and raising her face. He lowered his head and his mouth retraced the path his fingers had taken before coming to rest on soft lips, invitingly parted.

He had intended nothing more than a brief display of his genuine affection for this wonderfully caring young woman, but as he felt those soft lips tremble deliciously beneath his own, as he became acutely aware of the firm young breasts pressed against his chest, his need returned with an urgency, reigniting that fire of desire in his loins. Before he realised what he was doing, he had eased her into the bed beside him and was peeling away that last flimsy barrier of her clothing with hands that now shook slightly in their urgency to touch every last inch of her.

It must have been this loss of sight which had finely tuned his other senses, he decided, for never before could he recall touching skin so satiny-smooth, so beautifully unblemished. She was perfect. Her breasts reacted instantly to his caressing touch, hardening and inviting his lips. Her soft moans of pleasure as he ran his fingers down to the softly swelling hips was music to his ears, a delightful encouragement for further intimate caresses.

Not for an instant did it cross his mind to wonder why the hands which began to explore the triangular mat of dark hair covering his chest were trembling slightly; nor did he consider the very real possibility that the body which re-acted so deliciously to his gentle caresses might not be that of an experienced woman, but that of a hitherto untouched female who was responding quite naturally to a knowl-edgeable man's tender lovemaking. It was only when he eased himself on top and inside her and heard that betraying tiny cry of pain that the truth dawned on him. But it was all too late now: his need too urgent for him to stop.

'Why didn't you tell me, Mary?' he asked gently when at last he lay beside her once more, and cradled her head on his chest. 'Did I hurt you very much, my darling? Had I known, I—'

'Had you known, Richard,' she interrupted, 'I suspect you wouldn't have made love to me at all.'

He wasn't so certain. He wasn't a man accustomed to curbing his natural desires. A string of mistresses over the years had satisfied his needs, but he had never before tam-pered with innocence. Maybe if it had once occurred to him that she might be untouched he wouldn't have reached a point where he was incapable of stopping, but it was rather too late to question the wisdom of his actions now. There was only one course open to a man who possessed any degree of honour.

He brushed his lips lightly over her forehead. 'We'll be married just as soon as I can arrange matters.' He felt her stiffen. 'What's wrong, Mary? Don't you want to marry me?'

'More than anything in the world, Richard!' It was like a desperate cry from a loving heart. 'But—but you know next to nothing about me.'

'I know that you're one of the sweetest scolds I've ever met,' he told her laughingly. 'I also know that your hair is blonde and your eyes are blue.'

'Ah, yes,' she murmured, a distinct catch in her voice, as though she were finding it difficult to speak. 'That's always been your favourite combination, hasn't it, my Richard?'

'How do you know that? Has Sergeant Hawker been gossiping again?'

She didn't respond to this, but asked instead with that bluntness which so characterised her, 'Do you truly want to marry me?'

'Of course!' he answered without a moment's hesitation and only hoped his voice hadn't betrayed his grave misgivings. 'Besides, now that I've come into the title it's essential I produce an heir. And I've come to know you well enough in these past weeks to be certain you'd make a wonderful wife and mother. So, we'll take it as settled.'

There was no response.

When Richard woke again it was to discover himself alone and that portion of bed beside him quite cold. By the tramping of feet in the passageway outside his room—which sounded like a regiment of infantrymen parading up and down—he knew it must be morning, a morning he had been longing for and dreading by turns; a morning that, no matter whether he would see again or not, would change his life forever.

Raising his arms, he rested his head in his hands and gave vent to a heartfelt sigh. He was honest enough to admit that for a newly betrothed man he certainly wasn't experiencing untold joy; honest enough to admit, too, that Mary wouldn't have been his ideal choice for a wife. He liked her very well, probably more than any other woman he had ever known. She was both kind-hearted and amusing, and for all that she spoke with a pronounced West Country accent she was far from uneducated.

It had been she who had penned the letter to his London solicitors in response to the one they had sent informing him of his brother's tragic demise. He had also learned from Sergeant Hawker that she had spent many hours with him improving his reading and writing skills. But this, he was only too well aware, was hardly sufficient reason to suppose that she would make a suitable wife for a baronet. The truth of the matter was, of course, that she was totally unsuitable. She could have no notion of what was expected of her. Those vicious society tabbies would have a field day at her expense when they discovered her former station in life.

'But you know next to nothing about me.' He frowned suddenly as Mary's words echoed in his mind. It was true: he knew absolutely nothing about her life. She had received a good education. He knew this from the numerous conversations they had had when she had spoken intelligently on a wide range of topics. She might well be the daughter of some country parson or practitioner. If this did turn out to be the case then the outlook was not all doom and gloom. She could be moulded and taught the ways of his social class. Added to which, she must surely come from a family with sufficient means to have been able to afford to hire this house for several weeks. Was she the daughter of a wealthy merchant, perhaps? But it was pointless speculating, he told himself. He would discover all he wanted to know, and perhaps a great deal that he didn't, when she visited him next.

The door opening interrupted his thoughts. 'Mary?'

'No, sir. It's me.'

He recognised his sergeant's rough voice instantly and smiled. 'What brings you here so early, you old rogue? And what the devil's that confounded din?'

'The servants be moving some trunks, sir. Captain Munroe be leaving us this morning. We be the last two 'ere now.'

'Where's Mary?'

There was a tiny pause, then, 'She be a bit—er—busy

at the moment, sir, so she asked me to see to you. High time I took up me dooties again. I can get about well enough, even though the old knee's still a bit stiff. Now, sir, I'll just pop this towel round you and give you a bit of a shave.'

No sooner had this task been completed than the doctor arrived, and Richard, for once not having Mary there offering comfort and support, found himself grasping the bedclothes. Not once during any one of those many cavalry charges in which he had taken part could he recall being in the grip of such intense fear as he was in those moments when the bandages were removed and he opened his eyes for the first time since that never-to-be-forgotten last battle.

At first all he could detect were dark, blurred shapes. It was like trying to peer through a thick London fog, but then, blessedly, the mists slowly began to clear and the concerned face of his sergeant staring down at him gradually came into focus.

'I never thought I'd experience pleasure at seeing that ugly phiz of yours, Hawker. And I have to say it hasn't improved any since last I saw it!'

The sergeant, far from offended, laughed heartily as he moved across to the window so as not to impede the doctor's further examination. He looked down into the street below, his amusement vanishing as he gave an almost imperceptible nod of his head, and then watched as the carriage pulled away from the house.

'Where is Mary?' Richard asked again, making his eagerness to see her very evident.

Giving a guilty start, Hawker looked back across at the bed. 'She's—er—just this minute stepped out for a bit of air, sir.'

'Well, when she returns to the house tell her I'd like to see her.' Richard smiled at the choice of words. 'Tell her I'm longing to see her.'

The sergeant didn't respond, but he knew it would be only a matter of time before this gallant commanding officer realised there was something amiss.

The moment he had been dreading came early that evening when he brought Richard his dinner.

'Where is she, Hawker? Why hasn't she been to see me today?'

He saw little point in trying to conceal the truth any longer. 'She be gone, sir.'

'Gone? Gone where?'

'She be journeying back to England. She left in the carriage as soon as she knew you were back to normal, as yer might say.' He couldn't bring himself to add that it had been he who had signalled to her from the window.

Richard experienced such a maelstrom of conflicting emotions that it was several moments before he could think clearly. 'Did she say why she had to leave so suddenly?'

'Her old lady were right poorly, sir. Never once left 'er room in all the time we've been 'ere. Miss Mary must 'ave wanted to get her back 'ome before she weakened any more, I suppose. Don't think Miss Mary would 'ave stayed this long if she hadn't been nursing us lot.' Reaching into his pocket, he drew out a letter. 'Before she left, she asked me to give you this, sir.'

Richard almost snatched it from the outstretched hand and, ignoring his sergeant's reminder that he wasn't supposed to strain his eyes by reading for at least a week, broke the seal.

Dearest Richard, he read. *This is to say goodbye—a cowardly way of doing so, I know, but it is for the best. Had I seen you again I might have weakened and agreed to be your wife, which would have been a grave mistake for both of us. I know you felt honour bound to ask for my hand after what had taken place between us, but I cannot allow*

*you to make that sacrifice. I gave myself willingly, and do
not regret what happened, nor shall I ever. But how can a
marriage be a happy one, my darling, when the love is all
on one side? One day you will meet someone and fall in
love, and bless me for my actions of this day. God keep
you safe. Mary.*

Richard swallowed the hard lump which had lodged itself in his throat, and cast his eyes again over those words
written in a beautifully flowing hand, a hand which for
some obscure reason seemed oddly familiar. His Mary had
released him from his obligations, but did he want to be
freed? He wasn't certain, but knew that he couldn't leave
things this way. He owed that young woman so much. He
simply couldn't allow her to walk out of his life like this.
It was his duty to find her.

'She hasn't written down her direction.' He looked up at
the rather concerned face of his sergeant. 'Did she leave a
forwarding address, do you know?'

'That I don't, sir. Miss Mary left with all 'er servants.
There's only the Froggies 'ere now.'

'They're Belgians.'

'All the same to me, sir. Do you want I should fetch the
'ousekeeper?'

Richard nodded, but she wasn't able to help him.
Mademoiselle had never mentioned her address. The only
thing the housekeeper could suggest was that he wait until
her master returned from Italy at the end of the month, and
ask him if he knew where Mary resided in England.

But Richard was not forced to await the owner's return.
Tragically, a little over a week later, he was to read a report
in a newspaper of the passenger vessel *The Albatross*,
bound for Southampton, capsizing in mid-Channel.
Amongst those listed as missing, believed drowned, were
a Mrs and Miss Mary Smith.

Chapter Two

With all the exuberance of an excitable child, Lady
Dartwood uttered a shriek of delight as she watched the
carriage pull up outside the front entrance and saw a young
woman in a very fashionable fur-trimmed travelling outfit
step gracefully down the steps.

'She's here, Brin! She's arrived at last!'

'Will you stop jumping up and down that way!' her husband admonished with a passable attempt at sounding severe. 'For heaven's sake remember your condition!'

'I can hardly forget it, now can I?' Glancing down at the
rather large, figure-damaging protuberance at the front of
her gown, the Viscountess's expression managed to betray
dismay as well as a deal of motherly love for her unborn
child. 'And Elizabeth's so beautiful, too. I know you'll fall
instantly in love with her!'

The Viscount rose from the comfort of his armchair and
took his young wife gently in his arms. 'I promise I shall
like her for your sake, Verity. I know how very fond you
are of your old school friend. But you're the only girl for
me. How many times do I need to assure you of that?'

She rewarded him for his sound good sense, but quickly
extricated herself from his embrace as the door opened and

a young woman in her early twenties swept into the room and came tripping lightly towards them, looking so gracefully ethereal that the Viscountess couldn't help but feel a tiny stab of resentment, but hid it quite beautifully as she gave her friend an affectionate hug.

'I swear, Elizabeth, you get lovelier each time I see you. And slimmer, too!'

'And you are blooming, my dear Verity. The very picture of health!' Elizabeth then turned and held out one hand to the Viscount. 'How do you do, my lord. Your wife mentions you so often in her letters that I feel I have known you for years.'

'And I must reciprocate, Miss Beresford,' he responded, executing an elegant bow before releasing his brief hold of the slender, tapering fingers. 'My wife has spoken of nothing else since she received your letter accepting her invitation to be our guest.'

'How odiously stuffy!' Verity's expression of staunch disapproval drew spontaneous chuckles from both her husband and her friend. 'Now you must know that in my delicate condition it isn't very sensible to vex me. So let's have no more of this unnecessary formality!'

'In the circumstances it might be wise to indulge her, sir,' Elizabeth suggested. 'But only on condition,' she added, casting the most winning smile up at him, 'that you refrain from addressing me in any one of those repulsive abbreviations so widely used where my name is concerned. I cannot abide Lizzie or Eliza. And I'm not enamoured of Beth, either.'

The Viscount readily agreed, thinking what a graciously charming young woman Verity's friend was, her manners open and wonderfully unaffected, and by the time she had left them a short while later to dress for dinner, he had decided, without any further coaxing from his wife, that he liked Elizabeth Beresford very well.

'Why in heaven's name isn't that charming young woman married? She's not only extremely pretty, but intelligent too.'

Not in the least surprised that he had been captivated so easily by Elizabeth's engaging manner, Verity smiled with satisfaction. 'I honestly don't know, Brin.' The smile faded. 'I wouldn't be at all surprised, though, if it didn't have something to do with her upbringing. She had quite a miserable childhood. From odd things she has let fall from time to time, I gather her parents' marriage wasn't a happy one. I believe Elizabeth was quite close to her father, but didn't deal at all well with her mother. And as for that sister of hers…!'

'Mmm.' He glanced thoughtfully at the logs burning brightly on the hearth. 'I hope you've forewarned her that it isn't unusual for Lady Chiltham to pay us impromptu visits?'

Verity's sudden scowl betrayed her feelings quite beautifully. She disliked Elizabeth's sister intensely and considered Lord Chiltham a pompous nincompoop. The Chilthams, however, resided less than three miles distant and for the sake of neighbourly harmony she had managed to conceal her dislike whenever they had happened to meet.

'She was so spiteful to Elizabeth when they were children. Elizabeth never returned to school after a vacation without having acquired at least one livid bruise from that sister of hers.'

'It isn't uncommon for brothers and sisters to quarrel, my dear,' his lordship countered fair-mindedly.

'I realise that. But Evadne's seven years Elizabeth's senior. It was nothing short of malicious bullying.' A sudden gurgle of laughter escaped her. 'I'd like to see her try it now,' she went on, the wicked glint in her eyes betraying how she would relish the prospect of an unfriendly encounter between the sisters. 'Elizabeth has changed out of all recognition since she went to live with her grandmother. I think darling Evadne's in for a rather severe shock when she does see her again.'

'Well, Elizabeth certainly didn't strike me as a shrinking violet. She certainly is nothing like her sister, though, not even in looks.'

'Very true,' Verity concurred. 'She was painfully shy at school, but thankfully that's no longer the case. She appears to be remarkably resilient too, now. Which is a blessing considering her recent loss. I must say she seems to have got over her grandmother's demise very well.'

In this, however, Viscountess Dartwood couldn't have been more wrong, as Elizabeth's personal maid and lifelong devotee could have enlightened her if asked.

None knew better than Agatha Stigwell, who had been employed as nursemaid in the Beresford household, what a miserable existence her young mistress had endured in her formative years. She had witnessed, first hand, the petty cruelties the pampered Evadne had inflicted on her sister and had been appalled by the sheer indifference Mrs Beresford had always shown when dealing with her younger daughter. The only displays of affection and kindness Elizabeth had ever received had come from her maternal grandmother when she had stayed with her in Bristol, and from her father, but as his visits to the family home had been infrequent and of short duration, Elizabeth's periods of childhood happiness had been few and far between.

Agatha had never regretted the decision she had taken, after her master had died, in aiding Elizabeth in running away to her maternal grandmother. Elizabeth had seemed to blossom overnight under that wonderful old lady's constant loving care. Although, even then, weakened by years of ill-health, Mrs Smithson had been more than a match for Elizabeth's mother when she had come hotfoot to Bristol, demanding her daughter's return.

Agatha herself hadn't been privileged to overhear what had passed between Mrs Smithson and her daughter that day, but whatever the old lady had said, it had been sufficient to send Mrs Beresford on her way again rather abruptly. Agatha was honest enough to admit that she hadn't been sorry to see the last of her old mistress; honest enough to admit, too, that she had been completely unmoved when she had learned of Mrs Beresford's death two years later. What Miss Elizabeth had felt was difficult to judge. She certainly hadn't shed any tears over her mother's unexpected demise; but the poor girl had wept bitterly when her dear grandmother had passed away the previous autumn. She just hadn't been the same person since; but then, Agatha reminded herself, her young mistress hadn't been the same since their return from Brussels last summer.

'Why are you staring at me with that peculiar look in your eyes, Aggie?'

Unable to hold her young mistress's gaze, she went across the bedchamber to collect a shawl. 'You're imagining things, miss. I was merely thinking how sensible it was of you to accept Viscountess Dartwood's kind invitation. You've locked yourself away from the world for far too long. You know your dear grandmother didn't want that.'

'No, I know she didn't. She even begged me not to deck myself out in mourning.' A sigh escaped her. 'I kept that promise at least. I've never once even donned black gloves.'

Rising to her feet, Elizabeth remained only for the time it took to have the shawl arranged about her shoulders, and then went back down to the salon, where she had left her host and hostess earlier, to find them looking the picture of marital bliss, seated side by side on the sofa.

The Viscount rose at once and went over to the table on which several decanters stood. 'I believe Verity omitted to inform you that we're expecting another guest, a friend of mine from my army days, but I'm not quite certain just when he'll be arriving—it could be today, or tomorrow.'

He watched Elizabeth seat herself in one graceful, sweeping movement before handing her the glass of Madeira. 'You were in Brussels last year, on hand, as one might say, to celebrate that famous victory. And I understand from Verity that you stayed to nurse some of our brave soldiers back to health.'

'Yes, I was there,' she admitted in a colourless tone, 'but I saw little worth celebrating. The sight of that endless procession of carts, filled with the dead and dying, pouring into the city after the battle was over is an experience I shall never forget.' She shook her head at the all-too-vivid recollection. 'Where is the glory, sir, in all that waste of life…that suffering?'

Verity noticed a look of respect flit over her husband's features before he raised his head, his acute hearing picking up a sound from the hall.

'What is it, Brin? Has your friend arrived, do you think?'

'Yes, I believe so. I'll go and see.'

Verity waited until he had left the room before turning to Elizabeth with a rather impish smile. 'I never realised until a few moments ago how similar your shade of hair is to Brin's.' She studied her friend's beautifully arranged locks once again. 'Except, perhaps, yours contains a little more red. Why, you might be brother and sister!'

'I should have very much enjoyed having him as a brother. You're a lucky girl, Verity. He's a charming man.' She cast her grey-green eyes over the Viscountess in a swift appraisal, deciding that marriage and the prospect of imminent motherhood suited her very well. She looked glowing and so utterly contented with her lot. 'When is the baby due? Any time now, I shouldn't wonder.'

'Great heavens, no! Not for several weeks, unfortunately.' Verity noted the slight frown. 'I know I'm huge already. And to think I've still another month to go!'

Her pained expression vanished as the door opened and she watched her husband return with a tall and ruggedly handsome gentleman in tow. She had never met this particular friend of Brin's before and was instantly aware of his aura of powerful masculinity. So captivated was she by Sir Richard Knightley's spontaneous and most engaging smile, as her husband made the introductions, that she failed completely to notice the effect the very personable gentleman's presence was having on her friend.

With a hand which trembled slightly Elizabeth took the very sensible precaution of placing her glass down on the conveniently positioned occasional table beside her chair, before she foolishly disgraced herself by spilling the contents down the folds of her rich green velvet gown. No one's unexpected appearance could possibly have unsettled her more, but with a supreme effort at self-control she contrived to appear as composed as ever.

'There is absolutely no reason to introduce Sir Richard to me, Brin,' she interrupted when he turned, about to do just that. 'I knew him quite well when I was a child.'

Looking a trifle pale, but maintaining quite beautifully that self-assured air, she rose to her feet and even managed a semblance of a smile at the three rather startled expressions bent in her direction. 'It has been several years since you last set eyes on me, sir, so I'm not in the least offended by your all-too-evident bewilderment.' She held out her hand, which thankfully no longer trembled. 'Elizabeth…Elizabeth Beresford.'

He didn't utter 'Good Gad!' but the expletive hung in the air, none the less, drawing forth a gurgle of wicked amusement from the irrepressible Viscountess.

'I'm not in the least surprised, either, that you appear dumbfounded, sir, especially if you haven't seen her for some time. When I met up with Elizabeth again last year I could hardly believe that it was my old school friend sitting in that famous Bond Street modiste's.'

'Indeed, you are vastly altered, Miss Beresford,' he agreed in that attractive deep voice that she remembered so well, 'but I ought to have recognised you.' His dark eyes rested for a moment on the charmingly arranged rich red-brown hair before returning to the delicately featured face turned so enchantingly up to his. 'Unlike your sister, you always did bear a marked resemblance to your father. With your unusual colouring you are unmistakably a Beresford.'

'I cannot express strongly enough how relieved I am to hear you say so, sir,' she responded with feeling, before turning and bestowing such a dazzling smile upon the Viscount that Sir Richard experienced a most unexpected and rather unwholesome spasm of jealousy gnaw at his insides.

'Your darling wife, Brin, has recently remarked that we might well be mistaken for brother and sister. You must be aware that she has never been known to put a guard on that unruly tongue of hers. Before you know it, rumours will begin to spread and we shall find ourselves on the receiving end of some rather strange looks!'

He laughed heartily at this before offering her his arm and escorting her across the hall and into the dining-room. Verity, following with Sir Richard, experienced a deal of wicked satisfaction when she noticed that her husband's very personable friend seemed incapable of preventing his gaze from wandering in Miss Beresford's direction.

Elizabeth became increasingly aware of this fact too as the evening wore on but, unlike Verity, found nothing satisfying in those all-too-frequent dark-eyed glances. Never in her wildest imaginings had she considered the possibility that the Dartwoods' other guest would turn out to be none other than the man she had secretly, and quite foolishly, loved since she was a girl.

Calling upon that all-important inner reserve of self-control, she managed to conceal this all-too-painful truth. However, trying to behave towards him as she might have done any other acquaintance of long standing, with a kind of polite, friendly interest, inevitably took its toll. So, when Verity announced her intention of retiring early, Elizabeth wasn't slow in making her own excuses to leave the gentlemen to their own devices.

Managing, still, to retain that serene look that suggested she hadn't a care in the world, Elizabeth accompanied her friend up the staircase. She accepted with alacrity the Viscountess's invitation to come to her suite of rooms later so that they could enjoy a comfortable coze before finally retiring for the night, but the instant she entered the sanctuary of her own bedchamber her expression changed dramatically.

'Ha! I knew it. In a right fix you are, and no mistake!'

Elizabeth flashed her maid a glance of impatience. 'I might have guessed that you'd have got wind of his arrival. And don't stand there gloating! Come help me off with this gown!'

Completely undaunted by the brusque tone, Agatha helped her young mistress get ready for bed. 'What are you intending to do, miss? You mark my words, he'll find out.'

Elizabeth pulled a brush through her silky russet-coloured hair with impatient strokes as she stared at her maid through the dressing-table mirror. 'How can he possibly do that? Only you and I know. And if you ever reveal my secret, Aggie, I'll never forgive you!'

'Wild horses could never drag it from me, miss. You know that. But he's no fool. You might let something slip.' Her expression betrayed her concern. 'It might be best if you make some excuse to leave,' she suggested, but Elizabeth shook her head.

'I cannot deny that that solution is very tempting, but it won't answer. It would look most odd if I suddenly upped and left.' She gazed sightlessly at her own reflection in the mirror, her mind deep in thought. 'No, that course of action would certainly give rise to conjecture. And besides, I'm quite adept at keeping a guard on my tongue, and concealing my feelings. I've had years of practice, after all.'

She saw sadness replace the concern in her maid's dark eyes and gave her arm an affectionate squeeze before rising from the stool to collect her robe. 'I must confess, though, that I'm more than a little annoyed with the Viscountess. I think for friendship's sake she might have taken the trouble to forewarn me that this friend of her husband's was none other than Richard. But—' she shrugged '—annoyed though I am, I couldn't with a clear conscience desert her now.' A worried frown suddenly marred the perfect symmetry of her own brow. 'Have you by any chance caught sight of her ladyship since we arrived, Aggie?'

'I have that, miss. Spied her crossing the hall when you all went into the dining-room earlier.'

'In your expert opinion, when do you consider the baby will be born?'

'Any day now, I shouldn't wonder.'

'Just what I've been thinking!' The frown of disquiet grew more pronounced. 'The Lord only knows what kind of practitioner has been in attendance upon her ladyship. Some antiquated old fossil who hasn't picked up a medical volume in years, I shouldn't wonder. I can perfectly understand why Tom works himself into such a passion over the old-fashioned notions of many of his colleagues. It's a thousand pities he isn't here now!'

She moved across to the door, but turned back to enquire,

'I don't suppose you happen to know precisely where her ladyship's bedchamber is situated, by any chance?'

'Turn left at the end of the passageway and it's the second door on the right.'

Elizabeth, marvelling at her maid's quite remarkable ability for acquainting herself with the layout of strange houses within a relatively short space of time, went along to her ladyship's apartments and discovered the Viscountess sitting up in bed, supported by a mound of frothy lace-edged pillows. She received a warm smile and was invited to sit on the edge of the huge four-poster bed, but she remained standing, her eyes betraying her very understandable resentment at her friend's rather heartless disregard for her feelings.

Verity was not slow in perceiving the look. 'What is it, Elizabeth? What's wrong?'

'Why didn't you inform me that you had invited Richard here, too?'

The enquiry was uttered lightly enough, but Verity couldn't mistake the note of censure in the soft voice and was frankly puzzled by it. 'I didn't realise until a few days ago that he would be coming. Brin met up with him in London the other week and invited him to stay. Why, you don't object to his being here, surely? You seem to get along quite well.'

Elizabeth cast her a look of comical dismay. 'Sir Richard, my dear Verity, is the gentleman my parents wished me to marry. At least,' she amended with a rueful smile, 'my father certainly desired the match. Don't you recall my telling you that when we met in London last spring?'

In truth, she did not, although she vaguely recalled Elizabeth mentioning that there was someone she had refused to marry because she had been convinced they wouldn't suit.

'Oh, I am sorry! Does it make you feel so very uncomfortable…his being here, I mean?'

There could be no mistaking the genuine distress, the undoubted concern her friend was experiencing on her behalf, and Elizabeth found those slight feelings of hurt and annoyance ebbing away.

Accepting the invitation at last, she seated herself on the edge of the bed and gave her friend's hand a reassuring squeeze. 'I should be a liar if I said no. But you mustn't concern yourself on my account.' A wistful little smile hovered around her very attractive mouth. 'Richard, I should imagine, was as relieved as I not to be forced into the union.'

Verity subjected her friend to a rather long and thoughtful look, her husband's bluntly voiced amazement at Elizabeth's unmarried state echoing in her ears.

Yes, now that she came to consider the matter, it was most odd that Elizabeth had chosen to remain a spinster. The reason might well be what she herself had suspected: that Elizabeth recoiled at the mere thought of contracting a marriage so desperately unhappy as her parents' union had been. Or the answer might simply be that she had never as yet met a gentleman with whom she wished to spend the rest of her life. A sudden vision of Sir Richard—tall, muscular and perfectly proportioned—appeared before her mind's eye, drawing a rather puzzled frown to crease her forehead. If, in truth, Elizabeth had never married because she had yet to meet a man to her taste, then she must be very hard to please, for how many gentlemen were there as handsome and personable as Sir Richard?

She found herself unable to quell her rampant curiosity, and after a moment found herself asking outright what her friend had glimpsed in his character to give her a dislike of him.

'Oh, I don't dislike him, Verity,' she responded without

the least hesitation. 'Far from it, in fact. As you might have gathered earlier, I like him very well. I cannot see how any female could take such a well-mannered and intelligent gentleman in dislike.'

Just what I've been thinking myself, Verity thought, and said with that bluntness which was so much a part of her charm, 'Then, why in heaven's name did you refuse to marry him?'

Elizabeth, far from discomposed, smiled rather serenely. 'Because, my dear, I couldn't bear the mortification of going through life knowing that in the eyes of my husband I would always figure as second best.'

Verity's jaw dropped perceptively. 'Do you mean that he was in love with someone else at the time?'

'I wouldn't go as far as to say that, exactly,' Elizabeth responded after giving the question due consideration. 'But you must remember that it was our respective fathers who desired the match. They had been close friends since boyhood, and that friendship continued until Sir Percival Knightley's death. Richard was, in fact, my father's godson, and although my father's sojourns at our home were rare, he did occasionally bring Richard for a visit.'

She paused for a moment to stare blindly at one ornately carved bedpost. 'From a very early age I knew Richard preferred the company of my sister. Hardly surprising when one considers how very pretty Evadne was in her youth, whereas I... Added to which, they were of a similar age, Evadne being only a year his junior.'

'Are you trying to say that he wished to marry her?' The Viscountess not only looked astounded, but sounded it too, and Elizabeth couldn't prevent a gurgle of laughter escaping.

'Most young men who met my sister swiftly became infatuated. And Richard was no exception. I came upon them together in the shrubbery one day, and overheard Richard saying that he wished she were the one his father had wished him to marry... Then he kissed her.' Her amusement faded and the grey in her eyes seemed to intensify. 'I think that must rate as one of the lowest points in my life. But I made up my mind, then, that I would never marry unless I was certain of my future husband's regard for me.'

Verity shook her head in disbelief. 'And here I was thinking that Richard was a man of sound good sense. How could any gentleman of discernment prefer Evadne to you?'

'Why, thank you, my dear! You do my ego the world of good!' Elizabeth exclaimed, genuinely gratified by the compliment, but then became serious once more. 'You must remember, though, that this happened years ago. Richard himself wouldn't have been much above twenty at the time. And there could be no denying that Evadne was quite captivatingly lovely.'

The Viscountess lay quietly mulling over what she had learned, then her ever-lively and rather wicked sense of humour came to the fore and she suddenly gurgled with laughter, a delightful tinkling sound which echoed round the room.

'No wonder Richard looked so dumbfounded earlier, but he should have remembered that plain little cygnets grow into quite regal creatures. I think he'll consider it most fortuitous that he never married your sister. What a blunder that would have been!'

'My dear, there was never any question of that. Evadne might have liked him very well, but she was ambitious, and had set her sights high. She wouldn't have settled for less than a title, and Richard, you must remember, was a younger son... Which reminds me. I must offer my condolences. His brother's death was—must have come as a bitter blow. They were very close.'

She rose from the bed. 'And now I really must leave you, otherwise that very doting husband of yours will quite rightly take me roundly to task for keeping you from your sleep,' and, without giving her friend the chance to argue, whisked herself from the room.

Completely satisfied now that there had been no ulterior motive in Richard's invitation to this house, Elizabeth smiled to herself as she moved almost soundlessly along the red-carpeted passageway in the direction of her own room. She ought to have known that the darling Viscountess would never do anything so underhanded, nor indeed anything which might cause her old school-friend embarrassment. But this didn't alter the fact, Elizabeth reminded herself, that she must remain on her mettle throughout the time Richard was here, for just one unguarded look, just one ill-chosen word, might alert the far-from-obtuse Viscountess to the true state of her friend's rather foolish heart.

Rounding the corner, she stopped dead in her tracks and only just managed to prevent a gasp escaping as her eyes focused on the tall figure standing in the shadows only yards ahead. Her robe had fallen open and she didn't realise that, with the candles behind her, the nightgown which modestly covered almost every inch of her became virtually transparent. But Richard was instantly aware of the fact.

The gentlemanly thing to do, of course, was to bid a swift good night and retire to his bedchamber. He swiftly discovered, however, that he was first and foremost a man, and couldn't prevent his eyes from wandering over one of the most perfectly proportioned figures he had ever been privileged to see, dwelling with intense pleasure on the softly rounded curves and, oh, so tantalising shadows before forcing his eyes up to a sweetly curved mouth just begging to be kissed.

Only iron self-control kept him firmly rooted to the spot, but he was powerless to prevent that telltale husky note of desire from creeping into his voice as he said, 'Miss

Beresford, I thought you'd retired long since. I'm sorry if
I startled you.'

'Not at all, sir. It's entirely my own fault for wandering
about the place at this time of night.' He watched a tentative little smile briefly curl up the corners of that delectable
mouth as she glided towards the door leading to the bedchamber almost directly opposite his own. 'I shall bid you
good night, Sir Richard. I dare say we'll see each other
again in the morning.'

'Oh, yes, Miss Beresford,' he murmured as she disappeared into the room without another word, 'you can be
very sure of that…very, very sure.'

Chapter Three

Casting a far from appreciative eye round his allotted bed-chamber, Richard rose wearily from the bed and went across to the bell-pull. He felt decidedly unrefreshed, but was only too well aware that he couldn't blame his singular lack of sleep on unfamiliar surroundings, or on the four-poster bed which had proved both comfortable and roomy. Oh, no, the sole culprit for his insomnia lay not in this elegantly appointed room, but in the bedchamber almost directly opposite. And wasn't that damnably frustrating in itself?

Unable to suppress a crooked half-smile, he seated himself at the dressing-table. Even now, he still found it difficult to accept that the elegantly poised young woman who had introduced herself the evening before, with all the calm self-assurance of some Grand Duchess, was the same Elizabeth Beresford he had known years ago.

Mother Nature, he mused, had wrought nothing short of a miracle there. In the space of a few short years *she* had transformed an unappealing nonentity into something quite out of the common way. To say that Elizabeth was the most beautiful woman he had ever clapped eyes on would be a gross exaggeration, he knew, but there was no denying that she was quite captivatingly lovely, both face and figure a delightful vista to any gentleman of superior tastes.

He experienced yet again the stirring of desire as his mind's eye, for perhaps the hundredth time, visualised her as she had rounded the corner of the passageway the night before, seeming to float, not walk, towards him, like some enchanted, ethereal creature well above his touch. But this ought not to be the case, he reminded himself. By rights he ought to be able to touch that young woman whenever he desired; by rights she ought at this point in time to belong to him, body and soul; and he experienced a sense of acute disappointment, not to say resentment, that this was not the case.

Running slightly impatient fingers through his sleep-tousled dark brown hair, he cast his mind back over the years, trying to remember the last time he had set eyes on the young girl whom both his father and godfather had wished him to marry. His memory was hazy, but he vaguely recalled having glimpsed her at Henry Beresford's funeral, a forlorn and solitary little figure standing quite apart from her mother and vivacious elder sister.

It must have been a year or, maybe, two later, when he had been out in the Peninsula fighting for his country, that he had received that one and only letter from her. She had considered that they were no longer obliged to comply with the wishes of their deceased fathers, and had released him completely from any obligation he might still have been harbouring to marry her.

Honesty prompted him to admit that he had experienced immense relief after reading that missive. After all, what man in his right mind was wishful to tie himself for life to a rather drab and plump female who had seemed incapable of stringing more than half a dozen words together at any one time? Of course he had felt duty-bound to write back suggesting that they wait a year or two before finally coming to a decision. He had received no further communication from her and, truth to tell, he hadn't given Elizabeth Beresford a single thought during the intervening years... No, not one, until he had unexpectedly come face to face with her again the previous evening.

The bedchamber door opened and his valet entered, breaking into his far from satisfying reflections, and Richard managed with a modicum of success to put thoughts of Elizabeth aside. This relative peace of mind was destined not to last very long, however, for the first person he set eyes on when entering the breakfast parlour a short while later was none other than the sweet torment who had deprived him of so much sleep throughout the night.

As he seated himself at the table he experienced a rather irrational stab of irritation. He wasn't quite certain whether this stemmed from the fact that Elizabeth, bright-eyed and cheerful, betrayed all too clearly that she hadn't suffered from lack of sleep, or that she appeared on remarkably friendly terms with their host, who was still looking highly amused at something she had just said.

'I trust you slept well?' Brin enquired after a servant had supplied Richard's needs.

'Very,' he lied. 'You have a remarkably comfortable home here. It was a pleasure to sleep in a bedchamber where the fire didn't billow out smoke every five minutes. I really must attend to the chimneys at Knightley Hall. Several of the fireplaces there are quite shocking.'

'I recall a similar problem at my parents' home,' Elizabeth remarked, 'especially when there was an east wind. Thankfully, I'm not plagued by such a nuisance at my home near Bristol.'

Richard frowned slightly at this. He had assumed, quite wrongly it seemed, that she still resided in her childhood home in Wiltshire, although he vaguely recalled learning of her mother's demise a few years ago.

'I wasn't aware that you no longer resided in Wiltshire, Miss Beresford. Do you live with a relative?'

'I did reside with my maternal grandmother. Sadly, she died last autumn.' A veil of unhappiness clouded her eyes as she looked directly across the table at him. 'And may I offer you my belated condolences. Some time ago I learned of your brother's death. Such a terrible tragedy!'

Offering him no time in which to respond, Elizabeth rose to her feet and transferred her attention to their host, that spontaneous, sweet smile which had won his regard so quickly touching her lips. 'I shall pay a visit to Verity's room first. So, shall we meet in the stable yard—say, in half an hour's time?'

Watching her leave the room, Brin experienced, yet again, amazement at her continued unmarried state, and shook his head in complete bewilderment. 'I still find it difficult to understand why that lovely creature isn't married.'

The hand raising the fork to Richard's mouth checked for a moment. Yes, he ruminated, she most certainly ought to be. And if it wasn't for the fact that the contrary little madam had suddenly taken it into her head to go against her deceased father's expressed wishes, she would now be married to me!

Suddenly finding his appetite had deserted him, he pushed his plate aside and turned to his host as a thought suddenly occurred to him. 'Am I right in thinking that Miss Beresford's sister resides not too far from here?'

'Yes, about three miles away.'

In that case, why hadn't Elizabeth chosen to stay with her? Richard wondered. She could quite easily have visited her friend the Viscountess whenever she wished. Evadne must surely feel affronted knowing that her sister had preferred to stay here. Why, it was tantamount to a direct snub!

'I hope Verity has remembered to warn Elizabeth that Lady Chiltham is not an infrequent visitor,' Brin continued, and failed to notice his friend's rather puzzled expression. 'Apparently the sisters don't get along too well. But, then, you'd know all about that, I dare say, your being a friend of the family.'

'No, I didn't know,' Richard freely admitted, and was rather intrigued by this snippet of information. 'Up until yesterday evening I hadn't set eyes on either of them since the day of their father's funeral.'

'Well, no doubt you'll be given ample opportunity to renew your acquaintanceship with Lady Chiltham during your stay with us. As I've already mentioned, she's not an infrequent caller,' Brin responded, his tone betraying clearly enough that he could wish it were quite otherwise.

Not offering his friend the opportunity to enquire further into the reason behind the sisters' antipathy, Brin rose to his feet. 'I'm an appalling host, deserting you like this on your first morning here, but if I don't hurry and change, Elizabeth will be kept waiting.' He made to leave, then checked as a most obvious solution occurred to him. 'Why not join us? I'm taking Elizabeth on a tour round the estate.'

Richard needed no second prompting. Grand though it undoubtedly was, the estate was of precious little interest to him; Elizabeth Beresford, on the other hand, most definitely was. So he wasted no time in returning to his room to change into his riding gear, and accompanied Brin outside to the stables a short while later to discover Elizabeth, becomingly attired in a bottle-green habit, which seemed to emphasise those gorgeous red tones in her hair, already mounted on her ladyship's chestnut filly.

'You are a rare female, indeed,' her host remarked approvingly. 'One of the few I've ever known who can be on time!' He glanced briefly in Richard's direction, watched him mount the handsome bay, and then turned back to Elizabeth with a conspiratorial wink. 'You do realise that we're going to be made to look a pair of veritable whipsters in the company of the man who was reputed to be the finest horseman in Wellington's army.'

Elizabeth couldn't prevent a chuckle at Richard's pained expression. 'I am well aware of his prowess, sir. My father was not infrequently heard to remark that his godson could ride before he could walk.'

'A gross exaggeration!' Richard put in before either of them could utter any further absurdities at his expense. 'This is a fine animal you have here, Brin,' he went on, quickly changing the subject and giving the bay's neck a fond pat.

'I acquired him a couple of months ago. Yes, I'm rather pleased with him myself,' he admitted as they all trotted out of the stable yard. 'Do you still possess that brute you had with you in Spain?'

'Sultan…? Sadly, no. The poor old fellow was shot from beneath me at Waterloo.' Richard saw Elizabeth pale visibly, and cursed himself for an insensitive clod. 'I'm so sorry, Miss Beresford. We seasoned campaigners tend to reminisce at the drop of a hat and frequently forget we're in mixed company.'

'My fault entirely,' Brin interposed, feeling extremely guilty for raising the subject in the first place. 'Dashed thoughtless thing for me to have said, considering your own experiences in Brussels last year.'

'You do me too much honour, sir,' Elizabeth countered with a dismissive wave of her hand. 'Like so many other faint-hearted souls, my one and only desire after hearing that first distant rumble of cannon fire was to make a bolt for the nearest port.'

Brin didn't know which shocked him more: Elizabeth's frivolous, and far from truthful, response, or Richard's openly contemptuous smirk in reaction to it. He was about to set his friend straight on the matter when his thoughts suddenly turned in an entirely different direction as he spotted his steward, in the company of one of his tenants, approaching them.

'It looks as if my presence is required elsewhere.' He cast them an apologetic smile. 'Would you be good enough to accompany Elizabeth, Richard? Hopefully, I shouldn't be too long and shall catch up with you both later.'

Although he was far from content to remain for long in the company of a female whom, with a complete turnabout of his former opinion, he now suspected of being quite light-minded, he politely agreed, but Elizabeth swiftly began to rise in his estimation again when she proved herself to be a very competent horsewoman. She handled the far-from-docile filly with praiseworthy ease, her light hands, deceptively, in full control.

'I cannot recall ever seeing you ride before, Miss Beresford,' he remarked as they headed towards the western boundary of the estate.

At this, her lips curled into the strangest little smile. 'No, I don't suppose for a moment that you can, sir. But, then, I doubt there's very much you do remember about me.'

Although she had spoken lightly enough, without so much as a hint of pique in her soft and very pleasant voice, he seriously suspected that he had just received a reprimand and didn't know whether to feel amused or annoyed by it.

After a moment's deliberation he chose to be diverted. 'Ungallant though it is of me to confess to it but, no, I don't recall very much about you, ma'am. But, then, in my defence, I had little contact with you when you were a child, and it has been several years since we last met.'

'Seven, to be exact.'

Little baggage! Was she deliberately trying to set him at a disadvantage? Or was it simply that she refused to indulge in the gentle art of dissimulation? Again he found himself more amused than annoyed, and not just a little intrigued as well.

'Yes, of course, it was.' He risked a sidelong glance in her direction, registered with a feeling of irritation that she was looking perfectly composed and experienced the most overwhelming desire to penetrate that shroud of cool dignity which seemed to be wrapped around her and glimpse the real essence of the woman beneath. 'It was on the very sad occasion of your father's funeral. If my memory serves me correctly, that was the last time I saw your sister too.' He gazed intently at her delightful profile. 'I hope she is in good health?'

'Very, as far as I know.' She turned her head to look at him then, and couldn't prevent a smile at the quizzical lift of one dark brow. 'Ours could never be described as a close family, sir. I became estranged from both my mother and sister when I chose to live with my maternal grandmother. Evadne did take the trouble to inform me of my mother's demise, and I wrote to her last autumn informing her of our grandmother's passing, but apart from those two instances, there has been no communication between us, verbal or otherwise, for several years.'

Because he had been so close to his own brother, he felt rather saddened to learn this, and not just a little appalled at Elizabeth's seeming indifference to the state of affairs which existed between her and her sister. He decided, however, that it would be wrong of him to make a snap judgement on a situation about which he knew next to nothing, and changed the subject by enquiring if she now had a companion living with her to bear her company.

'No, I live quite alone, except for the servants, that is. Oh, and Aggie, of course! But I don't consider her a ser-

vant, even though she is my personal maid,' she explained
when he looked a trifle bewildered. 'You perhaps wouldn't
remember her, but she was employed in my father's household. She has known me since the day I was born, and is
quite touchingly devoted.' He found the rather wistful little
smile which accompanied the admission most engaging. 'I
must say, Sir Richard, it is rather wonderful having someone around who is so concerned for my well-being, but she
does tend to fuss over me like a mother hen.'

He tactfully refrained from voicing his staunch disapproval of a young lady of quality living alone and, as they
made their way along the high ridge which formed the
western boundary of his lordship's land, encouraged her to
talk about those years she had lived with her grandmother.

It didn't take him long to discover that she had been
touchingly devoted to her grandparent. She could not speak
highly enough of the lady who had, through sheer determination and hard work, built up a thriving company, own-
ing several sailing ships which had travelled to distant
points on the globe, and who had died one of the richest
women in Bristol.

As he listened he vaguely recalled his father once remarking on the fact that a substantial dowry was the only
thing that had made Elizabeth's mother acceptable to the
younger son of an earl. Many of the top Ten Thousand still
looked down on those who had any connection with trade,
and he found himself admiring Elizabeth's total lack of
snobbery or embarrassment over her maternal grandparent's humble origins. It was quite evident that she felt nothing but admiration for her grandmother's businesslike acu-
men, and didn't shy away from the fact that she owed her
comfortable existence, now, to that woman's hard-working
life.

'I wish I had had the pleasure of making her acquaintance,' he remarked with total sincerity when she fell silent. 'You make her sound a very interesting character.'

'Oh, she was! There's no denying she was a hard-headed businesswoman, as shrewd as they come, but there was a softer side to her nature too. She fell in love with my grandfather when she had just turned eighteen. Their marriage lasted such a tragically short length of time, less than six years, but she never married again, even though she received numerous offers throughout her life. She told me once that we were alike in that…that we were destined to love only once.'

For a brief moment he glimpsed a faraway look in her eyes, then she seemed to collect herself and looked at him with that completely unforced smile of hers, which never failed to reach her eyes, igniting a sparkle in those lovely grey-green depths.

'My apologies, Sir Richard. You must think my tongue runs on wheels. I've done nothing but chatter about myself since we began our ride.'

Drawing her filly to a halt, she gazed at the rippling stream gurgling its way along the shallow valley below. 'How beautiful it is here! Brin and Verity seem very contented in their new home, but they must find the landscape vastly different from their native Yorkshire.'

Richard, too, cast his eyes over the hilly terrain. 'The more I travel about this glorious land of ours, the more I come to realise that each county possesses its own individual charm and beauty.'

'Mmm.' Elizabeth frowned suddenly. 'I ought to travel more. It's a dreadful thing to confess, but I've never ventured further north than Gloucester. I've always wanted to visit Scotland, and I could take in other places on the way—the Peaks, and the Lake District, to name but two. Late spring or early summer would be the ideal time to travel, don't you agree?'

'Emphatically no, Miss Beresford!' he astounded her by responding in forthright tones. 'Your father was my godfather, so I suppose I'm the closest you've ever had to a brother. Therefore, I do not scruple to tell you that it would not only be extremely foolhardy, but grossly improper for you to embark on such a venture without the support and guidance of some male relative.'

He could easily discern a look of combined annoyance and astonishment in her eyes, and was not just a little surprised himself that he had tried to interfere in something which was, after all, none of his concern. He was surprised, too, and not just a little bewildered by the totally unexpected and overwhelming desire he was experiencing to protect this young woman who was quite evidently battling against the very understandable compulsion to tell him to mind his own business.

'I think, sir,' Elizabeth said with careful restraint, 'that it might be wise if we made our way back now. It doesn't look as if Brin will be joining us, and I think if we are left alone together for very much longer we shall be in the gravest danger of coming to cuffs.'

His response was to throw his head back and roar with laughter, which only succeeded in annoying her further, but by the time they had arrived back at the Dartwoods' charming country residence genial relations had once again been restored.

As she walked with Richard towards the house, Elizabeth was vaguely aware that there was a carriage standing in the courtyard, but gave not a single thought to the possible identity of the person who had called, until she entered her bedchamber and saw the disgruntled look on her maid's face.

'And what has put you out of temper this morning, Aggie? Had a difference of opinion with one of her ladyship's servants, have we?'

'To hear you talk, Miss Elizabeth, anyone would think I was the kind of odiously bossy female who always tried to rule the roost.'

'And so you are!' Elizabeth returned, never having put a guard on her tongue where Agatha was concerned. 'Well, out with it, then!' she encouraged when her maid regarded her in tight-lipped indignation. 'If it wasn't one of the servants then who, or what, has sent you into a fit of the sullens?'

'Her ladyship has a visitor,' Agatha unlocked her mouth to announce in tones of dire foreboding.

'Ha! I begin to see daylight.' Peeling off her habit, Elizabeth regarded the maid with an understanding smile. 'So, darling Evadne is here, is she? Well, we knew it would be only a matter of time.' A hint of mischief sparkled in her eyes. 'Do you know, Aggie, Wellington could have done with your services during the Peninsular Campaign. You would have made an excellent spy. You possess the most uncanny knack of discovering things with quite remarkable speed,' but Agatha refused to be diverted and looked at her mistress in some concern.

'Be careful, my lamb,' she urged. 'She were a nasty, malicious child. I know people can change over the years, but it's been my experience that they never do to that extent, unless forced to mend their ways.'

'Pray, don't concern yourself on my account.' Elizabeth was completely undaunted at the prospect of coming face to face again with the female who had bullied her quite mercilessly years before. 'You above anyone else should know that Evadne would never show herself in a poor light when in public. She will be all charm and social graces.'

A hard look, rarely glimpsed in her, suddenly took possession of Elizabeth's fine features. 'One viper in a family is more than enough. But if she is foolish enough to cross swords with me again, then she might be surprised at the venom I possess. My grandmother taught me well. I'm more than a match, now, for my beloved sister.'

Although Agatha said nothing further while she helped her mistress change her attire, she was still experiencing a deal of concern; but she was, as she had been told, fretting quite needlessly. When Elizabeth left the bedchamber and descended the ornately carved staircase she was complete mistress of herself.

In point of fact, her self-confidence had reached a new high. She had, after all, coped superbly with Richard's un-expected and rather unnerving presence in this house, not once betraying her true feelings for him. But it wouldn't do at all to become overconfident, she reminded herself, recalling vividly that moment earlier when he had dared to presume that he could dictate how she should go on. Such impudence! She had come perilously close to losing her temper, but that, she knew, would have been a grave mis-take. If she allowed anger to surface, what other emotions might she foolishly betray to the man whom she had adored since her girlhood?

A young footman opened the salon door for her and she couldn't prevent a smile at the anxious glance the Viscountess shot in her husband's direction before he rose to his feet. Richard rose also, and she thought she could detect a flicker of unease in his eyes before she transferred her gaze to the elegantly attired woman seated beside a total stranger on the couch.

If Lady Chiltham was experiencing shock over her sis-ter's drastically altered appearance she certainly betrayed no sign of it as she went rushing forward to embrace her warmly. Elizabeth, however, was far too experienced in the ways of her elder sister to be fooled by the false display of affection and, refusing to return the embrace, merely said, 'You are looking well, Evadne. Marriage and motherhood evidently agree with you.' The large cornflower-blue eyes

were as brightly sparkling as she remembered, but her sister
was betraying clear signs that she was rapidly approaching
her thirtieth year. Tiny lines were beginning to mar what
had once been a flawless complexion, and there was a definite hard, pinched look about the mouth that had once been
so softly inviting to members of the opposite sex. 'I trust
your husband and children are keeping well?'

'Clara and little Edwin go on very nicely, unlike their
poor papa who does tend to suffer from the gout from time
to time.'

An image of the obese Baron when last she had seen him
sprang before Elizabeth's mind's eye. He was not renowned
for depriving himself of his creature comforts and she
wouldn't be in the least surprised to discover that his girth
had increased over the years.

'Do the children resemble their father, Evadne?'

'Edwin does, certainly, but most say that Clara is the
image of her mama.' Lady Chiltham then prudently
changed the subject, before her sister could remark on the
fact that she had never set eyes on either her niece or
nephew, by introducing her to Mrs Westbridge who was at
present staying with them and who, it transpired, was Sir
Richard's nearest neighbour.

'Before you entered I was on the point of inviting Sir
Richard to dine with us on Friday, and sincerely trust that
you will accompany him.'

'I shall be honoured to act as your sister's escort, Lady
Chiltham,' Richard responded, thereby offering Elizabeth
no opportunity to accept or otherwise.

Evadne appeared genuinely pleased and smiled delight-
edly as she transferred her gaze to the occupants of the red
upholstered couch on the opposite side of the room. 'I fully
understand why your ladyship is disinclined to accept invitations at the present time,' she remarked, 'so shall not
press you, ma'am. I'm certain, though, that you'd have no

objection to my depriving you of my charming sister's company for just one evening.'

'Of course not,' Verity responded, having little choice, and could only hope that Elizabeth wasn't too disturbed at the prospect of dining at the Chilthams' home, but gained some comfort from the knowledge that Richard would be there too.

Conversation then became general, but Lady Chiltham, never having failed to adhere to the strict rules governing polite behaviour, rose to her feet a few minutes later as the socially acceptable time allotted for paying morning visits drew to a close. 'Would you be kind enough to escort me out to my carriage, Elizabeth?'

A wickedly mischievous look added an extra sparkle to a pair of grey-green eyes. 'Believe me, Evadne, nothing could afford me greater pleasure!'

The *double entendre* might have escaped Lady Chiltham, but Richard was very well aware of precisely what the younger sister had meant and cast a frowning glance at her slender retreating back as the three ladies left the room.

'Phew!' The Viscount put his fingers to his neckcloth as though it had suddenly grown uncomfortably tight. 'Well, that went rather better than we had dared to hope.'

Verity smiled. 'I must confess I was on tenterhooks, but I should have realised that Elizabeth would rise to the occasion.'

'You'll forgive me for saying so,' Richard remarked, delving into his pocket to draw out his snuffbox, 'but aren't you making rather too much of it? I understand the coolness between the sisters is of several years' standing, but I'm certain that, now they have been reunited, the breach will soon be healed. Lady Chiltham, at least, seems eager to make up their differences.'

Verity regarded him in open-mouthed astonishment for a moment. 'It's quite obvious to me, sir, that you know nothing about the matter. Elizabeth warned me before we even moved down here that her sister possessed two faces—one she keeps for public show, and a very different one for private. And Elizabeth doesn't lie.'

'I'm not so certain of that,' her husband responded unexpectedly, and she looked up at him sharply.

'What on earth do you mean, Brin?'

'It was something she said to me earlier,' he explained, looking decidedly puzzled. 'I recall clearly your telling me that Elizabeth's only reason for going to Brussels last year was to take care of her grandmother who was concerned for the welfare of her godson. Thankfully, he was amongst the lucky ones and came through the battle unscathed. We also both know for a fact that Elizabeth remained in Brussels for far longer than had been originally planned in order to nurse several wounded British soldiers. She mentioned that in the letter she wrote to you from Brussels last summer, remember? So why, when I brought the subject up, did she try to give the impression that it had been quite otherwise—that she had fled the capital shortly after the battle had begun?'

Richard transferred his gaze from the Viscount's rather puzzled expression to study the delicately painted box in his hand. Yes, he silently agreed, that was most odd. Perhaps, though, she was by nature very modest and didn't want her highly commendable acts of kindness to become generally known. Or, maybe, there was some other reason? She must have realised, surely, that Brin knew the truth already? So there could have been only one other whom she had been trying to mislead. His eyes narrowed. How very intriguing!

Before returning to his estates in Hampshire, he decided, clamping his jaws together in hard determination, he intended to get to know the delightful Miss Beresford a good deal better!

Chapter Four

Settling himself more comfortably in the corner of his well-sprung travelling carriage, Richard looked across at his intriguing companion with narrowed, assessing eyes. Although they had resided under the same roof for several days, he knew little more about Elizabeth Beresford now than he had after that first exploratory ride across Viscount Dartwood's estate.

It would be grossly unjust to suggest that she had deliberately gone out of her way to avoid him, because she most certainly had not. He'd spent many pleasurable hours in her company, either exploring the Devonshire countryside on horseback, or enjoying a hand or two of piquet in the evenings after dinner; but since that first ride across the estate, they had never once found themselves alone together.

Of course this went some way to explain why he'd been unable to discover anything further about the life she had been leading since leaving the protection of her family home; nor, indeed, what had induced her to seek sanctuary with her maternal grandmother in the first place. He could hardly question her in any great detail when in the company of either their host or hostess. To do so would give rise to the wildest suppositions, especially on the part of the sportive Viscountess, who was quite obviously as touchingly fond of Elizabeth as was that dragon-faced maid who always accompanied her whenever she took a stroll in the gardens.

Not that he believed this was done with the deliberate intention of thwarting his attempts to be alone with her, nor through any reasons of propriety, either. If that were the case, why hadn't Miss Beresford insisted on her maid accompanying her out this evening? After all, it was hardly considered correct behaviour for a young, unmarried female to ride in a closed carriage with a gentleman who wasn't a close relative without the support of some female companion.

'Something appears to be troubling you, Sir Richard,' Elizabeth remarked, turning her head suddenly and catching the frowning scrutiny. 'If it is the prospect of dining with the Chilthams which has brought on a bout of ill-humour, then let me remind you that it was you who accepted the invitation, not I.'

'On the contrary, I am looking forward to it.' He didn't add that it might offer the opportunity to discover why—and this was pure supposition on his part—she seemed disinclined to make up her differences with her sister. 'I'm rather surprised, though, that you chose to leave your maid behind.'

He had long since come to the conclusion that she was far from slow-witted and wasn't in the least surprised, therefore, to see a spark of mischief suddenly brighten her eyes. 'Sir Richard, let me assure you that you're in no danger of being compromised. Nor do I consider my reputation is likely to suffer by taking a short carriage ride with you. Besides which, I deemed it far more important for Aggie to remain at the house.'

She wasn't slow to recognise the unspoken question in

his eyes, either. 'It's my belief that the Viscountess is nearer her time than she supposes.'

His brow rose. 'I didn't realise, Miss Beresford, that amongst your many other accomplishments you were such an expert on childbearing.'

'Certainly not in childbearing, sir. But I have some experience of childbirth.'

Again his brow rose and he regarded her with amused interest. 'May I be permitted to know how you acquired this knowledge?'

'Unlike many young females of my class, I have not frittered away my time in sewing or painting water-colour pictures. During the past few years I have not infrequently accompanied Tom out when he has made calls.'

'Tom?' he echoed, totally bemused.

'Dr Thomas Carrington, a licentiate of the London College of Physicians.' Her lips curled into a warm smile, betraying clearly enough her regard for the doctor. 'His father was an apothecary and a close friend of my grandmother's. He died when Tom was little more than ten years old, and my grandmother virtually brought Tom up. She took him into her home, paid for his education and provided him with funds when he went to train in London. When he returned to Bristol he continued to live in my grandmother's house up until her death.'

Her sudden scowl revealed quite beautifully her feelings of intense annoyance, even before she added, 'He then considered that it would be grossly improper for him to remain there with me, and now resides in the far from comfortable rooms above his father's old shop.' She raised her hand in an impatient gesture. 'I've come to the conclusion that your sex can be quite foolishly stubborn at times!'

He decided that, as she seemed in an informative frame of mind, it might be wise to refrain from agreeing wholeheartedly with the actions the doctor had taken on her behalf, but could not resist remarking, 'And I suppose the experience you gained by accompanying Dr Carrington on those visits to his various patients over the years came in very useful when you were in Brussels last summer?'

Her expression betrayed her immediate understanding. 'I see! So you've been gossiping about me behind my back.'

'It was remarked upon that you nursed some British soldiers, certainly,' he admitted.

'And so did many others, sir,' she responded with yet another dismissive wave of her hand. 'My grandmother and I were in no way unique. Many opened their doors to the injured.' She looked at him steadily. 'I understand that you, too, were wounded and offered sanctuary. I trust you were not badly hurt?'

'As you see, ma'am, I survived.' Richard turned his head to stare out of the window at the rapidly fading light as he experienced again that all-too-frequent gnawing spasm of grief. Would thoughts of Mary Smith, and her untimely death, always remain a painful torment?

He forced himself to look back at Elizabeth again, saw that she was regarding him rather thoughtfully and decided it might be to his advantage to change the subject before she turned the tables on him and began to enquire too deeply into certain aspects of his past that he would far rather be allowed to forget.

Consequently, they continued the journey with him only raising topics as impersonal as the weather, which had in the past twenty-four hours grown markedly colder. Evidently, Elizabeth was feeling the drop in temperature, for he noticed her shiver and glance up at the dark early evening sky as she stepped down from the carriage, after it had drawn to a halt outside the front entrance of the Chilthams' imposing but rather gloomy greystone mansion.

The high-ceilinged, draughty hall was anything but inviting, but no fault could be found with the warmth of the welcome bestowed upon them by their hostess as they entered the drawing-room. Lord Chiltham, too, was urbanity itself, praising his sister-in-law on her charming appearance before introducing her to his youngest brother, Edward, who was at present residing with them and who, Elizabeth noted with a wry smile, was in the gravest danger of continuing the family tradition by doubling the size of his girth by middle age.

Several people had been invited to dine and the sumptuous meal, which included numerous courses and a wide variety of richly prepared dishes, as Lord Chiltham was not famed for his abstinence, was most enjoyable. Afterwards the ladies returned to the drawing-room and Elizabeth found herself seated beside the lady who had accompanied Evadne on her visit to Dartwood Manor two days before.

Apart from the fact that Caroline Westbridge resided in Hampshire, and happened to be Sir Richard's nearest neighbour, Elizabeth knew absolutely nothing about her. She had seemed rather ill at ease when she had made that visit with Evadne, barely uttering a word, while at the same time watchful.

This evening, however, she appeared far more relaxed and chatted away on a variety of topics before announcing quite unexpectedly, 'You are nothing like your sister, Miss Beresford.'

Elizabeth had heard this remarked upon too many times in the past to experience the least pang of jealousy. Although she held her sister in scant regard, she had to own that Evadne, even though not in her first flush of youth, was still an extremely pretty woman.

She glanced across the room to where her sister stood conversing with the Rector's wife and eldest daughter. Considering Evadne had borne two children, her figure was good, and although perhaps her complexion could no longer withstand close inspection, her blonde hair still retained its guinea-gold lustre.

'No, I bear no resemblance to my sister whatsoever. There's no denying that Evadne was the beauty in the family, and I must confess she has retained her looks remarkably well.'

'She certainly has,' Mrs Westbridge agreed. 'But I was thinking more of the difference between you in temperament.'

Although she had spoken levelly enough, there was something in the tone which puzzled Elizabeth. She had assumed that Mrs Westbridge was an old friend of Evadne's, but she experienced the oddest feeling, now, that this was far from the case.

'Have you been acquainted with my sister long, ma'am?'

'My husband was Lord Chiltham's cousin. We became acquainted through our husbands.'

'Was?' Elizabeth echoed.

'I've been a widow for five years.'

'I'm so sorry. I didn't know.'

'One grows accustomed, Miss Beresford. My son is my life now. He'll be going to university in the autumn, and I must confess I miss him dreadfully when he's away from home.'

'I see you two are getting along famously.'

Evadne's sudden interruption brought the little tête-à-tête to an abrupt end. It seemed to bring a cessation to Caroline Westbridge's friendly and easygoing manner too. Although she added one or two snippets to the ensuing conversation, she appeared to have grown tense quite suddenly, with that watchful, almost wary look returning to her eyes.

Elizabeth was not granted the opportunity to dwell on this rather puzzling circumstance, for a few minutes later the door opened and the gentlemen rejoined them. Evadne was in her element, and it rather amused Elizabeth to discover just how much pleasure her sister derived from playing the hostess.

There was no denying that she was extremely adept at the role, dismissing such mundane entertainments as cards or charades as commonplace, and encouraging most of her guests to join in one of her, now, famous treasure hunts. Only Lord Chiltham, the Rector and his wife refused to be tempted. Names were written on pieces of paper and placed in a bowl, and Richard, his being the first name to be drawn out, found himself partnered with Caroline Westbridge, which seemed not to displease either of them. The Rector's daughter was teamed up with the very handsome son of the local squire, which left Edward Chiltham to make up the last pairing with Elizabeth.

She was not too disappointed at this. Edward was an amiable enough young man, if a trifle light-minded, but the bright glint in his eyes, which suggested that he had been imbibing rather too freely of his brother's port, did cause her a moment's disquiet.

Handing each pair a folded sheet of paper on which was written their first clue, Evadne started each couple off at ten-minute intervals. Elizabeth and Edward were the last to begin and it didn't take Elizabeth very long to realise that she would be doing most of the searching and solving of clues on her own, as Edward appeared far more interested in reducing the levels in the decanters placed in the various rooms.

By the time she had discovered the whereabouts of the fifth clue, taped to the back of the mantel-clock in the Yellow Salon, Edward had succumbed to his excesses and had fallen sound asleep on the sofa; whereas Richard and Caroline, having satisfactorily completed the hunt in record time, were making their way back along the gallery towards the head of the stairs.

'Evadne is quite famous for her treasure hunts, and I

must say it does make a pleasant change from sitting down and playing cards.'

'Yes, most enjoyable,' Richard concurred. 'But I think someone should drop Lady Chiltham a hint to play her games only during the summer months. Some of these rooms are confoundedly draughty!'

Caroline laughingly agreed. 'I must say my bedchamber is not the most comfortable of rooms. Fortunately my visit this time is only a brief one,' she confided, smiling up at his handsome face.

She had been a close neighbour of the Knightleys for almost sixteen years. Richard had been little more than a boy when she had first gone to live in Hampshire with her husband. She had liked his brother very much, and Richard's sister-in-law had been a particular friend. Their deaths had upset her deeply; but she had never doubted Richard's ability to take his brother's place as head of the family. He had inherited the Knightley temperament, steadfast and reliable, and had already won the respect of his tenants and estate workers during the few short months he had been back in England.

'How long do you intend to remain in Devon?' His sudden scowl surprised her. 'I'm sorry, Richard. I didn't mean to pry.'

'No, no. I wasn't thinking that,' he hurriedly assured her, his attractive smile erasing the lines in his forehead. 'I really haven't given it much thought… Another week, maybe two.'

'Lord and Lady Dartwood seem a charming couple,' she remarked after a moment's silence.

'Yes, they are. I've known the Viscount for some time, of course. Before he came into the title he was in the army. We spent several years together out in the Peninsula. But this is the first time I've met his wife.'

'Am I right in thinking that she and Miss Beresford were at school together?'

'Yes, yes, they were. The Viscountess thinks a great deal of her.'

Caroline paused for a moment before descending the stairs. 'I had the pleasure of speaking to her earlier and thought her a most charming and likeable young woman.'

She chanced to glance up at him as he opened the drawing-room door for her and caught a look in his eyes, a strange mixture of tenderness and what appeared suspiciously like exasperation, and couldn't help but wonder whether the Dartwoods' hospitality was the reason he seemed disinclined to leave Devonshire, or something else entirely.

'How quick you have been!' Evadne exclaimed as they entered the room. 'I can see I'm going to have to make the clues more difficult in future.'

She then invited them to play a game or two of whist while they awaited the others. The Rector's daughter and her partner were the next to return; but half an hour later there was still no sign of Elizabeth and Edward.

Richard glanced up at the clock. It was getting quite late and he didn't wish to delay his departure too long. His coachman, no longer a young man, was not as dependable as he had once been, and might well lose his way on the unfamiliar roads. 'I think I'd better go in search of Miss Beresford,' he announced, rising to his feet. 'It's time we were taking our leave.'

Evadne, betraying a moment's alarm, rose also and drew him to one side. 'I haven't as yet been given the opportunity, but I was hoping to persuade Elizabeth to remain here with me tonight.' She couldn't mistake the surprised look in his eyes and smiled dazzlingly up at him. 'Yes, I'm sure, Richard, you have gathered by now that relations between my sister and me have not been—well, very good. And I wish to rectify this.'

She paused as though expecting a response, but when he remained silent, staring down at her almost quizzically, she added, 'Like most family disagreements, ours grew out of all proportion. My mother was deeply upset when Elizabeth suddenly took it into her head to live with our grandmother and, naturally, I took Mama's part. But I never intended the estrangement between Elizabeth and myself to continue all these years. So very unnecessary! So foolish!'

His expression changed instantly to one of approval. 'Far be it from me to throw a rub in your way, but I think it only right and proper that I go in search of her and inform her that I intend to leave.'

'Oh, no, don't do that!' Placing a restraining hand on his arm, she stared into his dark eyes with a look of entreaty in her own. 'She'll very likely wish to go with you, and I shall be denied the opportunity to speak to her alone. I cannot abandon my other guests, and was hoping to have a long talk after the others have gone. I cannot expect to heal the breach in five minutes and if, after she has heard me out, she is still determined to leave, then I shall return her safely to Dartwood Manor in my own carriage.'

In the face of these assurances Richard couldn't find it within himself to thwart her plans. He saw no earthly reason why he should remain, though, and after saying he would order his own carriage brought round from the stables, he made his farewells and went out into the hall.

As a young footman helped him on with his coat, Richard heard the sound of a door closing and turned in time to glimpse a flash of Elizabeth's dark blue velvet cloak before she disappeared down a narrow passageway. Where on earth was she going? he wondered. Evidently she had gone hopelessly wrong somewhere in the hunt, for all the clues and answers were to be found on the upper floor.

'Where does that lead?'

The footman turned his head in the direction of Sir Richard's pointing finger. 'The kitchen area, sir, and the cellar.'

'Good heavens! She has got herself hopelessly lost!'

'I beg your pardon, sir?'

'Nothing. Don't bother to order my carriage just yet,' he called over his shoulder as he set off across the hall. 'I'll arrange for it to be brought round later.'

The passageway was dimly lit and, like the rest of the house, prone to draughts. Picking up a candle off an old wooden table placed against the wall, he turned the corner, and was about to open the door on his left, when he saw a faint glimmer of light through an open doorway at the very end of the passage. Shielding the candle flame with his cupped hand, he approached the door and, seeing a series of stone steps, realised it must lead to the cellar.

'Miss Beresford,' he called. There was no response, so he descended the steps to the cold stone floor below. 'Miss Beresford, are you down here?'

'Sir Richard?' Her head appeared from behind one of the huge wooden wine racks. 'I see you had the sense to put on your coat, too. This house is abominably draughty. And it's absolutely freezing down here!'

'Very true. But what quite amazes me, my dear girl,' he responded as he moved towards her, 'is what you're doing down here in the first place.'

'The same as you, I should imagine. I'm looking for clues. I sincerely hope this is the last one. I'm rather tired of this game. It seems to have gone on for—'

Elizabeth caught herself up abruptly as the sound of the door being slammed shut echoed loudly round the cold stone walls. There followed the unmistakable grating of a key being turned in a lock, and Elizabeth looked up at Richard, the all-too-obvious question in her eyes.

'It would certainly seem so.' He removed a fleck of dust from his sleeve. 'How exceedingly tiresome!'

Elizabeth ran back up the steps and her groan as she tried to turn the doorknob was confirmation enough. 'What are we to do?'

'Wait until someone comes searching for us.'

He sat himself on the edge of a large wooden table. It creaked slightly beneath his weight, but he had every confidence that it would support him and began to swing one well-muscled leg to and fro, for all the world as though he hadn't a care.

'Aren't you coming up here to help me attract someone's attention?' Elizabeth paused in her pounding of the door to ask.

'No. But far be it from me to stop you making yourself hoarse and bruising your hands if you've a mind to do so.' The look she cast down at him left him in no doubt that she would have derived great pleasure from pounding her fists against him. 'I think I should warn you, though, before you become completely exhausted, that there isn't an earthly chance of someone hearing you unless he happens to be in that passageway. And it's quite obvious to me, at least, that the culprit has long since departed, or is profoundly deaf.'

'Yes, I suppose you're right.' After descending the steps again, she moved towards the table, a sudden frown creasing her brow. 'If you didn't come down here searching for clues, why did you come?'

'To bid you farewell. I was on the point of departure when I happened to catch sight of you disappearing down the passageway.'

'You were leaving?' Initially she experienced surprise, but then felt quite aggrieved. 'What...*without* me?'

He couldn't prevent a slight smile at this. 'Your sister

hopes to persuade you to stay the night. She's wishful to make up your differences.'

'Is she, indeed.' Elizabeth was decidedly sceptical. She would never trust her sister an inch, but at the same time would have granted her the opportunity to say her piece. 'I shall certainly listen to what she has to say, but I've no intention of remaining here all night.'

'Let us hope we're permitted a choice, my dear,' he responded drily and, easing himself off the table, held his candle aloft. 'In the meantime, we may as well make ourselves as comfortable as possible. There's no saying how long we'll be forced to wait before we're released from our temporary confinement.'

He discovered a pile of sacks in a crate and began to carry them across to the table. 'Spread these out. At least we'll have something soft to sit on. And, thankfully, we're not short of something to quench our thirsts, either.'

He began to inspect the wine racks while Elizabeth placed the sacks neatly over the table. 'If I know anything of butlers, there's sure to be an opener here somewhere. Ha! Here it is, ready for his secret tipple, but no glasses, I'm afraid. Still,' he shrugged, 'one cannot expect every creature comfort.'

He rejoined her at the table and, after helping her to climb upon it, settled himself down on the sacks beside her. The opening of the bottle was accomplished easily enough, and he offered her the first taste, smiling at her grimace as she foolishly took rather a large swallow of the excellent old brandy.

Her eyes watered and it was a moment or two before her throat had cooled sufficiently for her to speak. 'How long do you think we've been down here?'

'Ten…fifteen minutes, maybe.'

'It shouldn't be too long then, surely, before we're missed?'

'I wouldn't have thought so, no.' He cast her a glance of approval. How thankful he was that she was quite calm and matter of fact about it all. He might well have found himself trapped here with some hysterical female, prone to fits of the vapours! 'It's very likely that your partner has already set up the alarm.'

'Edward?' She couldn't help chuckling at this. 'I doubt it. I left him sleeping off his excesses on the couch in the Yellow Salon.'

'Yellow Salon?' he echoed. 'What the deuce were you doing in there? In fact, I still don't understand why you came down here. All the answers to the clues were to be found on the upper floor.'

'How very odd!' She looked nonplussed for a moment, then shrugged. 'Well, unless we were hopelessly out with the solution to the first clue, I can only assume there must have been two sets. All our answers were found in the rooms on the ground floor. We never ventured upstairs at all. Where are you off to now?'

Richard had eased himself down from the table and began searching abut the cellar once more. 'I'm looking for more candles. Yes, here they are. I thought I recalled seeing some. We may as well try to keep as warm as we can.'

Elizabeth watched in some amusement as he began to light the candles and place them on the floor around the table. 'I feel like a sacrificial lamb placed on the altar,' she quipped, looking down at the semicircle of light.

There wasn't so much as a ghost of a smile round Richard's mouth, however, and the look in his eyes as he raised his head was faintly disturbing. 'That, my dear girl, is precisely what you shall be if we're not rescued soon.'

Chapter Five

Richard cast a jaundiced eye up at the faint morning light filtering through the metal grating at the grimy window. The novelty of enforced confinement having long since worn off, he could only chafe over the amount of time they had already spent in this freezing prison and broodingly ponder over how much longer they would be forced to remain. Surely the servants must be up and about by now? He flexed the fingers of his right hand. He could hardly feel them, or his toes. The candles had long since guttered, but he was loath to move to find replacements.

Transferring his gaze to the tousled mass of hair cascading over his shoulder, he managed a smile. At least Elizabeth had kept his left side warm. Unused to strong liquor, she had eventually succumbed to the effects of the brandy and had been sleeping soundly for the past two or three hours. He could have wished for more comfortable surroundings for their first night together; would have expected a more intimate contact. The next time they lay together it would be in the soft comfort of a large bed, he decided, experiencing immense pleasure at the delightful prospect.

Raising his eyes once more, he gazed about the depressing, dank cellar. Forced confinement was hardly the most conventional way to acquire a wife, but he didn't doubt that they would deal extremely well. It felt so right, somehow, having this young woman lying beside him.

She murmured suddenly, and after a few moments moved her head against his shoulder and opened her eyes. It was quite obvious that she was still half asleep, for she gazed up at him in a kind of half-dazed bewilderment and frowned as though she couldn't quite bring his features into focus. Then she sat up abruptly, virulent colour suffusing her cheeks.

'Richard! What in the world...? Oh, yes, of course, I remember... Oh, my head!'

'If you have a hangover you've only yourself to blame,' he told her with a merciless lack of feeling. 'If you will consume half a bottle of brandy, what do you expect?'

'Was it as much as that? Dear me!' She tried to appear shamefaced, but failed quite miserably. 'Oh, well, at least it kept me warm.'

Swinging her feet to the floor, she swayed slightly, but regained her balance almost at once when Richard's long-fingered hands gripped her shoulders, steadying her. She was about to reassure him that she was perfectly all right when she detected a distinct noise in the passageway. Richard heard it too and, jumping off the table, was halfway up the cellar steps before she had a chance to move.

Pounding his fist on the door, he called out, but only silence answered him. He tried again, louder this time, and his efforts were rewarded.

'W-who be that?' a frightened voice enquired from the other side of the door.

'Sir Richard Knightley. Lady Chiltham's sister is here too. Let us out at once!'

A long silence, then, 'I can't sir. I ain't got no key. Only Mr Quimper 'as a key to the wine cellar, sir.'

He looked down at Elizabeth with raised brows. 'Who the deuce is Quimper?'

'The butler, I should imagine. I expect he's that seedy little man with the shifty eyes who admitted us to the house yesterday evening.'

'Sounds delightful!' Richard murmured, failing completely to bring an image of the servant to mind. He turned back to the door. 'Are you still there, girl? Good! Go and find this Quimper and tell him to let us out at once.'

'Has she gone?' Elizabeth asked eagerly.

'Yes, but whether she does as bidden is not so certain. Sounded half-witted to me.'

But here he did the young servant girl an injustice, for a few minutes later they both heard the key being placed in the lock, and then the door, blessedly, swung open.

A sea of astonished faces greeted them as they emerged from their temporary prison, but Elizabeth was far too relieved to be freed at last to concern herself with gaping expressions; and Richard, raising his quizzing-glass, cast his eyes over what he suspected was the entire staff, his keen gaze seeking the one who fitted Elizabeth's rather unflattering description. He spotted him at last, half-hidden by the cellar door.

'Ah! Quimper, I presume?'

'Y-yes, sir.' He seemed more stunned than all the rest of the servants put together. 'I cannot imagine how this happened...how you came to be locked—'

'Yes, yes! We'll no doubt sort that out later,' Richard cut in impatiently. 'What Miss Beresford and I need is to sit before a fire and thaw out. Escort us to the nearest one at once!'

'But that's in the kitchen, sir!' he informed him in patent disapproval, but Richard was in no mood to pander to the outraged feelings of a high-ranking servant.

'I don't care if it's in the wash-house. I just want warmth, Quimper. And now!'

By the time Richard had seated himself on a hard wooden bench placed in front of the kitchen range, and had consumed half the contents of a cup of piping-hot coffee, he was feeling more himself. Really, he was becoming quite soft, he reflected. Quite spoilt, in fact! During these past months back in England he had quickly grown accustomed to every comfort and luxury. The disagreeable night spent in that cellar was as nothing when compared to the privations he had been forced to endure during his years in the army, and yet here he was thinking himself quite ill-used.

He cast a quick glance at Elizabeth, seated on the bench beside him, and experienced a tiny stab of irritation. Apart from the fact that most of her hair had escaped its confining pins, no one observing her would suppose for a moment that she had just spent possibly the most uncomfortable night of her life. Here she was chatting away merrily to the cook, complimenting her on the excellent dinner served the night before, just as though she hadn't a care in the world! Did nothing ever daunt that young woman?

The patter of footsteps drew his attention and he looked up to see Lady Chiltham peering over the metal handrail. The face beneath the fetching lace cap was quite pale with mortification, but there was something rather more than stunned disbelief glinting in the depths of those cornflower-blue eyes as she hurried down the last few steps towards them.

'I just couldn't believe it when Quimper informed me.' She rounded on the hapless butler who was trying to make himself as inconspicuous as possible. 'How came you to lock them in the cellar, you fool?'

'It's hardly fair to place the blame on any of the servants,

Evadne,' Elizabeth put in before her sister had a chance to berate the major-domo further.

'At least, not all the blame, certainly,' a voice from above corrected, and Elizabeth raised her eyes to see Caroline Westbridge staring down at them with a very thoughtful expression on her kindly face. 'After all, Evadne, it was you who assumed that Richard had left with your sister. Might it not have been wise to make sure?'

Lady Chiltham looked decidedly ill at ease, but regained her composure almost at once. 'Yes, of course it would. But when I was informed that Elizabeth's cloak was missing I quite naturally supposed that she'd left with Richard. What defeats me completely,' she continued, transferring her gaze to the pair on the bench, 'is what you were doing in the cellar in the first place.'

'From what I can make out,' Richard said before Elizabeth had a chance to open her mouth, 'Miss Beresford seemed to have been engaged in a completely different hunt from the rest of us.'

Once again all eyes turned in Lady Chiltham's direction. 'Well, I don't see… Oh, dear! I must have inadvertently given you the wrong first clue. We had a treasure hunt here at Michaelmas, and that did include a venture down to the cellar. I asked the servants to leave all the clues in place, as I fully intend to use them again at Easter when we're expecting quite a large party of guests.' No one could have appeared more contrite. 'What an ordeal for you both!' She paused for a moment before adding, 'Where, by the way, is Edward? Don't tell me he's still down there!'

'He never was there.' Elizabeth's eyes twinkled with amusement. 'What a comedy of errors! I left Edward asleep on the couch in the Yellow Salon. For all I know he's still there.'

'Go and see, Quimper,' Evadne ordered before turning back to her sister. 'I cannot apologise enough. What an uncomfortable time you must have spent. What I cannot understand, though, Sir Richard, is why your coachman didn't apprise us of your continued presence here.'

'Perhaps if you were to take a look out of the window, Evadne,' Mrs Westbridge remarked, having by this time joined the group by the fire, 'the reason might become very clear. There must be four inches of snow covering the landscape. I remarked upon it last night, after the Rector and his family had departed. Don't you remember? I'm sure Richard's coachman must have assumed that his master had decided to spend the night here in view of the deterioration in the weather.'

'You're possibly quite right, Caroline,' he agreed, rising to his feet. 'But I don't intend spending another night here. My apologies for my incivility, Lady Chiltham, but what I need, and possibly your sister too, is a bed, breakfast and a bath, but not necessarily in that order. So if you would be kind enough to order my carriage brought round from the stables, we'll not trespass on your hospitality further.'

'Of course, it shall be attended to at once.' She reached out to place a reassuring hand on his arm. 'The sooner things get back to normal, the sooner this whole unfortunate episode can be forgotten.'

Elizabeth was very well aware of just what her sister had been so delicately trying to impart: in a roundabout way Evadne had been assuring Richard that he must not feel himself under any obligations whatsoever to do the honourable thing. And, of course, she was absolutely right!

Elizabeth was not insensitive to the very unfortunate position in which they now found themselves. Richard had behaved like a perfect gentleman, which was no more than she would have expected of him; and she had treated him just as she might some elder brother, successfully, as always, keeping her feelings firmly under control, although if the truth be known it had caused her a moment's disquiet when she had woken to discover herself in his arms.

It would be foolish to imagine that the happenings of the previous night would not be spread abroad. Although her sister, Elizabeth didn't doubt for a moment, would be discretion itself, there was nothing servants enjoyed more than a juicy snippet of below-stairs gossip. No doubt it would be the talking point of the neighbourhood for some considerable time to come, but she was more than able to put up with that for the duration of her stay in Devonshire. What she could never reconcile herself to was the knowledge that a gentleman had been compromised into offering her the protection of his name. She would never contemplate an offer of marriage on such grounds, least of all one from Richard.

Just what he thought about the whole unfortunate episode was difficult to judge, but as he never alluded to it once throughout the entire journey back to Dartwood Manor, she assumed with a deep sense of relief that he, like herself, considered the sooner the unfortunate episode was forgotten the better.

Trying to catch up on lost sleep and writing several letters kept her in her bedchamber for most of the day, so it wasn't until early in the evening when she went down to the salon where her host and hostess always sat before dinner that she realised that she had been rather naïve to suppose that Sir Richard would conveniently forget the whole unfortunate affair.

The instant she entered the room the conversation ceased abruptly and Brin, after a quick glance in his friend's direction, looked faintly embarrassed; but his wife, never having been one not to speak her mind, said, 'Richard has just been telling us what befell you last night. Brin and I naturally assumed you'd decided to stay over because of the weather. If only we'd known!'

Resolute, but slightly disappointed that Richard had chosen not to keep his own counsel, Elizabeth joined the little group by the fire. 'Yes, one could almost believe it was a conspiracy,' she remarked, little realising that she would come to regret her joking response, 'with my sister, her servants and Sir Richard's head groom all involved in a devilish plot to keep us prisoners in a freezing cellar.'

Richard looked far from amused. 'I would certainly never suspect my coachman of such a thing. Obadiah Hodge has been with my family for more than forty years.' His frown grew more pronounced. 'And that's just the trouble. He's getting too old now to tool a carriage for any great distance. He's extremely forgetful and frequently takes the wrong road. But how do you tell a devoted servant, who sat you on your first pony, that he's not up to his work any longer without hurting his feelings?'

'Yes, old retainers can be a problem,' Verity agreed, and Elizabeth almost sighed with relief at the change in conversation, but she was sensible enough to realise that this respite would not last very long.

Throughout dinner she was conscious of the furtive glances her host and hostess, and occasionally Richard, cast in her direction. She felt like a rare specimen in a jar being examined and assessed. She knew it was going to be only a matter of time before the conversation returned to the happenings, and possible repercussions, of the previous night, and was determined to formulate some well-rehearsed speech to put an end to the matter when it was raised again.

Her thoughts, however, took an entirely different and unexpected turn when she and Verity returned to the salon, leaving the gentlemen to their port. No sooner had the tea things been brought to the room than Verity suddenly gave a tiny cry, and placed a hand to her side.

'Oh, dear,' she murmured when the pain began to subside. 'The little one seems rather lively this evening,' and Elizabeth was instantly alert.

Coaxing Verity to return to her room, she helped her back up the staircase. No sooner had they entered the bedchamber than Verity uttered a further gasp, and then looked faintly embarrassed when she suddenly found herself standing in a pool of water.

'Oh, no, it cannot be!' she cried in distress. 'It's too soon!'

'Your baby evidently doesn't think so,' Elizabeth countered and went across to the bell-pull.

Meg, her ladyship's very efficient young maid, was not slow in answering the summons, but it was Elizabeth, calm and collected as ever, who issued instructions. Directing the maid to inform his lordship that his child was on the way and that it might be wise to summon the doctor, she then requested the abigail to go in search of Aggie.

Within minutes Agatha had arrived and aided her mistress in helping the Viscountess into her night-gown and making her as comfortable as possible in the large bed.

'I forgot you once mentioned you had experience in such things,' Verity said as her friend examined her. 'How very comforting it is having you here!'

Elizabeth's spontaneous smile would have reassured anyone, but Agatha was instantly aware that all was not as it should be when her young mistress turned away from the bed a moment later, an unmistakable frown of concern erasing the smile. Agatha had had a deal of experience in looking after newly born infants, but nowhere near as much as her mistress in delivering them, and drew her to one side.

'What is it, Miss Elizabeth?' she whispered. 'What's troubling you?'

'The baby isn't quite in the correct position for birth, Aggie. I do hope the doctor doesn't delay too long in getting here.'

Meg returned to inform them that a footman had been despatched for the doctor but, unfortunately, also disclosed that the weather had deteriorated again and that it was snowing quite heavily. Within the space of an hour the wind had picked up strongly, gusting round the stone walls of the mansion with increasing ferocity. It certainly didn't improve Elizabeth's peace of mind to learn that the footman had returned without the doctor. He had apparently been out on another call, but his housekeeper had assured the servant that she would inform Dr Phelps of the happenings at Dartwood Manor as soon as he came home.

It became quite evident as time went on that the doctor was disinclined, or perhaps unable, to venture out again on such a wild night. It also became quite obvious that her ladyship was becoming increasingly distressed by the very real possibility that her husband would foolishly go himself for Dr Phelps.

Beads of perspiration were glistening on Verity's forehead, and her hand felt clammy as she held her friend's wrist in a viselike grip. 'Elizabeth, you must stop him! He wouldn't dream of sending a servant out again on a night like this, but he'd go himself...I know he would! You can deliver the baby...I have every faith in you. Promise me you'll prevent Brin from going himself for the doctor!'

Elizabeth looked down into her friend's wildly anxious eyes for an endless moment, then nodded. 'You have my word, Verity, that your husband shall not leave the house this night.' She turned to her maid. 'Aggie, look after her ladyship until I return.'

Delaying only for the time it took to pay a brief visit to her own room in order to collect a small bottle from the medicine chest which she always carried with her whenever she travelled, she went back down to the salon. Richard and his lordship rose at once, their expressions betraying their all-too-evident anxiety.

'How is my wife? When's that damned doctor going to get here!' the Viscount snapped, forgetting to put a guard on his tongue in his distress. 'If he doesn't arrive soon, I'm going for him myself.'

'I'll accompany you,' Richard didn't hesitate to assure him, but Elizabeth had been prepared for that and merely smiled to herself as she moved over to the decanters.

'Yes, I was hoping you would. But why not fortify yourselves for the journey by partaking in a glass of brandy first?'

Without waiting for a response she poured out two large measures and, concealing her actions, poured half the contents of the small bottle into one of the glasses. 'Drink up, gentlemen,' she encouraged after handing them the glasses. 'You'll need something warm inside you on a night like this.'

To her immense satisfaction both tossed the brandy back without a second prompting. Brin was halfway to the door when he suddenly swayed slightly and placed a hand to his head.

'Quickly, Richard, help me get him over to the sofa!'

He was at her side in an instant and together they managed to get Brin on the couch before he succumbed completely to the effects of the drug.

For a few moments Richard looked down at his friend, unable to account for this rapid slide into unconsciousness, then realisation dawned and he reached for the empty glass his lordship had placed on a table. 'What the deuce are you about, Elizabeth!' he demanded after detecting the faint sweetly smelling odour.

'I'm doing my level best to make the ordeal ahead as easy as I possibly can for the Viscountess. She has enough to concern her without the added burden of worrying over her husband's safety.'

Completely unmoved by the continued expression of staunch disapproval on Richard's face, she gently positioned the Viscount's head on a cushion and covered him with a blanket. 'Neither you nor Brin would send a dog out on a night like this, and yet you were both foolish enough to contemplate venturing forth yourselves.' She turned towards him again, giving him back look for look. 'Have you seen just how bad it is out there? It's impossible to distinguish the roads from the verges. Even if you did, by some miracle, manage to reach the doctor's house without having an accident, there's no guarantee that you'd find him at home, or that you could persuade him to return here with you.'

He knew she was right: it was madness to attempt that four-mile journey in what was nothing less than a howling blizzard. 'What else can we—I do?'

'You can ensure that Brin doesn't attempt to leave. I've given him as much of the drug as I dare, but he's a man with a strong constitution. There's no saying just how long he'll remain asleep. Should he wake, I rely on you, Richard, to keep him here.'

He looked at her closely for the first time and saw the unmistakable signs of strain in her young face. 'What is it? What's wrong?'

She hesitated for a moment, uncertain whether to confess her fears or not, but then decided that she desperately needed this man's support and said, 'The baby isn't lying in the correct position for birth. I might be able to move it. I've watched Tom perform this feat often enough; have even successfully made the attempt once myself. But if I can't...'

'If you can't?' he prompted, and he watched a moment's fear flicker in her eyes.

'The baby isn't small. If I'm unable to turn it, and Verity becomes exhausted, then I shall be forced to bring it into the world by other means... I've witnessed that, too, on more than one occasion.'

In two giant strides he had bridged the gap between them, and took such a firm grip of her upper arms that she winced. 'Elizabeth, you can't! The mothers always die.'

'That isn't strictly true,' she countered, calling upon her superior knowledge in this particular subject. 'The first recorded Caesarean operation successfully performed in this country occurred during the last decade of the previous century. And I've witnessed Tom perform it successfully once.' She thought it prudent not to add that she had also been present on two occasions when the mothers had died, but something in her expression must have given her away.

'It's too risky, Elizabeth, and you know it.'

'What choice do I have?' The anguish in her voice was heartrending. 'If I leave it too long we might lose them both.' With a supreme effort she managed to break free from his hold. 'If I'm forced to use the knife, and my friend dies, then I shall find myself in very serious trouble, but I would far sooner face the consequences of my actions than do nothing—' she cast her eyes down at the sleeping Viscount '—and have to face that man again.'

Richard watched her leave, mingled anxiety and frustration gnawing at his insides. For the first time in his life he felt totally inept. He was incapable of doing anything positive to aid that brave young woman who would possibly be putting her own life at risk this night. All he could do was that very small thing she had asked of him and ensure Brin remained in the house. But at first light he would go for the doctor himself and bring him back, by force if necessary. He glanced at the clock. It was a fair few hours until dawn, though, and all he could do in the meantime was wait and pray.

Placing two more logs on the fire, he sat himself in the armchair and watched the logs hiss and crackle and burn away to almost nothing before replacing them with two more. Time dragged interminably, each minute seeming like an hour. There were moments when he almost wished Brin would wake and revile him. At least it would relieve the tension of waiting alone; might ease that raw pain of torment that continued to gnaw at his insides with ever-increasing fierceness.

The howling wind slowly lessened in strength and the silence was broken by an occasional murmur from his lordship, but Elizabeth had performed her task too well. The Viscount didn't begin to stir until after the mantel-clock had chimed six, and it was a further hour before he became fully conscious.

'Dear God! What on earth were we drinking last night?'

Richard watched him swing his feet to the floor and cradle his head in his hands. The actions reminded him vividly of Elizabeth's the previous morning when she had done much the same thing. A rather rueful smile curled his lips. He was beginning to think that he would never be allowed much rest while he remained in this part of the country. He hadn't enjoyed a decent night's sleep since he arrived!

Brin raised his head from his hands to stare at the logs on the hearth, and Richard knew by the sudden widening of his friend's eyes that memory had returned.

The Viscount rose rather too abruptly and was forced to grip the back of the sofa for support. 'My God... Verity! I must go to her!' But Richard had other ideas, and easily arrested his friend's progress to the door.

Any husband with a modicum of feeling would betray deep anxiety at such a time, and Brin's distress over his wife's well-being was only natural, but Richard's concerns were for quite a different person. If the Viscount burst into the bedchamber at the wrong moment, he would do far more harm than good. He had to be stopped!

'I sincerely trust you are not proposing to indulge in a bout of fisticuffs, gentlemen.'

Richard, lowering the fist which had been aimed at the Viscount's powerful jaw, swung round to see Elizabeth framed in the doorway. She had removed her apron and looked as neat as wax, without so much as a single strand of hair out of place.

The Viscount, taking advantage of his friend's loosened grip, easily broke free and took an urgent step towards her. 'Verity...? Has the doctor arrived?'

'No...but your son has.'

'My...?' He swallowed in an attempt to move the sudden obstruction lodged in his throat. 'Is he...?'

'He's a fine, healthy young fellow, sound in wind and limb,' she assured him, knowing the question he couldn't bring himself to ask.

'And Verity?'

'Tired, but that's only to be expected. See her by all means, but please do not remain too long. She needs to rest.'

'And so do you, my darling girl,' Richard said gently when Brin, almost running from the room in his eagerness to see his wife and new-born child, had left them.

Taking her arm, he guided her to the chair he himself had sat in for that interminable length of time. 'What a night you must have had! Did you need to...?'

'No, thankfully. The baby decided, with a little coaxing from me, that he would aid his mother by getting into the correct position. After that, it was a simple matter of waiting.'

He couldn't prevent a smile at the matter-of-fact tone. Anyone listening to her might be forgiven for thinking that she had done nothing more arduous than turn the pages of a novel for the past eight hours, but he had long since come to the conclusion that she possessed a masterly knack of always appearing outwardly calm.

Thrusting his hands deep into his breeches' pockets, he stood before the fire and stared down at the rapidly dying embers. The outcome of the night had been a joyous one, but it could so easily have been vastly different, so very tragic for all concerned. But he would never have allowed her to take the consequences on her own. Strangely enough, he felt responsible for her; just as any husband would for his wife. And his wife was precisely what she must become in the not-too-distant future, he decided firmly. So the sooner that stubborn, adorable little witch was brought to realise this fact the better!

He turned, about to broach the subject which had occupied his thoughts almost to the exclusion of everything else for the past twenty-four hours, only to discover that the future Lady Knightley, having succumbed to the tense pressures of the night, had fallen sound asleep.

Smiling tenderly, his eyes devoured the lovely contours of her face. Well, perhaps it might be wise to declare himself at a more appropriate time, he mused and, without disturbing her, very gently picked her up in his arms.

He was halfway to the door when he checked, his smile fading as he detected the distinct fragrance of lavender-and-rose water in her hair. The delicate perfume was achingly familiar... But where and when had he detected that sweetly smelling fragrance before?

Chapter Six

Viscountess Dartwood turned her head in the direction of the window where her friend stood holding the Honourable Arthur Gerald Charles Carter. Her baby seemed quite content to be cradled in those infinitely capable and comforting arms and to listen to that soft singsong voice talking absolute nonsense, telling him that he was born during one of the worst blizzards Devonshire had ever known, with him howling louder than the wind itself after he had taken his first breath.

How completely natural Elizabeth looked holding a baby, she mused. She really ought to have children of her own. She would make the most wonderful mother... But first, of course, she must become a wife!

A tiny crease of consternation furrowed her brow as she pondered over the few days since the birth of her son. Elizabeth had spent much of her time in this room. Verity couldn't deny that she had been pleased to have her company, but she couldn't rid herself of the disturbing suspicion that Elizabeth's attentiveness hadn't stemmed from a wish to prevent her friend from becoming bored, but from a desire to avoid a certain someone's company as much as possible. The reason for her doing so, of course, was abundantly obvious: she was avoiding the declaration that she knew he would make.

She had broached the subject of a possible union between Elizabeth and Richard when her husband had paid her a visit late the previous evening, but Brin had said that nothing had been decided upon as far as he knew. Elizabeth, of course, could do no wrong now in his eyes, and he had strictly forbidden Verity to become involved in something which had absolutely nothing to do with them. As far as he was concerned Elizabeth was an intelligent young woman who ought to be allowed to make her own decisions without pressure or interference from anyone else.

And he was absolutely right, of course. But why did Elizabeth seem disinclined to accept an offer of marriage from a gentleman whom she obviously liked very much? Surely love would grow from the mutual respect they had for each other?

The door opened and Agatha, looking as grim-faced and purposeful as ever, came striding into the room to collect her charge.

'I thought it wouldn't be too long before you came to reclaim him,' Elizabeth remarked, reluctantly handing over the precious bundle. 'You just cannot bear to be parted from him, can you?'

'I'll have to get used to it, won't I,' was the terse response. 'The new nurserymaid arrives tomorrow, and I've no intention of interfering.' She sniffed loudly. 'I wouldn't have any reason to be jealous, though, if someone else was to furnish me with a babe or two to look after.'

Verity suddenly found the nails on her left hand of immense interest, but couldn't resist saying when Agatha had left them, 'Not that she isn't perfectly right, of course. You would make a wonderful mother!'

Only too well aware where this conversation would eventually lead, Elizabeth came slowly towards the bed.

Her expression was as serene as ever, but there was an unmistakable thread of steel in her voice as she said, 'Let me make it perfectly clear here and now that I haven't the slightest intention of accepting an offer of marriage from a gentleman who feels himself in honour-bound to offer the protection of his name because of an unfortunate episode over which he had no control and, I might add, during which he couldn't have behaved with more propriety.'

Verity agreed fully with her friend's sentiments, but refused to leave matters at that. 'Richard certainly doesn't appear to be averse to a union between you. Quite the opposite, in fact!'

'Really?' There was a decidedly sceptical arch to Elizabeth's left brow. 'Although I have been acquainted with Richard for a number of years, I would be the first to admit that I do not know him very well. Nevertheless, I wouldn't have suspected him of being the garrulous sort who doesn't balk at discussing his most private concerns with all and sundry.'

The Viscountess had the grace to blush at this. 'You know full well that he hasn't spoken a word to me on the subject. I've set eyes on him only once since the baby's birth. I don't believe he's broached the subject with Brin, either,' she admitted. 'It was the impression I gained on the last evening we all dined together when he disclosed what had befallen you both at your sister's house. And if,' she went on, not giving her friend a chance to respond to this, 'you weren't afraid that he would make you an offer, why have you been doing your level best to keep out of his way as much as possible?'

Elizabeth couldn't help but smile. There was absolutely nothing amiss with her friend's understanding, but it was rather a pity that she spoke in such a no-nonsense fashion, thereby giving the recipient of her staunchly voiced opinions little room for manoeuvre. She decided, therefore, that it wasn't in her own best interests to seek sanctuary with her friend this time, and went over to the door.

'Perhaps because I believed that, given time, Richard would come to realise that there's absolutely no need for him to make such a sacrifice on my account,' and with that she left the room, but not before she had heard the far-from-ladylike derisive snort in response.

Not that Verity wasn't perfectly correct, of course, Elizabeth mused, making her way back along the passage-way to her own room. She had been avoiding Richard's society as much as she could. If the truth be known, though, the reason wasn't that she feared he would make her an offer: unfortunately, that was all too inevitable; but she did fear that she might foolishly give way to the deepest yearnings of her heart and accept him.

She reached the door of her bedchamber, then paused, her hand on the doorknob. But this was no answer, she told herself roundly. Unless she intended skulking in her room for the remainder of her stay, like some frightened rabbit, then she must start behaving normally. It was ridiculous to suppose that she could avoid him indefinitely. Sooner or later he would get her on her own, and from somewhere she must find the strength to refuse him. She'd done so before, she reminded herself. So she was quite capable of doing so again!

Determination added an extra spring to her step as she continued along the passageway. As she descended the stairs she saw the butler crossing the hall, and after learning that both his master and Sir Richard had gone out for a ride, she went into the library to pass the time until their return by reading a book. She had just made her selection from the wide and varied choice when the butler entered to inform her that Mrs Westbridge had called.

Elizabeth thought it rather strange that he should choose to apprise her of this fact, unless, of course, he was uncertain whether his mistress would be willing to receive visitors so soon after her confinement. Elizabeth, however, experienced no such doubts. 'It's quite in order for your mistress to receive visitors,' she assured him. 'I'm certain her ladyship will be delighted to see her.'

'You misunderstand, Miss Beresford. Mrs Westbridge is wishful to see you.'

How very odd, she thought, but didn't hesitate to request him to show the lady in, and moments later Mrs Westbridge, dressed in a very becoming carriage outfit of dull yellow, and appearing much younger than her thirty-six years, swept into the room.

'Forgive this intrusion, Miss Beresford,' she began, after Elizabeth had politely asked her to sit down, 'but I'm leaving Devonshire today and felt I had to see you before commencing my journey home.'

More intrigued than ever now, Elizabeth gave the unexpected caller her full attention, wondering why this lady, with whom she was barely acquainted, should be so wishful to see her. She wasn't left in ignorance for long.

'I gather from things Evadne has from time to time let fall that you and she are not upon the best of terms.' She paused for a moment, but when Elizabeth continued to regard her in silence, she smiled before adding, 'That, of course, is your own affair and has nothing whatsoever to do with me, but I considered it only fair to warn you—although that is perhaps too strong a word…make you aware of something rather puzzling.'

'Warn me about what, ma'am?' Elizabeth prompted, when her unexpected visitor fell silent.

Mrs Westbridge didn't respond for a moment, and for the first time since entering the room appeared slightly ill at ease. 'About your sister, Miss Beresford.'

'Evadne? Why? What has she done?'

'It isn't so much what she has done as what, I strongly suspect, she intended to do.'

Although Elizabeth felt loath to discuss a member of her family with a woman who was a virtual stranger, something in her visitor's tone caused a feeling of disquiet and she was prepared to listen to what she had to say.

'I think I had better begin by recounting certain curious events which took place on the evening of the dinner-party. It was quite some time after Richard had left, or so we had believed, that your sister made enquiries about your continued absence. It did occur to me at the time that it was rather strange that she didn't merely ring for a servant and request a search for you. She went out of the drawing-room herself and returned a short time later to inform us that you had left with Richard.'

She regarded Elizabeth steadily, her eyes never wavering for an instant. 'Now, this I did find most odd. I had been favourably impressed by your polite, open manner, Miss Beresford, and thought it rather strange that you hadn't taken the trouble to bid us all farewell before your departure, but it wasn't until the following morning, after I had discovered that you and Richard had been locked in the cellar, that I began to piece together the rather curious happenings of the previous evening, and swiftly came to the conclusion that your enforced confinement had been far from the innocent mistake I had believed it to be.'

She paused for a moment to untie the strings of her reticule. 'No one could have doubted your sister's genuine distress when she discovered you both seated in her kitchen. However, not long after you and Richard eventually departed, I happened to be passing Evadne's bedchamber and overheard her berating the butler again. "You fool, Quimper! You ought to have made certain," I distinctly heard her say. This in itself was not suspicious, but her next words most definitely were—"Your bungling has ruined all my plans."

'Unfortunately that was all I managed to hear, as a maid emerged from one of the other rooms, but it was enough. Something made me go back downstairs to the drawing-room. The servants hadn't had a chance to tidy up in there. Which was most fortuitous, for in the wastepaper-basket, where your sister had deposited them the night before, I found these.'

After delving into her reticule, she reached forward and deposited several small pieces of slightly crumpled paper into her interested listener's lap. Elizabeth frowned as she examined each one in turn. 'But they're all blank, Mrs Westbridge.'

'And yet on those our names were supposed to have been written.'

The implication was all too obvious. 'So we didn't find ourselves partnered that way by mere chance, but by design,' Elizabeth remarked after a moment's intense thought. 'To be precise...my sister's design.'

'Exactly! And I do not now believe, although I have no proof, that it was a mere accident that you were given a different set of clues to solve, one of which would eventually take you down to the cellar.'

'Where someone was keeping watch, waiting to lock the door once I was safely inside,' Elizabeth murmured, gazing at an imaginary spot on the wall behind her very informative visitor. 'And, unless I much mistake the matter, the person who should have been locked in the cellar with me was none other than Edward Chiltham.'

'That is what I believe, Miss Beresford. No one would think to question Edward's continued absence on the night of the dinner-party. It is not unusual for him to succumb to his excesses and retire early. The mistake Evadne made was to suppose her brother-in-law might curb his usual overindulgence because she had other guests present.'

Drawing together the strings of her reticule, Mrs Westbridge rose to her feet. 'No doubt you find all I've told you rather difficult to accept. What prompted her to lock you in the cellar in the hope of forcing a union between you and her brother-in-law, I can only wonder at.'

'Her actions do seem rather difficult to understand.' Elizabeth's voice was soft and as smooth as silk. 'No doubt, though, she had her reasons.'

Mrs Westbridge looked as though she were about to say something further, then seemed to think better of it and moved across to the door, but turned back to add, 'I would deem it a great favour if what we have discussed in this room goes no further. My visit to this house, of course, would not be considered unusual in the light of the recent happy event. Might I also request that you pass on my sincere congratulations on the birth of their son to Lord and Lady Dartwood.'

Elizabeth thought the request for secrecy rather odd, but didn't hesitate to agree, and after Mrs Westbridge had left, she remained in the house only for the time it took to toss the evidence of her sister's perfidy into the fire and to make a brief visit to her room in order to collect her cloak.

This was the first time she had ventured out of doors since the morning of darling little Arthur's birth. The early March sun was doing its best to rid the landscape of those last stubborn pockets of white, the only lingering evidence of the unseasonably late snowstorm which had swept the county three days before.

After taking a leisurely stroll round the perimeter of the Dartwoods' fine country residence, she wandered along the path that traversed the formal gardens at the back of the mansion, and then decided to walk a little farther to explore the shrubbery. Here, she discovered definite signs that spring was not too far away, but it was rather too early for any of the shrubs to be in flower. She swiftly found her interest in her surroundings fading and her mind returned to that rather informative and most unexpected visit of Mrs Westbridge's.

She shook her head, not in disbelief, but in wonder at her sister's continued acts of malice. One might be forgiven for supposing that a woman rapidly approaching her thirtieth birthday would have long since outgrown acts of childish spite; but Evadne was a law unto herself. Perhaps if she hadn't had ample experience of this darker side to her sister's character she might have been inclined to dismiss Mrs Westbridge's suspicions as ludicrous, but sadly she knew her sister's nature too well.

A tiny chuckle escaped her as she absently kicked at a pile of rotting leaves on the path. No wonder Evadne had looked so ludicrously crestfallen when she had seen Richard, and not Edward, sitting before the kitchen range. But it truly was the most foolish and ill-conceived attempt to force two people into wedlock. And why should she have wished to compromise Edward in the first place? Certainly not through any consideration for her sister's future well-being. That much was certain! Elizabeth mused, before she forced herself to consider seriously just what might have prompted her sister's underhanded scheming.

Evadne's marriage had taken place a few months before their father's death. She had by that time attained her majority, and had received from the age of sixteen numerous offers for her hand, all of which she had refused. Many a brow had risen when she had quite surprisingly become betrothed to Lord Chiltham, a man almost twenty years her senior. He would hardly have been considered by any romantically inclined young woman as an ideal partner: he was portly and not remotely good looking; but he was an amiable enough soul who possessed both title and wealth;

and social position, of course, had always featured very strongly in Evadne's evaluation of a suitable mate.

Perhaps during the ensuing years, though, she had come to repent her choice; had come to regret putting the pursuit of social standing above the attainment of those more tender emotions. Maybe her twisted mind had nurtured the hope that the sister whom she had always despised would suffer the same fate: a loveless union with a great lump of a man who was not precisely witless, but who was certainly not academically over-furnished. And who better to fill that role than the young man who was yearly turning into a mirror image of her unprepossessing husband?

The sound of footsteps on gravel drew her out of her not unamusing reflections and she turned, the wry smile curling her lips swiftly fading. Curbing the childish inclination to dive into the shrubbery in the slim hope that he hadn't spotted her, she studied Richard's elegant, long-striding gait as he approached. The sight of him in riding garb, which seemed to emphasise the breadth of shoulder and the strength of his well-muscled legs, was enough to send the most hardened female's heart a-fluttering. It certainly did little to restore her composure recalling being told that he had carried her, sound asleep, up to her room on that eventful morning not so long ago, and it took a monumental effort to raise her eyes to his when at last he stood before her.

'I'm pleased to see that you have risked a venture out of doors at long last for a breath of fresh air.'

He was probably being rather sarcastic, but she decided to give him the benefit of the doubt. 'It was too fine a morning to waste,' she responded, thankful that her voice betrayed none of her inner turmoil. 'Did you have an enjoyable ride?'

'Yes, but I would have found it more pleasurable if you had accompanied us.' He couldn't prevent a smile at the becoming little blush which added extra colour to the perfect complexion. 'Perhaps if the weather continues fine you'll grant me the pleasure of escorting you out tomorrow?'

As her brain for some inexplicable reason seemed unable to function sufficiently quickly for her to think up a reasonable excuse to refuse, she had little choice but to acquiesce to the invitation.

'You cannot imagine how relieved I am to hear you say that, Miss Beresford! I was beginning to dwell on the rather lowering possibility that you found me a bore. And with good reason!' He slanted a mocking glance. 'You have, after all, made it abundantly obvious that you've been doing your level best to avoid my company.'

Mortified that her actions had been so obvious, but more determined than ever, now, to put an end to the rather embarrassing predicament in which they now found themselves, she said, 'Sir Richard, I cannot deny that I have done my level best to keep you at a distance these past days. In view of the unfortunate happenings which took place at my sister's house, sooner or later the question of a marriage between us would need to be broached, and it was rather foolish of me to try to avoid the inevitable. I now feel that the matter ought to be brought out into the open and settled without delay so that we can continue our sojourn here without awkwardness or recriminations.'

'What a very sensible young woman you are, Miss Beresford! I applaud your sentiments.' Arresting her further progress along the path by placing a restraining hand on her arm, he turned her round to face him squarely before taking a firm and yet surprisingly gentle hold of her hands. 'I shall not insult your intelligence by feigning ignorance of the present delicate situation. Nor shall I risk causing further offence by requesting a little time to consider the very generous offer you have just made and, therefore, have no hesitation in telling you that I shall be extremely honoured to become your husband.'

'W-what?' She gaped up at him in astonished incredulity, her thoughts in complete turmoil. 'Sir, you misunderstand. I wasn't...I never meant...I wasn't suggesting for a moment that we...'

She was so deliciously confused that he had to curb the almost overwhelming desire to take her in his arms and add to her discomfiture by ruthlessly kissing her. Then he felt the fingers in his tremble slightly, and the desire to tease her further instantly vanished.

'My dear young woman, I am very well aware of what you were trying to say.' Releasing one of her hands, he reached for her chin and forced her to look up into his face. 'Not many hours after first meeting you again, I had begun to realise that at last I had found a woman with whom I could quite happily spend the rest of my life. The more I was in your company the more I grew to like and to admire you, Miss Beresford.'

Elizabeth gazed up at him in wonder, not daring to believe what she was hearing, and yet what she saw mirrored in those wonderfully sincere dark eyes of his almost made her heart turn a somersault.

'In the normal course of events I would have wished to give you more time to come to know me a little better. For my part, I have no doubts, and refuse to be thwarted in my desire to achieve what I truly believe would turn out to be an admirable match because of a rather foolish occurrence over which neither of us had any control.

'Therefore, Miss Beresford...Elizabeth, would you do me the very great honour of becoming my wife?'

Chapter Seven

To be married to a man who was both thoughtful and generous, as well as being well blessed in both face and figure, was surely every young woman's dream, Elizabeth reflected, tossing her book aside and leaning back against the mound of frothy white pillows.

Her marriage had taken place the week before by special licence. There had been absolutely no reason at all for such unseemly haste, except that Richard, surprisingly insistent, had seen no reason why they should wait and had brushed aside all those small arguments put forward for delaying the ceremony until late spring. She couldn't prevent a wry little smile as memory flooded back. Almost from that deliriously happy moment in the grounds at Dartwood Manor, when she had accepted that rather touching proposal, it seemed that her life had been taken over by a will far stronger than her own.

Within days she had been whisked back to Bristol, where Richard had left her while he journeyed to London to obtain a special licence. His return to her home the following week had sent her poor servants into a whirl of activity, for he had insisted on departing for Hampshire without delay. She had then been deposited for propriety's sake in Caroline

Westbridge's home, where she had spent the night, and the following day the ceremony had taken place in the tiny church nestling in the picturesque village just beyond Knightley Hall's boundary wall.

Everything had happened so fast that she still felt somewhat bemused by it all, frequently wondering if she would wake to find the whole thing had been nothing more than a delightful dream. But no, it was real enough, she assured herself, smiling tenderly down at the ring on her finger. That simple gold band was wonderful proof that she was now Lady Knightley, married, surely, to one of the most charming men in the land. Her smile slowly faded. Yes, she was married right enough...but as yet no wife.

Fleetingly her eyes moved in the direction of that connecting door. Not once since her belongings had been placed in this room had that door been opened. Richard had delicately touched upon the fact that, considering the speed with which their marriage had taken place, he was prepared to give her time to accustom herself to her new role in life. He had been all kindness and consideration, attentive to her every need. Since the day of their marriage they had spent almost every daylight hour in each other's company, riding across the estate, receiving the occasional visitor and eating their meals in relaxed comfort; but their nights had been spent apart.

She was very conscious of the iron control he was exerting over himself. She had glimpsed on more than one occasion a look in his eyes that betrayed rather more than warm regard. She was far from the naïve little innocent Richard evidently supposed her to be. During her years in Bristol, when she had eagerly gone about helping Dr Thomas Carrington in his work, she had acquired a deal of experience in human behaviour. She had been offered numerous opportunities to witness the results of happy marriages. Sadly, she had glimpsed the tragic results of failed ones, too, where discontented husbands had sought their pleasures elsewhere, many venturing into the more noisome parts of the city, where they risked far more than just their health by associating with women of a certain calling to satisfy their carnal desires.

She wasn't foolish enough to suppose that Richard hadn't satisfied his needs over the years with a string of experienced mistresses, but there was no reason for him to continue to do so now. She was more than willing to take on all the duties of a wife, and knew quite well just what was expected of her in the marriage bed. But how in the world could she assure him of her willingness to comply without appearing vulgarly immodest to a man who would, perhaps, expect her to find the whole act of procreation quite repugnant, at least at the beginning?

Seeing no immediate solution to her present predicament, and not being a young woman to worry unnecessarily over a problem that would no doubt resolve itself given time, Elizabeth decided, as she wasn't in the least tired, to write a letter to Viscountess Dartwood. She had promised faithfully to do so on the morning she had left Devon, but somehow her days had been so busy that she just hadn't found time to put pen to paper.

Tossing the bed covers aside, she padded across the thickly piled carpet to the wardrobe and took out her robe. As she went to place her arms in the sleeves she rather clumsily caught one of the scent bottles on the dressing-table in the robe's silken folds, sending the tiny glass container tumbling to the floor.

With a cry of dismay she bent to retrieve it before the entire contents had seeped into the carpet. It was a lovely, delicate fragrance when used sparingly, but half a bottle wafting through the air was quite another matter. She was about to go across to the window to let in some much-needed fresh air when the connecting door was unexpectedly thrown wide and her husband came striding into the room.

'Are you all right, Elizabeth? I heard you cry out. You're not feeling unwell, I trust?'

She was touched by the evident concern for her welfare, but couldn't resist saying, 'No, but I shall very soon become asphyxiated if I don't get some air.'

He was puzzled for a moment, then the powerful odour hit him too. 'Phew! Yes, I see what you mean!' He obliged her by throwing both windows wide. 'It smells like an opera dancer's boudoir in here.' The rather unfortunate comparison was out before he realised just what he was saying. 'I'm so sorry, my dear,' he apologised, slanting a look of comical dismay. 'I shouldn't have remarked on such a thing in the presence of a lady.'

'You have experience of such places, sir?' she enquired, one finely arched brow raised in hauteur.

He realised he would probably be digging himself into a deeper hole, but was about to apologise further when he detected an unmistakable glint in her eyes. 'Elizabeth, you little baggage!' Reaching for her shoulders, he gave her a playful shake. 'You weren't offended in the least.'

She dissolved into laughter, a delightful, infectious gurgling sound, and he found himself laughing too. Then, without quite knowing how it happened, he found he had his arms about her. It was one thing keeping a tight rein on his passion when she remained at a discreet distance, but quite another when every contour of that lovely slenderness was pressed so enticingly against him. Iron resolve crumpled beneath an uncontrollable surge of desire and he lowered his head to capture her lips with a hunger that left little doubt of his urgent need of her.

Elizabeth was hardly aware of being led towards the bed. The removal of her clothes was executed with such consummate skill that before she knew what had happened she was lying naked beside him, bathed in a pool of candlelight. Eyes, darkened by desire, swept over her in a slow, intimate appraisal, from cascading russet curls to slender white thighs, before hands and lips explored the silky smoothness of her skin with infinitely gentle and well-remembered caresses. No words of love had ever passed his lips, but no man could be so tender and be totally devoid of that sweet emotion.

The conviction swept aside that last barrier of restraint. She began to caress him in return, a little tentatively at first, but then with an increased confidence. His throaty moans of pleasure acted like a stimulant, fuelling her own passion, so that when, finally, he eased himself on top and inside her she instinctively moved her body to meet his in perfect harmony, one entity spiralling ever upwards to the heady delights of blissful fulfilment.

Supreme contentment which follows a perfect union left Elizabeth floating on a cloud of euphoria, but her rapid return to earth was as unexpected as it was painful. She sensed a change in him, even before she opened her eyes to see him staring down at her with an almost frozen expression on his face.

'What is it, Richard?' She touched his cheek with gentle fingers. 'What's wrong?'

Thrusting her hand away, he scrambled up from the bed, as though her nearness, now, was abhorrent to him. Snatching up the robe which earlier he had let slip to the floor, he shrugged himself into the strikingly patterned crimson brocade. 'Not that a strumpet like you, madam, would blench at the sight of a man's naked torso, but one of us at least should strive for a modicum of decency in this sordid union of ours.'

The totally undeserved name he had called her smote her like a physical blow, and his contemptuous look made her feel even more vulnerable, and ashamed of her own nakedness. She reached for the covers which he had carelessly tossed aside, only to have her wrist captured in a bone-crushing grip.

'It's a little late for a display of maidenly modesty now! You should have considered that stratagem earlier at the crucial moment, instead of behaving like a wanton.' His lips curled into a cruel sneer as he watched a surge of colour rise from the base of her throat. 'My God, you're good! I'll give you that. How long did it take you to perfect that little trick?'

Elizabeth could only stare up in disbelief at eyes hardened by anger and loathing. He looked like a madman. In fact, he must be insane, she thought. Why else would a man turn from gentle lover to cruel tyrant in a matter of minutes?

'Richard, what's wrong?' She was desperately striving to remain calm, but that wasn't easy when in the presence of someone who looked as though he might unleash his wrath in a display of physical violence at any moment. 'What have I done? I don't understand.'

'But I do…and only too well. Where is the evidence of your lost virginity?' His cold, accusing glance swept the crumpled sheets. 'I certainly didn't take it, so who did? And how many tumbles have you enjoyed since? A dozen… two…a hundred?'

Suddenly she understood what had wrought this drastic change in him. He believed her a woman of easy virtue, and his anger was not unreasonable. It was foolish to have remained silent on certain important happenings in the past for so long, but she'd hardly been granted the opportunity to explain during these last two hectic weeks and, truth to tell, she simply hadn't given the matter a thought since leaving Devon.

'Richard, I'm so sorry.' At last he released the cruel hold

on her wrist, and she didn't hesitate to reach for the covers. 'I should have told you before the wedding, but—'

'But you were sensible enough to realise,' he interrupted in a voice as cold as steel, 'that if I'd had the smallest inkling that you were far from chaste, then there never would have been a question of a marriage between us.'

'That isn't true! If you'd only allow me to explain,' she pleaded. 'It happened once, Richard.'

But he was in no mood to listen, his cruelly mirthless shout of laughter proof enough of that, even before he said, 'My dear, you take me for a fool. You didn't acquire your experience from one coupling. No!' he rasped, holding up his hand in an arresting gesture when she tried to reason with him further. 'Don't nauseate me with more lies.'

Completely lacking his usual grace, he swung away and began to pace the room like a prowling beast just waiting to strike. 'I can see it all now.' His voice was even, but edged with venom. 'I've been a damnable fool, but you played your part well, madam wife. I'll give you that. Right from that first night in Devon you had your strategy well planned, offering a tantalising glimpse of rose-tipped breasts and slender shapely thighs. What red-blooded male would not have been bewitched!'

Had he taken a moment to glance at her he couldn't have failed to notice the look of total bewilderment on her face, but he was too wrapped up in his own hurt and anger to care what effect his accusations were having on her, and kept his eyes firmly glued to the floor.

'Ye gods! And to think it never once crossed my mind to suspect that the evening spent at your sister's home had been carefully planned, planned down to the finest detail by you and that sister of yours.'

He did take the trouble to glance across the room at her then and saw a look of horror in her eyes, like that of a terrified animal caught in a trap with no possible means of escape; but he was far from finished with tormenting her yet.

'I recall clearly that there was a time years ago when you couldn't bring yourself to accept me as a husband, but no doubt my coming into the title made me an entirely different proposition.' The cynical twist to his mouth was a further cruel taunt. 'Well, madam wife, you have achieved your objective... But you have yet to know the man who comes with the title.'

Some detached part of her brain registered that on this point, at least, he was right—the man with that hard, intractable look in his eyes was a stranger; nothing like the friendly, carefree youth she had known years before; nothing like the charming man who had spoken such endearing words in a Devonshire garden not so very long ago. This man was as cruelly unjust as the accusations he had levelled at her and, she suspected, just as false.

'Why did you ask me to become your wife, Richard?' she forced herself to ask in a voice that sounded nothing remotely like her own.

The softly spoken enquiry seemed momentarily to surprise him, but the hateful smirk remained. 'Why does any man in my position marry? I require an heir. I believed that in you I would be getting a virtuous woman, admirably suitable for the wife of a baronet. A ludicrous error of judgement on my part, but I shan't be foolish enough to make any more.'

He came slowly back towards the bed, but Elizabeth, numbed by merciless reality, was now oblivious to the darkly threatening expression, and the continued hard-edged tone of his voice as he added, 'There can be no happiness now in this union of ours, but wedded we'll stay. When I can bring myself to touch you again you will fulfil your duties as my wife. But first I shall demand proof that you're carrying no other man's spawn. It would be unfortunate, therefore, if our activities between the sheets this night bore—er—fruit, for I should never believe the child was mine.'

He paused for a moment to study her closely. She was not staring at him but at some distant spot, with such a look of complete desolation in her eyes that he experienced uncertainty and a surge of pity, but quickly had the momentary weaknesses under control and hardened his heart.

'In the meantime, however, I have no intention of depriving myself of my own bodily needs, and shall seek my pleasures elsewhere. I shall leave for London in the morning, but you will remain here.' Once again he regarded her for a moment in silence, then stalked over to the door. 'During my absence you will behave with propriety... Woe betide you, madam wife, if news reaches me to the contrary!'

Elizabeth was only vaguely aware that he had left the room. For endless moments her eyes remained glued on that imaginary spot, her happiness, all hopes for the future, now ashes at her feet. Then she lay back against the pillows, but sleep, which might have brought a temporary respite from the ice-cold desolation gripping her heart, never came.

The candles in their sconces had guttered one by one, and then the first light of a new day filtered between the gap in the curtains. She wasn't certain whether the man in the next room had slept or not, but she was suddenly aware of the sounds of footsteps, of doors opening and closing and of a low murmur of voices. It seemed no time at all before something heavy was being dragged along the passageway. Then her bedroom door was thrown wide and the numbness which seemed to have taken possession of her with an ever-increasing intensity slowly began to subside and a degree of feeling, of nightmarish reality, returned.

'Has he gone, Aggie?'

Nodding, the maid closed the door quietly and came over to the bed. Her rather harsh-featured face seemed, for once, less severe and those dark all-seeing eyes betrayed more than just a modicum of disquiet.

'It's finished, Aggie…it's ruined.' A solitary tear hovered for a moment on the dark lashes before running down one pale cheek. 'I thought he loved me. What a fool I've been! If he had cared for me at all he would never have said—believed such things,' she managed to confide before great racking sobs shook her body and she found herself cradled in a pair of loving arms.

Agatha didn't attempt to check the flow, for the hurt, she knew, was better out than in, but it was a hurt that could—should have been avoided. She guessed what must have taken place the instant she had learned that Sir Richard had given orders for his trunk to be packed, and she couldn't help but feel that her young mistress had only herself to blame for the despair she was now feeling.

'You should have told him the truth from the beginning, but you would have your way. And look where it's brought you.' Absently she began to stroke the silken red-brown hair. 'He were bound to realise, my lamb. A man of experience wouldn't be easily fooled.' She felt the slender body stiffen. 'You think your Aggie didn't know. Oh, my lamb, I've known since that night,' she admitted, softly. 'I heard you get up and go to him, and you didn't return to your bed until almost dawn. You shouldn't have left Brussels without telling him the truth—that it was you who had nursed him so tenderly all those weeks.'

Easing herself away a little, Elizabeth looked into her maid's worried eyes. 'You know why I couldn't tell him. I didn't want his gratitude, Aggie. I knew he didn't love me, just as I'd known years ago when I wrote to him…

But I believed he had come to care for me during our stay in Devon.'

'He does love you, my lamb. Anyone can see—'

'No!' Elizabeth cut in, virulent anger suddenly thrusting aside the searing pain of hurt. 'He doesn't love me…he never has. He admitted as much. He married me for the sole purpose of producing an heir, and for no other reason.'

In silent dismay Agatha watched her young mistress walk over to the window and stare out at the park for what seemed an interminable length of time. She appeared to have regained her composure, but when, eventually, she did turn her head to glance across the room, the look of undisguised hatred in the depths of her eyes made Agatha's blood run cold.

'He wouldn't even grant me the opportunity to try to explain everything to him. He was determined to think the worst of me—even accused me of being a wanton, a woman of experience.' Her shout of laughter was mirthless. 'I could almost wish that that were true, Aggie, for it has brought me nothing but sorrow being his, and his alone. Well, let him think what he likes, for he shall never learn the truth from me, now! Let him take his pleasures where he may—the longer the better—for he shall never touch me again…that I swear!' The green in her eyes seemed to intensify. 'He said that I had yet to know the man I had married… Well, he has yet to know the woman he took to wife.'

Chapter Eight

If one or two eyebrows were raised at Sir Richard Knightley's unexpected arrival in the capital, no more than a casual remark here and there was passed about a newly married man deserting his bride so soon after the nuptials had taken place. Perhaps it was nothing more than urgent business which had brought him to town, or maybe he was arranging his honeymoon abroad, something that he had had precious little time to organise considering the speed with which the marriage had taken place.

Those who initially gave the unconventional behaviour any thought at all expected him to be gone within days. When, however, he betrayed no signs of a speedy return to Hampshire and, furthermore, began to accept invitations for events taking place rather later in the Season speculation quickly grew, and the rumour that Sir Richard had already come to repent his rather hurried marriage began to circulate.

Lady Knightley herself, being something of an enigma, only added to the rife conjecture. No one seemed to know very much about the new bride, not even Sir Richard's close friends, a circumstance the tattle-mongers considered most odd. She was well connected, of course—the Earl of

Eastbury's niece, and according to him a very pleasant 'gel', although rumour had it that he hadn't set eyes on her himself for several years.

Her sister, of course, was none other than Lady Chiltham. What a pity the Chilthams had decided not to come up to town this Season! Dear Evadne was always so forthcoming; and hadn't it been remarked upon by her very good friend Lady Hartley that Evadne was not precisely jubilant over her sister's marriage to the Baronet?

Naturally, Sir Richard's tight-lipped attitude only fuelled the gossip-mongering. He was as uncommunicative with his close friends, most of whom had served with him in the army, as he was with any society hostess who tried to coax a little information out of him. It didn't help to quash rumours when he began to indulge in flirtatious behaviour with several highborn ladies; and, when he was seen on several occasions entering a certain house owned by a lady who was not averse to more intimate, if discreetly conducted, relationships, most of Society began to assume that Sir Richard's marriage, if not one of convenience, had speedily proved to be an unmitigated disaster.

As the weeks passed Sir Richard continued to keep his own counsel. In public he behaved with that easy charm of manner which had always endeared him to those leading ladies of society; but, when in the privacy of his own home, he became quite a different person: moody, withdrawn and having recourse to the brandy decanter rather more frequently than was good for him.

It was only to be expected that his own servants found the present situation rather hard to understand: their new mistress in the country; their master in town, and behaving in a way that did him little credit. Medway, who had been placed in charge of the town residence by Sir Richard's brother several years before, and who hoped one day to take Mr Finch's place in Hampshire when the ageing butler eventually retired, quickly quashed the below-stairs tittle-tattle. He was both diligent and loyal and would never dream of gossiping about Sir Richard's private affairs, but that didn't prevent him from wondering himself just what had brought about this drastic change in his master.

He was emerging from the library, after having refilled the brandy decanter yet again that day, when a sharp rap of the door-knocker echoed loudly round the hall. He knew well enough that his master didn't wish to be disturbed that evening and, therefore, had no hesitation in informing the distinguished visitor, whom he recognised instantly, that Sir Richard was not receiving.

'He'll damned well receive me!' was Lord Dartwood's forthright response to this intelligence and, brushing past the startled servant, stepped into the hall. 'There's no need for you to announce me,' he went on, handing over his hat and gloves. 'Where is he? In the library?'

'I thought I told you I didn't wish to be disturbed, Medway,' he heard his master say before the library door was firmly closed.

'You might not wish to be,' his visitor countered, 'but you're most certainly going to be.'

'Brin?' Peering round the wing of his chair, Richard blinked several times in a vain attempt to reduce the effects of his overindulgence and clear his vision a little. 'What the deuce brings you to town?'

'You took the words right out of my mouth,' the Viscount responded, glancing fleetingly at his friend's half-finished brandy before going over to the decanters and helping himself to a glass. 'Business is what brings me to town.' Without bothering to wait for an invitation, he sat himself down. 'But from what I've been hearing since my arrival, it certainly isn't business keeping you here.'

He cast a critical eye over his friend's dishevelled appearance. His cravat was crumpled, there were one or two stains down the front of his shirt and he looked in urgent need of a shave. 'It's perhaps just as well that Elizabeth is in Hampshire if half the reports about you are true.'

Richard kissed the tips of his fingers in an exaggerated gesture. 'The ample charms of the delicious widow are enough to induce any red-blooded male to stay.'

The Viscount's lip curled. 'So it is true. My God, and you haven't been married five minutes!'

'But minutes were all it took for me to discover I'd been tricked—deceived by my, oh, so very lovely but not-so-virtuous wife.'

'What the deuce are you talking about?'

It was Richard's turn to sneer now. 'Isn't it obvious? Elizabeth didn't come to the marriage bed—how shall I put it?—*virgo intacta.*' Even in his far-from-sober state, he could see his friend was stunned. 'How would you have felt if you'd discovered you were not the first man to enjoy your wife's charms? Elizabeth swears it happened only once.' The unpleasant sneer grew more pronounced. 'But how can I believe her? How can I believe anything she says after the way she deceived me, after the way she, with the help of that sister of hers, tricked me into marriage?'

The injustice of the last remark drew Brin's head up. 'If you truly believe that then your wits must be addled. She told Verity that she would never accept a proposal of marriage from a man who believed himself to have been compromised.'

'Then why did she accept me?'

Brin didn't even take a moment to consider the answer. 'I suspect, Richard, it was because the poor deluded girl believed you loved her. You certainly gave Verity and myself that impression before you whisked Elizabeth away from Devon in such romantic style.'

Finishing off his brandy, he placed the empty glass on

the table before rising to his feet and staring down at his friend in some concern. It had been a mistake to come here; he realised that now. In Richard's present condition it wasn't likely that he could be made to see sense, and Brin feared that, if he remained, he might end by raising his fist to a half-drunken man, but he couldn't resist one final attempt to make him see sense.

'Perhaps if I'd discovered Verity wasn't chaste, I would have felt as bitterly resentful as you do now. But remaining here will solve nothing, Richard. It's my belief that Elizabeth loves you deeply, but if you should discover that you cannot find it within yourself to forgive and forget her past indiscretion, then it would be better for you both to terminate the marriage before more misery is caused.'

Richard didn't attempt to respond, nor did he attempt to show his friend out. He merely stared blindly down at the empty hearth, his tortured mind once again plagued by painful memories and bitter regrets. He wasn't so inebriated that he couldn't appreciate Brin's sage advice. After all, it was no more than he had been telling himself since his arrival in town.

A heavy sigh escaped him. Had he really been so unjust? Had hurt and bitter disappointment clouded his judgement? He closed his eyes, trying desperately to blot out the heart-rending image of his wife's lovely face when last he had seen her; of the look of sheer desolation in those beautiful grey-green eyes of hers. No matter how well he had succeeded in hoodwinking Society as a whole, he had found precious little enjoyment, precious little solace here in London. Even those times spent in the voluptuous widow's bed had not succeeded in erasing Elizabeth from his mind, and during the past week he had experienced no desire to visit Lady Torrington at all. Their brief liaison was over. It was to his shame that it had begun in the first place.

Yes, Brin was right: remaining in London was achieving

nothing. If, as his friend suspected, Elizabeth had agreed to become his wife because she loved him, then all was far from lost. It might take him a long time to come to terms with her deception, but he still cared enough to try.

Rising rather unsteadily from the chair, he gave the bell-pull by the marble grate three hard tugs, and almost at once the door opened. 'Make the necessary arrangements, Medway. I leave for Hampshire in the morning.'

Richard arrived back at Knightley Hall the following afternoon. At first everything seemed quite normal, as lovely and tranquil as ever. The lawn at the front of the house had been recently cut, there wasn't a weed to be seen in any one of the numerous flower beds, nor on the paths, and the early May sunshine seemed to enhance the golden warmth of the mansion's deep yellow stone, making the whole place feel so wonderfully welcoming.

As he approached the front entrance the door was thrown wide and he knew at once that all was not as it should be by his butler's grave expression as he came out to meet him.

'Thank goodness you've returned, sir! I wanted to send word to you, but was informed that you weren't to be told.'

'Told what, Finch?'

'About the mistress, sir. Very poorly she is.'

Richard looked at the ageing retainer sharply. 'What's wrong with her?'

'Typhus,' Finch responded in a whisper, as though to speak the dreaded word aloud were to sign his lovely young mistress's death warrant.

Sublimely disregarding Finch's warning to keep well clear of the sickroom, Richard bounded up the staircase and, after a perfunctory scratch on the door, entered his wife's room to see the faithful Agatha seated beside the bed with some sewing resting in her lap. Betraying a moment's surprise at his unexpected appearance, she rose at once and he could see instantly that she was looking tired and drawn through lack of sleep.

'How long has she been ill, Aggie?' he asked, having fallen into the habit before leaving Devonshire of using his wife's pet name when addressing the maid.

'Almost a week, sir.'

Without another word Richard strode across to the bed and placed a gentle hand on his wife's forehead. She was burning hot, her cheeks a feverish scarlet against the whiteness of the pillow. She murmured something and moved her left hand as though wanting to brush his away. It was such a pathetically weak and helpless gesture that he experienced a surge of compassion, swiftly followed by a veritable torrent of self-disgust as his eyes focused on the solitary ring on her third finger.

It was he who had slid that plain gold band into position and the reason he had done so was quite simply that he had desperately wanted her as his wife. There had been no question in his own mind of a forced union between them because of what had occurred that night at the Chilthams' house, and he had felt fairly certain that she had felt the same, no matter how many times he had tried to convince himself to the contrary during his stay in London.

She was without question a lovely, desirable young woman who possessed many fine qualities, but, even so, he would never have sought her hand in marriage if it hadn't been for the undeniable fact that for the first time in his life he had fallen deeply in love.

Perhaps this depth of feeling went some way to explain his cruel and unreasonable attitude on the night before he had left for London. Any man would feel deeply hurt and resentful at discovering the woman he loved so much had played him false, but this was a poor excuse for his behaviour. He had allowed battered feelings to override common sense. She had wished to explain, but his confounded pride would not even grant her that small courtesy. Pray God he was allowed to make amends for his cruelly insensitive attitude!

'Why didn't you send for me at once, Aggie?' His voice, edged with censure, sounded rather harsher than he had intended, but she held his reproachful gaze steadily, and he knew the answer even before she said,

'She wouldn't hear of it, sir. Said it wasn't necessary to disturb you.' Her young mistress's sentiments had lost a little something in the retelling, but Agatha couldn't bring herself to repeat, 'Don't you dare to send for that black-hearted demon, Aggie! Let him rot in London with his filthy whores!'

Sir Richard regarded her rather quizzically for a moment, but thankfully didn't probe further, and after a moment asked how his wife had managed to contract the dreaded scourge.

Once again Agatha found herself in something of a quandary. She had no intention of being disloyal by disclosing that her mistress had been behaving quite out of character, almost like a thing possessed, galloping about the countryside alone on her husband's most spirited mount, not caring what happened to her.

'She was wont to explore the surrounding countryside, sir. One day about three weeks back she came upon a village some five miles distant, and learned of a family in trouble. Poor folk they were, sir, with no money for doctors and the like. Lady Knightley has never been one to turn the other way when she sees folk in trouble. She purchased medicines and visited every day. The widowed mother and youngest child were very poorly, sir. The little girl died, but the mother was on the mend when my lamb goes and takes the sickness.'

Her lip trembled, but she managed to keep her emotions

firmly under control. 'She knew the danger she were in, sir, but refused to put anyone else at risk. She went nowhere near your little niece, and kept clear of the servants, having her meals brought up here on a tray, but she couldn't stop me tending her. I've kept my distance from the others too, sir, since my mistress took sick.'

He regarded her with the utmost respect. 'Well, you cannot continue to nurse her on your own. You're worn out, Aggie. From now on we'll take it in turns to sit with her. Go and get some sleep. We'll talk again later.'

She seemed to debate within herself for a moment, then went slowly to the door, but turned back to add, 'I did take it upon myself to send for Tom, sir. Sent an express to Bristol three days ago.'

'Tom?' he echoed, not realising for a moment to whom she referred.

'Dr Thomas Carrington. A fine young physician he be. He'll come, sir. I know he will. If anyone can pull my little lamb through, he can!'

Richard wished he had her faith, and during the next few hours there were occasions when he began to think that nothing short of a miracle would save his wife. In his most despondent moments he would tell himself that he had precious little experience of sickrooms, and that her condition probably looked far more serious to him than, in fact, it was. When she moved her head, in vain attempts to find a cooler spot on the pillow, all he could do was bathe her face with water scented with lavender, which brought vividly to mind his own convalescence in Brussels the year before and with it bittersweet memories of Mary. He had lost that wonderful young woman through no fault of his own, but that had not stopped him suffering the most searing pangs of guilt during the past months. How much deeper would the pain of guilt eat into him if he were to lose Elizabeth too? Had stupid pride not induced him to desert her, she wouldn't be in this condition now.

An unexpected knock on the door pierced his mood of black gloom, and Finch entered to inform him that a gentleman by the name of Carrington had called.

'Furthermore, a gentleman who refuses to be kept waiting in the hall,' a deep, authoritative voice announced from somewhere behind the butler, and a moment later a tall, powerfully built young man with overlong, waving light-brown hair and a pair of piercing clear grey eyes came striding purposefully into the room, almost thrusting Finch aside as he did so.

Richard rose from the chair and found his outstretched hand taken for a moment in a firm clasp. 'Thank you for coming so swiftly, Dr Carrington. Did you journey in a hired carriage?' At the brief nod of confirmation, Richard turned to his butler. 'Have Dr Carrington's baggage brought in and pay the post boys, and then arrange for one of the maids to wake Miss Stigwell. Also inform Cook that there will be a guest for dinner, and have a bedchamber made ready.'

'As close to this one as possible,' the doctor added before going across and seating himself on the bed.

Richard watched the butler leave the room and then turned his attention to the young man who had already begun to examine Lady Knightley.

Thomas Carrington was unlike any other doctor Richard had ever seen before. He was young, twenty-seven—eight, at most—with a tall, lean and athletic figure, kept finely honed by moderate eating and hard work, no doubt. The waving hair reached the collar of a coat that was both unfashionable and slightly worn in places. His rather shabby appearance gave one to suppose that his practice in Bristol was not precisely lucrative, but if this were the case, then it certainly wasn't through a lack of medical expertise, for he carried out a brief examination with faultless efficiency.

With a sound of impatience Dr Carrington glanced at the bandages on Elizabeth's arms, evidence of the bloodletting performed by the local physician the day before. Then he placed his hand on her forehead and gently raised each eyelid in turn.

'Elizabeth. Elizabeth, come, wake up,' he commanded in a voice that was both gently coaxing and imperious. 'Come, my little love. Open your eyes. It's Tom...your Tom.'

Richard stood as though turned to stone. Anyone listening to the doctor might be forgiven for thinking that the young woman lying in the bed was his wife, such was the unmistakable note of tenderness in the deep attractive voice. The most dreadful suspicion began to take root, and it certainly didn't help restore his peace of mind to see Elizabeth's eyes flutter open and to see a hand weakly raised to the doctor's cheek.

It was perhaps just as well that Agatha chose that auspicious moment to re-enter, for Richard was battling with the almost overwhelming desire to grasp that worn collar firmly, haul Dr Carrington from the room and kick him down the stairs.

'Ah, Aggie, well timed!' A boyish smile erased the serious lines in the young doctor's face. 'Come over here and lend a hand. And while you're about it you can tell me what this young madam has been doing to herself.'

'Perhaps, when you've finished examining my wife, you would care to join me in the library?' Without giving Dr Carrington time to respond to the curtly spoken suggestion, Richard swung round on his heels and left the room.

Trying desperately to control the rising anger, and marshal his wildly conflicting thoughts, he went down to his library and poured himself a stiff drink. The conviction that there was something rather more than mere friendship between Elizabeth and the young physician refused to be quashed, but by the time the doctor had joined him he had at least managed to regain a modicum of control over his temper.

'It's typhus right enough,' Dr Carrington confirmed without preamble as he accepted the glass held out to him and sat himself in a chair. 'The good news is that it's a milder form of this scourge. Her head aches continually and she's more feverish at nights, but that's only to be expected.'

This brought some comfort, but anxiety still remained. 'But one of the people my wife took it upon herself to nurse died,' Richard pointed out.

'Yes, so Aggie informed me. A little girl, I understand.' One of the doctor's broad shoulders rose, but the shrug didn't seem one of indifference, more that of inevitability. 'Bad diets and lack of hygiene make the poor much more vulnerable to disease. Thankfully, Elizabeth is not of that class.'

He paused for a moment to savour his wine, but his clear grey eyes never wavered from Sir Richard's face. 'I should like to remain for a few days. I don't envisage any complications arising, but one can never be one-hundred-percent certain. However, it would be most unethical for me to treat your wife without you informing your own practitioner that you have sought a second opinion, sir.'

Richard didn't even take a moment to consider. No matter what suspicions he might still be harbouring he felt, like Aggie, that one could put complete trust in this young man's abilities. 'I shall inform him of my intention today.'

'Very well. I shall, you understand, be able to remain only three days, four at the most. I cannot desert my other patients for long. Aggie, of course, is extremely capable, but Elizabeth can twist her round her little finger.' A sudden frown creased the high, intelligent forehead. 'Whilst I remain the little wretch will do as she's bidden. She'd not dare to do otherwise! But when I'm gone, Sir Richard, I rely on you to ensure that she takes the medicines I've prescribed. She isn't going to recover from this overnight.'

'You may rely on me, Doctor.'

'I was certain I could.' Tut-tutting, Thomas Carrington stared broodingly down into the contents of his glass. 'Of course, I was expecting something of the sort to happen sooner or later, and I blame Mary for it.'

'Mary?' Richard experienced that all-too-frequent spasm of pain. Would the mere mention of that particular name always affect him so deeply?

'Elizabeth's grandmother, Mrs Mary Smithson. Didn't you ever meet her?'

'No, I was denied that pleasure,' Richard responded, suddenly recalling those moments in church when they had exchanged their vows. 'Elizabeth's second name is Mary. She must have been named after her grandmother, I suppose.'

'Very likely,' Dr Carrington responded without much interest. 'As I was about to explain, the old lady spoilt Elizabeth quite shockingly during the six years they lived together. Mary worshipped the ground her granddaughter walked on. There wasn't anything she wouldn't do for the girl; refused her absolutely nothing. Still...' he shrugged one broad shoulder again '...there's some excuse, I suppose, when you consider the life the poor girl endured before she lived with Mary.'

Richard was instantly alert. 'Yes, I've heard mention of that... Didn't get on too well with her sister, so I understand.'

'You don't know the half of it, sir.' He muttered something unrepeatable under his breath. 'I hope to God I never come face to face with that sister of hers!'

Richard regarded him keenly. It was evident to anyone of the meanest intelligence that the doctor was touchingly fond of Elizabeth, and yet there was naught of the lover in his manner when he spoke of her. 'You're very fond of my wife, aren't you?'

The doctor's rare and rather charming smile flashed out. 'Yes, very,' he freely admitted. 'She's the nearest I've ever had to a sister.' He then fell into a reminiscent mood, recalling the many times he had been forced to take her out on his visits, simply because she would only have followed him had he not done so. He spoke of their years together at Mary Smithson's house with gentle affection, his voice tender for the most part, but occasionally spiced with disapproval at what he considered Elizabeth's frequently headstrong behaviour.

As Richard listened intently to the softly spoken reminiscences, he became increasingly convinced that there had never been anything deeper than a loving brother-sister relationship between his wife and the young practitioner; and by the time he retired to his bed that night he was not only beginning to like Dr Carrington very well, but admire him too.

During the following days Richard was more than happy to leave his wife's well-being in the doctor's capable hands; although Dr Carrington spent a great deal of time in the sickroom, Richard was offered numerous opportunities to enjoy his company. His admiration and liking for the serious young man rapidly grew, and he became increasingly convinced that such a dedicated and gifted person ought to be offered every assistance to better himself. But climb the professional ladder Dr Carrington could not if he remained in his present situation.

During the many hours they spent together, Richard discovered that Mrs Smithson had left Thomas a sum of money in her will, but by his rather shabby appearance it was quite obvious that he hadn't spent a penny of this bequest on even modest luxuries. His dedication to the poor of Bristol was commendable, but the poor couldn't afford doctors' bills, and Richard suspected that Thomas had been tapping into this inheritance just to survive. Although the bequest had been substantial, it wouldn't last forever, and Richard couldn't help but feel that the money could be put to better use. The doctor was a young man with radical opinions, but his views would never achieve recognition if he didn't gain the respect of his peers, and the only way to achieve this end was to become accepted and respected by people of Sir Richard's own social standing.

On the day of Thomas's departure, Richard suggested that they go out for a ride. Thomas had ridden out with his host on several occasions and, as he was a great believer in fresh air and regular exercise, readily agreed. It was only when he found himself a short while later, seated astride his borrowed mount before a charming red-brick house, located in the centre of the thriving market town some three miles distance from Knightley Hall, that he began to think there was rather more to this excursion than a final enjoyable ride out together.

He cast his companion a penetrating glance, wondering why on earth he should have wished to come here, before dismounting and tying the reins to the metal railing. 'Yes, a very attractive property in an ideal position, I should say, Richard,' he remarked, having dropped all formality during their first evening together. He followed his silent host up the short path to the front entrance. 'Who owns it? A thriving lawyer, perhaps?'

'No, I do,' Richard responded, drawing a key from his pocket and unlocking the door. 'My father had it built for one of his aunts. Great-aunt Matilda was a dear soul, and much loved. Being extremely kind-hearted, my father was prepared to take an interest in her well-being, but was not prepared to endure her incessant prattling up at the Hall. Consequently, this house was erected at a discreet distance. She outlived him by some ten years, as it happens. For some reason my brother couldn't bring himself to sell the place and, since Great-aunt Matilda's demise, the property has been rented out from time to time. As you can see, at present it awaits a new tenant…and I sincerely hope that you will take up that position.'

Offering his rather astonished companion no opportunity to respond, Richard commenced a guided tour of the excellently maintained property, which offered all the creature comforts, while at the same time explaining the reasoning behind his unexpected suggestion.

Without interruption Tom listened intently to all the arguments put forward for his removal from Bristol and his setting up of a new country practice, and when Richard led the way back down the stairs to the large front parlour, he said in his usual no-nonsense and practical way,

'I'd find little time for entertaining morning callers, and this room would make an excellent apothecary's shop. It could be fitted out quite easily. It would have the added benefit, of course, of inducing people who might not otherwise make the attempt to come to the doctor's house, where the physician might be on hand to diagnose precisely what ailed them.' He sighed. 'It's tempting, Richard, I can't deny it, but I have patients in Bristol who are in desperate need of my services. There's no one else to whom they can turn.'

'Tom, there are poor everywhere, even here,' he countered. 'Are the needs of poor country folk less than those in the towns? Had there been a practitioner with a ha'p'orth of fellow feeling in him in this area, Elizabeth would not be suffering now.'

The truth of this hitting him quite forcibly, Tom went over to stand by the window. The street was busy with many townsfolk going about their daily business. He quickly caught sight of a child who had obviously contracted rickets in infancy. A moment later a man of about his own age went by, dragging his left leg which, Tom suspected, had been broken at some time, and badly set. Yes, Richard was only too right: the poor were everywhere.

'Would you give me a week or two to think it over?' he said at length. 'I'm not unappreciative of the opportunity you've given me to set up a practice here and move into this house at a ridiculously low rent, but I have many considerations to take into account.'

'Take all the time you need,' Richard assured him, but Tom shook his head.

'No, I'm accustomed to coming to decisions quickly. A week will suffice, two at the most.' He regarded his companion with a deal of respect. 'I wondered why Elizabeth, who shares a deal of my views, should have suddenly upped and married a peer of the realm… But I rather think, now, that I'm beginning to understand.'

But I am not at all certain why she did, Richard thought, turning abruptly to lead the way out of the house. But I mean to find out!

Chapter Nine

Releasing her breath in a heavy sigh of discontentment, Elizabeth, decidedly lacking her usual grace, slumped down on the *chaise-longue* in her bedchamber. By the quite painless act of lowering her eyelids it was a simple matter to blot out her elegant surroundings. Would that she could erase so easily the painful truth of her present situation!

During those weeks of her illness Richard couldn't possibly have shown more consideration for her well-being. Since the day of Tom's departure he had made a habit of visiting this room several times a day. At first she had felt highly resentful, deeming his presence nothing more than an unwanted intrusion, and she had certainly made her feelings quite plain by frequent bouts of ill-humour; but as the days had passed she had grown accustomed to his visits, even if she had been unable to bring herself to greet his arrivals with any degree of enthusiasm.

There was no denying that she hadn't made an easy patient, she mused, managing a semblance of a smile. The illness, naturally, had brought with it a lowness of spirits, but the disease could not be held entirely responsible for those frequent swings in mood: one moment accepting her lot with a kind of resigned, placid indifference; the next, bitterly resentful, when nothing anyone said or did seemed to please her. Poor Aggie had had a deal to contend with, and Richard, too, for that matter, for he had not infrequently been on the receiving end of some barbed remark, and had even had the occasional object hurled in his direction.

But she had absolutely no excuse now for behaving like some overindulged, unruly child. She was, perhaps, a little thinner than she had been before her illness, but getting stronger with each passing day. There really was no reason now for remaining in her rooms. She was no danger to others any longer, and so she really ought, she supposed, to think about resuming her duties once again as mistress of this house... But how many of Lady Knightley's duties was she willing to resume?

She couldn't deny that she still felt a deal of resentment towards her husband. His cruel, unjust accusations remained firmly embedded in her memory, just as surely as if each bitter word had been branded there with a red-hot iron. The hatred that had consumed her on the morning of his departure to London had long since ebbed away, leaving discontent and mistrust at every thing he said and did in its wake. She had times without number tried to convince herself that she no longer cared for him in the least, that he had completely destroyed the deep love she had once borne him, but if that were the case, why then had she felt such searing pangs of jealousy when she had learned from one of their not-so-pleasant neighbours about the light-skirt his name was being linked with in London? And why had she felt so bitterly resentful yesterday when he had unexpectedly announced his intention of returning to the city that morning?

The bedchamber door opened and she turned her head to see Agatha, carrying Juliet in her arms, enter the room. This was the first time for several weeks that she had seen the little girl and her bright smile of recognition and squeal of delight did Elizabeth more good than a dozen bottles of the very best tonic could possibly have done.

'There! I said she wouldn't have forgotten you,' Agatha announced, plumping the two-year-old infant down on her mistress's lap.

Instantly Juliet reached up a hand to Elizabeth's hair, which was loosely dressed and cascading about her shoulders. 'Ouch! I see your manners haven't improved any, young lady,' she admonished gently, trying to free the silken strands from the podgy clenched fingers. 'And you're certainly heavier. We'll need to put you on a diet at this rate.'

'The master spoils her. And you, too, for that matter,' Agatha proclaimed with a loud sniff of disapproval. 'The poor man has the patience of a saint, so he has!'

Elizabeth, knowing only too well what lay at the root of the disapprobation, raised her eyes from Juliet's cherubic face and fixed them on her maid's displeased countenance. 'I do realise, Aggie, that for some time I haven't been quite myself; if, during my recent illness, I've been less than fair in my dealings with you then I can only apologise and thank you for your forbearance in putting up with my megrims.'

Now, this was much more like her darling Elizabeth of old, so considerate to others' feelings! A smile pulled at her nutcracker mouth, but Agatha easily suppressed it and continued in the same censorious tone as she said, 'It isn't me you should be apologising to. You didn't hurl that soup bowl or that glass of lemonade in my direction. Any other man would have taken a birch-rod to you, ill as you were!'

Elizabeth wasn't so successful at suppressing a smile, wicked though it was. The glass of lemonade she had hurled had narrowly missed his head, but the soup bowl, depending on whose viewpoint you happened to take, met with more success, its contents ending up down the front of her husband's immaculately cut blue superfine jacket.

'He shouldn't have been forever badgering me about eating my meals,' she offered in a feeble attempt to justify her appalling behaviour. 'For heaven's sake, Aggie, he was enough to try the patience of someone with the most placid of temperaments! He never entered this room without demanding to know whether I'd eaten my food or taken my medicine.'

'Well, of course he did!' Agatha countered in defence of her absent master for whom she had acquired a deal of respect during the weeks since his return from London. 'He was desperately concerned about you. Any fool could see that!'

Elizabeth didn't need reminding of this but, unlike Aggie, who evidently looked upon him as some kind of paragon of all the virtues, she was suspicious of his motives. After all, his reputation had certainly been liberally stained during his weeks away from Knightley Hall. How much more might his character have been blackened had he remained in London to enjoy the widow's charms whilst his wife had been in Hampshire, and so desperately ill?

She came out of her musings to discover her maid regarding her rather quizzically. 'I am hardly in a position to apologise to your master, now am I, Aggie?' she pointed out with a touch of asperity. 'He returned to the metropolis yesterday, or had you forgotten?'

'He's back now,' was the surprising response. 'Arrived about half an hour ago.' She turned and went out of the room, thereby hiding the wickedly satisfied smile that this time she was unable to suppress.

Reports of Sir Richard's amorous activities during his spring sojourn in the capital had also come to Agatha's ears. One of the parlourmaids, whose sister happened to be in the service of that acid-tongued Lady Pentecost—whose home, unfortunately, was not four miles distant from Knightley Hall—had been indiscreet enough to spread rumours of her master's rather disreputable behaviour. Agatha had known by the sudden change in Elizabeth's behaviour that she also had got wind of her husband's unfortunate liaison with the sophisticated widow and, during those two weeks before she had taken the sickness, she had betrayed more than just angry discontent. No matter how often Lady Knightley had tried to convince herself that she no longer cared for her husband, Agatha knew better, for where there was no love there could be no jealousy and her poor young mistress had been—and still was, for that matter—suffering from a surfeit of that particular emotion.

Not that Agatha considered there was any need to be remotely jealous this time. After all, Sir Richard had stayed away only one night. She doubted very much that he had taken the trouble to visit his light o' love, but even if he had, it stood to reason that the widow's charms had offered insufficient inducement to remain in the capital.

Elizabeth, too, had swiftly come to the same conclusion, but she was not permitted to dwell on this rather puzzling circumstance. Juliet, having slipped to the floor, was making a beeline for those fascinating little bottles on her aunt's dressing-table, and Elizabeth was too occupied in trying to keep the little girl out of mischief to dwell in any great depth on her husband's behaviour.

They were engaged in a game of peek-a-boo when the bedchamber door opened again. Thinking that it was Agatha returning in order to collect Juliet for her afternoon nap, Elizabeth didn't look to see who, in fact, had entered until Juliet, suddenly uttering a squeal of delight, padded across to the door, and she peered round the end of the *chaise-longue* to see the little girl being held in a pair of strong, muscular arms.

It was difficult in the extreme trying to convey the im-

pression that one had returned to the elegantly poised and
sensible young woman of yore when one was on one's
hands and knees, peering round an item of furniture as
though one had been caught red-handed in some slight misdemeanour. It certainly did little to restore a modicum of
self-possession to see a pair of dark brown eyes regarding
her with a kind of amused interest, either. Fortunately help
arrived in the form of Agatha who entered to collect Juliet,
and the brief interruption offered Elizabeth the opportunity
to rise to her feet and put to rights her slightly dishevelled
appearance.

'I didn't expect you back so soon,' she remarked lightly
in an attempt to break the uncomfortable silence when
Agatha had left them. No response, however, was forthcoming and the amused gleam in his eyes seemed more
than ever pronounced. 'I thought you would remain away
for several days.'

'My business was accomplished quickly, so there was no
reason for me to remain in town.' He detected the scornful
look which for just one unguarded moment glinted in the
depths of her eyes, and decided it might be wise to change
the subject. 'During my brief time away you seem to have
improved vastly.'

This was the first occasion he had seen her dressed in
anything other than one of her night-gowns for what
seemed a considerable time. She looked utterly charming
in the simple sprigged-muslin gown, and appeared much
younger, too, with her lovely russet-coloured locks cascading loosely about her shoulders. 'As you deem yourself
strong enough to indulge in playful games with our niece,
perhaps you might consider resuming your other duties?'

Ever watchful for any slight change in her mood, he was
instantly aware of the sudden tension in her, even before
she took a hasty step behind the couch, for all the world
like a frightened child who expected to be severely repri-

manded. He was well aware of what lay behind the sudden panic, and didn't hesitate to reassure her.

'I don't expect you to resume all your duties immediately, of course, only those you feel—er—able to undertake.' The wary look remained in her eyes and he couldn't forbear a smile as he went over to the door. 'Perhaps you would care to accompany me down to the library? I called at the receiving office on my way home and there are one or two letters for you.'

This was the first time that Elizabeth had ventured out of her bedchamber since she had become ill. She felt suddenly very vulnerable as she led the way down the stairs, and it took a monumental effort not to run back to the sanctuary of her bedchamber, but by the time she had seated herself at her husband's desk in the pleasant book-lined room, and was halfway through reading a letter from her dear friend Viscountess Dartwood, she began to feel more relaxed in the house which she had loved from that moment when she had first stepped into the hall. Nevertheless, she seemed unable to stop herself from casting the odd furtive glance in her husband's direction just to check what he was doing.

Richard unexpectedly rose from his chair, startling her, and without asking poured her a glass of wine. 'Here, drink this,' he ordered. 'It might help to calm you.'

'I'm perfectly all right,' she assured him, but accepted the filled glass, all the same.

'In that case stop staring at me as though I were a serpent about to strike. What does your friend Verity have to say?' he asked, deciding that channelling her thoughts in a different direction might be beneficial. 'I trust they are all well down there in Devonshire?'

'Very. Little Arthur, apparently, is growing rapidly.' She kept half an eye on him as he moved round the desk, suddenly conscious of how tall and strong he was. Even the powerful masculinity he exuded, which had in the past attracted her, now seemed a threat in itself.

She gave herself a mental shake, determined to appear outwardly calm in his presence, at least. 'Evidently you wrote apprising them of my illness.'

'Yes, I did. Verity was all for coming here to see you, but I managed to dissuade her. Perhaps a little later in the year we can invite them to stay?' He watched the slender, tapering fingers raise the glass to her lips. She was still a little thinner than he would have liked, but apart from that, and this sudden and totally unnecessary diffidence in his company, she appeared to have got over her recent illness remarkably well.

'Perhaps in the autumn you would care to accompany me to the capital? We need stay only a week or two, but it would grant me the opportunity to introduce you to a number of people who are wishful to make your acquaintance.'

She didn't respond, but always vigilant for any slight change in her, he didn't miss the sudden veil of contempt that passed over her strikingly pretty features. He didn't doubt that his associating with a certain widow had come to her ears, but now was not the time to offer an explanation about an affair which ought never to have taken place, and which, although she was not to know it, had ended weeks before.

'The subject of a future sojourn in the town house,' he continued in a conversational way, 'brings me to another matter I wish to discuss with you. It concerns Finch's replacement.'

This drew her eyes to his. 'Is he leaving us, then?'

'My dear, he has turned seventy. You must have noticed how badly he suffers from rheumatism. It's high time he was pensioned off. The servants are your department, and

I don't wish to interfere, but if you would prefer that I broached the subject with him then, of course, I shall.'

'Yes, yes, I would prefer that you spoke to him.' It was a cowardly way out, perhaps, but she didn't feel up to such a distasteful task just yet. She was very fond of the ageing retainer who had from the day she had become mistress of this lovely house always shown her the utmost respect. But Richard was right—it was pitiful to see the poor man coping with the stairs so many times during a day.

'He has been with your family for so many years that I think the suggestion of his retirement would be better coming from you. I'd hate him to think that I have found him wanting in any way. But at the same time, like yourself, I consider the position would be better served by a younger man.'

'Very well, I shall deal with it. I think Medway, who is in charge of the town house, would be the ideal replacement. I'll send for him. I should like you to see him first before I offer him the position here. If for any reason you take him in dislike, or think him unsuitable, then we can always look elsewhere for a new butler.'

'I'm sure I shall find him perfectly satisfactory, but send for him by all means,' she agreed, thinking how natural it seemed discussing such topics with him. She felt the tension in her ebbing away, but sadly the rapport between them was not destined to last for very much longer.

'I could wish that my other rather unenviable task might prove to be as easy. Hodge,' he explained when she cast him a questioning glance. 'It's high time he retired, too. I should have replaced him soon after I returned here last year.'

'Then why didn't you, Richard?'

'Oh, I don't know,' he responded, running impatient fingers through his hair. 'I suppose I didn't want him to think that I held him in any way responsible for my brother's

GET FREE BOOKS and a FREE GIFT
WHEN YOU PLAY THE...

Lucky 7

Just scratch off the silver box with a coin. Then check below to see the gifts you get!

SLOT MACHINE GAME!

YES! I have scratched off the silver box. Please send me the 2 free Harlequin Historicals® books and gift for which I qualify. I understand I am under no obligation to purchase any books, as explained on the back of this card.

349 HDL DFT4

246 HDL DFT3
(H-HB-OS-11/01)

NAME   (PLEASE PRINT CLEARLY)

ADDRESS

APT.#   CITY

STATE/PROV.   ZIP/POSTAL CODE

7	7	7	Worth TWO FREE BOOKS plus a BONUS Mystery Gift!
🍒	🍒	🍒	Worth TWO FREE BOOKS!
♣	♣	♣	Worth ONE FREE BOOK!
🔔	🔔	🍒	TRY AGAIN!

Visit us online at www.eHarlequin.com

Offer limited to one per household and not valid to current Harlequin Historicals® subscribers. All orders subject to approval.

© 2000 HARLEQUIN ENTERPRISES LTD. ® and TM are trademarks owned by Harlequin Enterprises Ltd.

The Harlequin Reader Service® — Here's how it works:

Accepting your 2 free books and gift places you under no obligation to buy anything. You may keep the books and gift and return the shipping statement marked "cancel." If you do not cancel, about a month later we'll send you 6 additional novels and bill you just $4.05 each in the U.S., or $4.46 each in Canada, plus 25¢ shipping & handling per book and applicable taxes if any.* That's the complete price and — compared to cover prices of $4.99 each in the U.S. and $5.99 each in Canada — it's quite a bargain! You may cancel at any time, but if you choose to continue, every month we'll send you 6 more books, which you may either purchase at the discount price or return to us and cancel your subscription.

*Terms and prices subject to change without notice. Sales tax applicable in N.Y. Canadian residents will be charged applicable provincial taxes and GST.

death. He happened to be tooling the carriage at the time of the accident. Thankfully, he managed to jump clear before it tumbled down the ravine.'

'Do you think the accident might have been avoided if a younger man had been in charge of the equipage?' she asked gently, and instantly he shook his head.

'No, I don't. I visited the spot where it happened, a narrow stretch of road, twisting and turning with a steep drop on either side. Hodge reacted instinctively. But that doesn't alter the fact that he's not up to the job any longer. He's so damnably forgetful. Why, look at what happened when we dined that night with your sister. Any servant worth his salt would have taken the trouble to enquire whether or not we had decided to remain for the night, instead of dropping off to sleep inside the carriage and forgetting all about us.'

She was instantly on her guard, with every nerve end in her body suddenly growing taut. 'That, perhaps, was a little remiss of him. But you can hardly hold him to blame for the unfortunate repercussions of that night.'

He looked across the desk at her searchingly. It had never been his intention to allude to that particular incident at all, or what had been the outcome, but now the subject had been raised he decided it would be rather foolish to try to pretend that what had happened between them had never taken place. Surely it would be better to thrash their differences out now so that a new beginning could be embarked upon without recriminations on either side?

'I don't blame Hodge for what happened between us shortly after our marriage had taken place, Elizabeth.'

'No,' she responded levelly. 'You blame me.'

'Not entirely, no,' he countered, holding her suddenly hard-eyed scrutiny. 'Neither of us is entirely blameless. Do you think my anger so unreasonable after what I had discovered about you?'

For a moment he thought she would stubbornly refuse

to answer, but then she said in a voice that was all the more disheartening because it betrayed no emotion whatsoever, 'Perhaps there was some slight justification for your behaviour. But we cannot change the past, even if we should wish to.'

Rising to her feet, she went slowly to the door, but turned back to add rather unexpectedly, 'You were certainly right about one thing, Richard. My sister did intend that I should spend that night in her cellar. It's my honest belief that she hoped to force me into marriage... But you were most certainly not her choice for the groom.'

Richard was too stunned by the admission to think clearly for a few moments, and by the time the full import of what she had disclosed had permeated his brain she had already left the room.

Going across to the decanters once again, he felt that it was he, now, in need of some urgent fortification. Carrying the glass of Madeira back over to the window, he stared sightlessly across his many acres of delightful rolling park land while his mind went over the events during their stay in Devonshire.

So, Elizabeth had at last admitted that the night they had spent in the Chilthams' cellar had been planned; contrived, seemingly, not by herself, but by her sister. And there was little doubt in his own mind that Lord Chiltham's brother ought to have been the one to bear Elizabeth company during those hours of confinement, and not he. His eyes narrowed, but not against the sun's bright afternoon rays. When, precisely, had Elizabeth uncovered her sister's despicable plot? She hadn't suspected initially; of that he felt certain. But, assuredly, at some point during their stay in Devon she had discovered her sister's perfidy.

He doubted very much that Evadne had admitted to it herself. She hadn't once taken the trouble to pay a visit to the Dartwoods after the night of the dinner-party, not even to congratulate them on the birth of their son. Might she have written Elizabeth a letter confessing her sins? Somehow he doubted it. From what he had learned from Verity and Brin, and more recently from Thomas Carrington, he now had a pretty shrewd notion of Lady Chiltham's true character. She was a deviously cunning woman who would never admit to any misdemeanour in a letter, where it might be used against her at some later date. No, he doubted that Elizabeth had learned the truth of the matter from her sister... So who on earth had the informant been?

He was destined not to discover anything further that day nor, which added to his frustrations, during the following few days. Although Elizabeth resumed her duties as mistress of Knightley Hall with praiseworthy efficiency, she retained that air of reticence whenever she found herself alone with him, but at all other times her behaviour was exemplary.

When they dined together she was always politely conversational and when they made or received visits from neighbours her manners were faultless. He couldn't fail to notice, however, that whenever he assisted her in and out of the carriage her hand would rest in his only for the briefest of moments before it was withdrawn rather abruptly, and she would never remain alone with him for longer than was absolutely necessary.

It would, he knew, be highly detrimental to hint that he was wishful for more intimate relations between them to begin again, even though with every passing day he was finding it more and more of a strain to keep his desire for her firmly under control. It was patently obvious that she mistrusted him now; clear, too, that she had every intention of remaining aloof and keeping him at a distance. Any fool could see that she was nowhere near ready for a resumption of all her wifely duties, and until he had once more managed to rekindle her respect and regard, he must remain understanding and, most of all, patient.

But as the days turned into a week, and then a second, he looked for any slight change in her attitude towards him in vain. Despondency took a firm hold, and he began to think that they would never again live together as man and wife; that she would never completely forgive him for his outburst on that never-to-be-forgotten night, nor for his wanton disregard for her feelings in trying foolishly to find solace for a short while in another woman's arms. Having her so close and yet not daring to risk more than a fleeting contact was more than flesh and blood could withstand, and he was rapidly reaching the point where he despaired of ever rekindling her love when help came from an unlooked-for and most unexpected quarter.

He had not forgotten the need to attend to several of the chimneys at the Hall. The long, warm summer days continued, and it was the ideal time to put this problem to rights. On the morning the sweep and his apprentice arrived Richard rode out early to visit a tenant. Finch, who was quite surprisingly looking forward to his retirement, knew precisely which chimneys were causing concern and directed the sweep to the various rooms.

It was getting close to lunch time when the house echoed with several terrified, pitiful squeals. Elizabeth, writing a letter to Viscountess Dartwood, was seated in the small parlour at the back of the house, which she had turned into her own private study. Clearly hearing the commotion, she went out into the hall to investigate and saw several of the servants huddled round the door leading to the large salon, all peering into the room with apparent rapt interest.

'What on earth is going on, Finch?' she demanded after a further bout of squealing emanated from the salon.

'It's the climbing-boy, my lady. He's disinclined to clean another chimney and the sweep is being rather forceful.'

'Stand aside!' Elizabeth ordered in a hard-edged voice none of the servants had ever heard their kind-hearted mistress use before, and instantly a path was cleared for her to march resolutely into the room in time to see the sweep raise a clenched fist to deliver a further stinging blow to his pathetically sobbing apprentice.

'Don't you dare to hit that unfortunate child again!' Her voice now was icy cold, brooking no argument.

The sweep automatically lowered his fist and stared across the room for a few seconds at the elegantly poised young woman with the commanding voice and the look of revulsion on her pretty face. Then he smacked his thick wet lips together before twisting them into an insolent smirk.

'Now, ma'am, don't you be a-fretting yourself over this young varmint. Jem 'ere needs a cuff or two to make 'im do 'is work.'

Walking slowly towards the overweight, obnoxious individual whose watery eyes betrayed his evident fondness for spirits, even before she was close enough to smell the strong odour of gin about his person, Elizabeth glanced briefly at the cringing child still held firmly in the massive hand. 'Unhand that child at once!'

'Now, ma'am, don't you be a-fretting—'

'There's no need to repeat yourself!' she cut in sharply. 'I heard you clearly enough the first time.'

The grasp loosened sufficiently for the boy to break free and he didn't hesitate to scurry away like a whipped pup, cowering and trembling with fright. Elizabeth looked him over from head to foot. He was a skinny waif of humanity. His clothes were little better than rags, ill-fitting and torn, and beneath the liberal coating of soot and grime she could clearly detect the many bruises and weeping cuts on his painfully thin limbs.

'Come here, child,' she said, softly coaxing and, after a

wary moment when he continued to knuckle his eyes, he took several tentative steps towards her.

Gently raising his shirt, she saw to her horror the clear evidence of ill-treatment: evil red criss-cross welts covering his back. 'Did you do this?'

'Ee be a lazy good-for-nothin',' the sweep growled, casting the child a look which boded ill for him once they had finished their work, and were away from this house and this lady who, despite her youthful appearance, looked as though she might cause a deal of trouble for hardworking folk with her soft-hearted, pernickety views. 'I do right by the lad. Ee's got no cause to complain. When ee do work, ee do get fed proper.'

'Fed? Why, the child's half-starved!' She glanced down briefly at the boy's rather unlovely snub-nosed face. 'How old is he?'

'Ee be ten now, I reckon, or thereabouts. Got 'im from the orphanage two year ago.'

'My God! It's a wonder the poor boy's survived all this time in your tender care!' Elizabeth took her eyes away from the sweep's bloated countenance to glance briefly at the hearth, where several pieces of wood had been placed. 'Why has kindling been put there?'

'Just a little persuasion, like. Do 'elp 'im do 'is work a mite quicker, as yer might say.'

Elizabeth had heard reports of such wicked practices, but up until that moment she couldn't bring herself to believe that a member of the human race could be so mercilessly cruel. Her contemptuous glance swept the man from head to foot, bringing a deeper hue to his normally ruddy complexion.

'He shall not climb another chimney this day, nor ever again!' she announced, determination hardening her pleasant voice. 'Pick up your belongings and leave this house! The boy shall remain here.'

Jem looked up at Elizabeth in a kind of wonder-struck reverence, not quite able to believe that anyone could stand up to his brutal master, least of all a woman, and not daring to hope that in this fine house, of all the unlikely places, he had found a guardian angel who was willing to rescue him from his hitherto miserable existence. His master, on the other hand, saw matters in a far different light, and the belligerent look Jem had seen all too often sprang into the sweep's soulless black eyes.

'I'll leave when I've bin paid for me work, and not until,' he ground out, waving his massive fist threateningly. 'And I'll leave wi' 'im an' all. Ee be my apprentice, and I got me rights.'

'And what rights might those be?' a deep voice queried from the doorway, and Elizabeth, experiencing untold relief, turned to see her husband sauntering in his graceful way towards them.

One glance at the trio standing in front of the large marble grate would have been enough to give Richard a fairly shrewd idea of what had been taking place in his absence, even if he hadn't happened to overhear the latter exchanges between his wife and the sweep. Elizabeth, with the child frantically clutching one of her slender white hands, was regarding him with a look of combined pleading and defiance; and the sweep, who found himself now having to deal with a far more formidable opponent in the form of the master of the house, had evidently decided that it might be wise to adopt a different tack, and had begun to wring his hands together in a subservient and quite nauseating way.

'Your good lady wife, m'lord, being a mite overnice in 'er notions, as yer might say, and not 'aving much experience o' the 'ard life us poor folks be forced to lead, seems to think the boy 'ere be 'ard done by. Which I tell you plainly ee ain't. So, if you just lets us carry on wi' our work, m'lord, we'll be on—'

'What is your name, my good man?' Richard interrupted in a faintly bored tone while removing a speck of fluff from his sleeve.

'Archibald Barton, Master Sweep, at your service, sir,' he responded with the most inelegant attempt at a bow Richard had ever had the misfortune to observe.

'Well, Master Barton, loath though I am to disabuse you, but my wife has had a deal of experience of the life endured by the unfortunate poor, and knows the difference between doing a hard day's work for one's keep and being forced to endure malicious cruelty which borders on slavery.'

Swiftly realising that Sir Richard was not going to prove to be the sympathetic ally for which he had hoped, the sweep dropped the obsequious pose. 'Ee be my apprentice and I gots me rights! I can deal wi' 'im as I like.'

'Not so very long ago a certain person engaged in the same profession as yourself was swiftly disabused of that erroneous belief. He was imprisoned for causing his apprentice's death. The chief magistrate presiding at the trial felt that apprentices had their rights, too, and, being a Christian soul, could not find it within himself to condone such wanton acts of cruelty as lighting fires in hearths to encourage climbing-boys to do their work.'

Richard glanced briefly at the kindling in the hearth before returning his gaze to the sweep whose mien was suddenly chary. 'Our local magistrate is a gentleman with similar views. Do you happen to be acquainted with Sir William Carmichael?' His lips twitched as the sweep visibly blanched. 'Ah, yes! I suspected that your paths might have crossed at some time or other. I think it behoves me to have a word or two with my good friend Sir William on this poor unfortunate child's behalf, but until that time I shall relieve you of your apprentice's companionship.'

He waited a moment or two to allow the sweep to digest this threat fully before adding, 'Now, pick up your belongings and leave. My butler will provide payment for any work already carried out.'

Elizabeth waited until the sweep, muttering a string of oaths under his breath, had left the room before turning to her husband with a look of dawning respect in her eyes. She had known, almost from the day of her arrival at the Hall, that those working in the house and on the estate held their master in high esteem. His concern for his workers' well-being was unimpeachable, but she had not been quite certain in those first few moments after he had entered the room whether he would be willing to display the same altruism towards a being who, in all fairness, had no right to expect it.

'Oh, Richard, how very glad I am that you arrived when you did!' she exclaimed with real gratitude. 'I was experiencing the most lively dread that that hateful man would take this poor unfortunate child away by force.'

'Most would agree that he would have been well within his rights to do so, my dear,' he responded with a wry smile before turning his attention with scant enthusiasm on to the scrap of humanity he had been instrumental in saving from a life of purgatory, short though that may well have turned out to be.

'What's your name, boy?'

'Jeremiah. But erryone calls me Jem, m'lord.'

'When you address me you call me sir, not my lord. And why do you keep scratching that way?'

Jem, who was still retaining a firm hold on Elizabeth's fingers, was putting his other hand to necessary use, alternating beneath his shirt and in his hair. 'I got crawlers, sir. Al'ays 'ad crawlers.'

This rather alarming intelligence sent Elizabeth into whoops of laughter, and her husband, with a look of acute dismay, striding purposefully over to the bell-pull. Finch

appeared in answer to the summons and was quickly despatched for the dependable Miss Stigwell.

'You observe this child, Aggie,' Sir Richard said when
she entered a few minutes later. 'He's no doubt hungry and
would appreciate some food. But first he's in the most urgent need of a bath. He has a deal of unwanted livestock
about his person.'

'Oh, my gawd!'

'Precisely what I thought myself, Aggie,' he responded,
casting his still highly amused wife a dour look. 'When in
your estimable opinion you consider him fit to mix with
the human race, find him something suitable to wear. There
are trunks full of old clothes in the attic. Then take him
down to the kitchen and feed him.'

'Will you be able to find him work on the estate?'
Elizabeth asked when Jem, though rather reluctantly, had
left the room with Agatha.

'I expect so, but just precisely what eludes me for the
moment.'

Smiling with gentle warmth, Elizabeth bridged the distance between them and, without the least hesitation, placed
her hand on her husband's sleeve. 'It was very kind of you,
Richard, to help the child that way. When he's older I'm
sure he'll appreciate what you have done for him, just as I
do now.'

He placed his hand over hers, and for the first time in
what seemed a very long time she made not the least attempt to draw hers away.

Chapter Ten

Elizabeth paused in the act of placing another flower in the vase and glanced about her husband's library. Except for that one and only time, she had always felt extremely comfortable in this room. Which was most strange when she came to consider the matter, she decided, for this room, above any other, seemed to retain its master's powerful aura long after he had left it.

Not that she considered her husband's masculine strength a threat any longer. It was now a little over three weeks since he had suggested that she resume her duties, and she had accompanied him down to this room. She couldn't deny that for a time she had feared he might use that superior strength of his in an attempt to force her into acceding to all that was expected of her as his wife. After all, he had cruelly admitted that the only reason he had married her was to beget an heir.

That, above all those other terrible things he had said to her that night, remained a constant torment, for she had truly believed, when he had made his proposal in Devonshire, that he had loved her. She shook her head, uncertain what to believe any more. Perhaps, though, Aggie was right and he did love her. If that was the case, then she could well understand why he had become so bitterly angry when he had believed she had played him false. Added to which, his considerate behaviour towards her during these past weeks gave her every reason to hope that his feelings for her went rather deeper than mere regard, but he had never put his feelings into words, and until she was absolutely certain in her own mind of the state of his heart, she could not bring herself to lie with him again, at least not willingly.

As though by a natural progression of thought, she began wondering why, in fact, he hadn't demanded his rights as her husband? Her health was no longer a bar to a resumption of intimate relations, and there was no denying that Richard was a virile man, not accustomed, she suspected, to curbing his natural desires. Surely he didn't still suspect her of carrying another man's child? If that were the case then it would be a simple matter, surely, to consult Aggie, with whom he had become wondrous close, and she would swiftly disabuse him. It was possible, of course, that he was satisfying his bodily needs elsewhere. His affair with the vivacious Lady Torrington had, she truly believed, ended, for he had never made a further return visit to the capital. There was always the distinct possibility, though, that he had a paramour living nearby, but somehow she doubted this, though of course she couldn't be completely certain.

She couldn't deny that she remained bitterly resentful over his affair with Lady Torrington, but was honest enough to admit, now, that she must shoulder her share of the blame for his seeking solace in another woman's arms. If she had been totally honest with him from the start, this rather unfortunate beginning to their marriage might have been avoided. So many foolishly kept secrets! So many things which ought to have been explained, not only concerning herself but others, too. Granted the right opportunity, she would willingly tell him everything... But it was, now, a case of the right opportunity arising.

The sound of voices in the hall pierced through her sombre reflections, and moments later the library door swung open and her favourite neighbour swept into the room.

Since her arrival in Hampshire she and Caroline Westbridge had become firm friends. Caroline was the only one, apart from the Rector and his good lady wife, who had paid regular visits during the early part of Elizabeth's illness. Richard had not permitted anyone to visit the sickroom itself until he had been certain that all risk of contamination had passed, but that didn't alter the fact that Caroline had put her own health at risk by merely entering the house.

'I must say, Elizabeth, you look positively blooming this morning! The colour is back in your cheeks, so you've absolutely no excuse whatsoever not to attend my summer ball on Saturday evening.'

'I have every intention of being there,' she assured her. 'From what I've learned from Richard the event has long since become one of the county's most celebrated, and not to be missed.'

'A slight exaggeration, but I believe it is enjoyed by many. My poor dear Giles did so love the summer—the hotter the better! Came from spending so much of his early life in India, I suppose. Since his death I've continued the tradition of holding a ball in high summer, though I must confess there have been some years when the heat has been quite oppressive.'

She glanced across at the large oak desk, where Elizabeth had positioned the beautifully arranged vase of flowers. 'Where is Richard hiding himself this morning?'

'He went out quite some time ago. Very secretive he was about where he was going, too. But he did say he would be back in good time for our morning ride. We've taken to riding out together daily,' she explained. 'Which, I suppose must have something to do with my improved appearance.'

Caroline was highly delighted to learn that they were spending so much time together. It was the only way, surely, to put right whatever it was that had caused that sad and most unexpected rift between them.

When news had reached her of Richard's rather surprising departure for London all those weeks ago she, like so many others, had thought it rather strange that he should pay a visit to the metropolis so soon after his wedding had taken place, leaving his lovely young wife behind; but hadn't really given his actions any more thought until rumours began to circulate of his association with Lady Torrington. Even now she still cringed inwardly at the memory. She had been here, sat in this very room, when that malicious Lady Pentecost, whose reputation as a spiteful tabby had been well earned, had called and had announced, with quite malicious intent, that Sir Richard's name was being linked, and not without good reason, to that of a certain attractive widow.

Caroline had always been very fond of Richard, but he had certainly plummeted in her estimation that day. During these past weeks he had retrieved his position somewhat. His devotion to Elizabeth's well-being throughout her illness had been quite touching to witness; but she still found it hard to understand why any man who was blessed with such a charming and lovely young wife should seek his pleasures in the arms of a notorious houri who was certainly not in her first flush of youth.

She had gained a slight insight into what might have brought about the rather unexpected rift between them during one of her visits a few weeks before. Elizabeth had still been keeping to her room at the time and in a mood of despondency had let fall that Richard had believed that she, together with her sister, had planned his incarceration in the Chilthams' cellar. Caroline had urged her to tell him the truth, and took the opportunity, now, of asking if her advice had been taken.

'Yes, I did broach the subject once, but whether he believed me or not is quite another matter.'

'But surely you mentioned that it was I who had discovered the truth?'

'No, I didn't,' Elizabeth freely admitted, casting her friend a fond smile. 'You particularly asked me not to repeat our conversation of that day. Don't you remember?'

Caroline dismissed this with an impatient wave of her hand. 'Richard's believing the truth is far more important than my rather ridiculous request. Tell him that you discovered your sister's underhandedness from me.' She was silent for a moment before adding, 'And talking of darling Evadne...have you heard from her recently?'

'My dear Caroline, I've mentioned on more than one occasion that we are not close. I have had no contact, written or otherwise, since I left her house on the morning after that very eventful dinner-party.'

Caroline didn't attempt to hide her surprise at this intelligence. 'But...surely you informed her of your intention to marry?'

'No, I did not, but Richard did. And I believe he wrote informing her of my recent illness; she didn't bother to write back enquiring how I was going on... But then, I never expected her to.'

'Well, I've heard from her. She wrote to me last week, informing me that she has invited herself to my ball. She'll be arriving sometime this week, but just when, I'm not perfectly sure.'

It was abundantly obvious from the distinct lack of enthusiasm in her voice that Caroline was not precisely overjoyed at the prospect of having Lady Chiltham as a guest, so why on earth hadn't she simply written back putting her off? This was not the first time that Caroline had betrayed her lack of esteem for Lady Chiltham. Almost from the first time they had met Elizabeth had gained the impression that Caroline disliked Evadne excessively, and yet she continued to visit Devonshire two or three times a year, and never attempted to prevent the Chilthams from visiting her.

'Although you are far too well-bred to pull my darling sister's character to shreds in my company, Caroline, I do realise that you have as much regard for her as I do myself. Precious little! So I cannot help wondering why you make a point of seeing her so frequently.'

The shrug in response was not so much one of indifference as resignation. 'There are reasons, my dear,' she admitted, and looked for a moment as if she might say something further, but then suddenly appeared to think better of it and hurriedly rose to her feet.

'Heavens above! Is that the time? I really must be going. I want to pay a visit to Melcham. I've heard that a young doctor has set up a practice there. I think I'll pay him a visit. If I like the look of him I shall certainly call upon his services in the future when it becomes necessary. Like yourself, I consider Dr Fieldhouse a pompous nincompoop.'

This piece of good news, for they were in desperate need of a second doctor in the area, diverted Elizabeth's thoughts from the previous topic of conversation. 'I might pay him a visit myself within the next few days,' she remarked, accompanying her favourite neighbour outside to the waiting carriage. 'I'd like him to take a look at Jem. Not that I think there's much wrong with the boy that a good and plentiful diet won't soon put to rights. But after the hard life the poor child has been forced to endure, one cannot be absolutely certain.'

Caroline knew all about the plight of the unfortunate climbing-boy, and the reasons why he had been rescued by the Knightleys. 'You haven't come to regret your act of charity yet, I see.'

'Oh, no! Well, at least I haven't,' she amended with an impish smile, 'but I'm not quite so certain that Richard feels as I do. It was only to be expected that, after years of nothing short of slavish hardship and privation, young Jem would display a deal of exuberance now that his shackles have been removed. But I'm afraid his natural high spirits didn't meet with Cook's approval, so he has been relegated to the stables. It was rather fortunate that Hodge, the head groom, took such a marked shine to the boy. He's become a kind of surrogate grandfather, and has Jem sleeping in his room above the stables.'

'Let me know how he's progressing when you come to the ball. I doubt I shall find the time to visit again before then. There are several guests staying for the weekend, so I'm afraid I am going to be rather busy.'

Smiling fondly, Caroline climbed into the carriage, but Elizabeth's smile in response faded the instant the vehicle moved off. For a few moments she followed its progress along the sweep of the drive and then returned indoors and went directly up to her room to change into her habit.

Without waiting for Richard's return she collected a suitable mount from the stables and set off in the direction of one of her favourite spots on the estate. There were no signs of an immediate break in the weather, which had remained hot and dry for over a week, and by the time she had arrived at the small copse, where a stream gurgled its way beneath the shading canopy of branches, she was already feeling the effects of the mid-July sun's intensely warm rays.

Leaving her mount to champ contentedly on the sweet grass in the shade, she made use of one of the trees blown down in the severe gales which had swept the county the previous January. For a while she sat silently drinking in the peaceful beauty of the spot, where it was not uncommon to see the odd wild creature emerge from the undergrowth to refresh itself in the stream's clear, sparkling water, but it wasn't long before her mind began to dwell on the visit earlier of that person who had become quite dear to her.

Caroline was without doubt one of the most warm-hearted, even-tempered people one could ever have the pleasure of meeting. She seemed to get along with most people very well. There was little doubt in her mind now, though, that Caroline disliked Lady Chiltham intensely. Elizabeth didn't find this in the least difficult to comprehend, for Caroline was far too astute not to have realised long ago that Evadne's sweet smiles and friendly overtures were merely a façade.

'People can change over the years, but it's been my experience that they never do to that extent...'

Aggie's word came back so clearly, bringing with them vivid and highly unpleasant recollections from the distant past. As a child Evadne had attained the utmost pleasure in allowing others to take the blame for her misdemeanours. Elizabeth recalled numerous instances when she had been punished by her mother for what had, in fact, been her sister's malicious acts. Evadne had enjoyed nothing more than wielding power: having a hold on some poor unfortunate, whereby he or she was forced to do precisely as she asked or risk a secret being revealed. Could this be the case with Caroline? Was Evadne privy to something that Caroline would prefer not to become generally known...? But what?

The most obvious explanation, of course, was that some time during her marriage Caroline had foolishly indulged in a fling with another man, but somehow that possibility didn't ring true. From things Elizabeth had learned since living in Hampshire, it seemed that the Westbridges had been the most devoted couple. Caroline had been devastated by her husband's most unexpected and tragic demise, and it had been only her loving devotion to their sole off-spring's well-being which had instilled in her the strength and determination to carry on with life during those early months after her husband's accidental death. Supposing, though, that exposure as an adulteress was the Sword of Damocles Evadne held above Caroline's head—why after several years of widowhood did it still matter so much? She frowned, perplexed. No, that wasn't the explanation; she felt certain of it. There was something, though…but what?

The sound of hoofbeats broke into her disturbing thoughts, and she turned her head to see her husband, astride the handsome grey that had taken the place of the mount shot from beneath him at Waterloo, cantering up the slight rise towards her.

'Why didn't you wait for my return?' he asked, not attempting to hide his disappointment because she had chosen not to do so. 'I haven't said or done anything to upset you, have I?'

'Of course not!' She waited for him to sit down beside her, and didn't attempt to move when she felt one strong muscular thigh brush against the folds of her habit. 'To be honest with you, I had something on my mind and left the house without thinking.'

'Oh?' He was instantly alert. 'Anything I can help you with?'

'You might be able to, yes.' She was staring straight ahead, and didn't notice the sudden look that softened his eyes as they studied her profile. 'How well did you know Giles Westbridge? What kind of man was he?'

The unexpected enquiry surprised him slightly, but he didn't hesitate to satisfy her curiosity. 'He was a good deal older than myself. My brother Charles knew him rather better than I did, but I always got on very well with him.

He was a large, amiable sort. He acquired his wealth out in India where he lived for some years. When he came back to England he met Caroline and purchased Heathfield House within a few years of their marriage. He was a bit of a gambler by all accounts. Evidently Lady Luck favoured him, for he always seemed very plump in the pocket. He invested a considerable amount in a friend's venture in South Africa which has paid dividends. Caroline will never need to worry her head over financial matters.'

She digested this in silence for a moment, then said, 'He was discovered slumped over his desk in the library, so I understand. The bullet had entered his heart, so I assume death was instantaneous.'

'I was in Portugal when it happened, but from what Charles told me later, Westbridge had been cleaning his pistol at the time. Everyone assumed that he had been rather careless and hadn't realised the thing was loaded.'

'And no one suspected foul play or suicide?'

'Giles Westbridge hadn't an enemy in the world. There were no signs of a forced entry. And as far as suicide is concerned—' Richard shook his head '—what reason could there have been? If my memory serves me correctly, Lord and Lady Chiltham were staying at the house at the time. They both spoke to the magistrate. The verdict was accidental death.'

'So, my sister was there, was she? How very interesting.'

Richard studied her closely and saw a decidedly calculating look in her eyes. 'Why do you find that circumstance so intriguing, Elizabeth?'

'Because I very much fear that darling Evadne has some kind of hold over Caroline—something she uses to make our very amiable neighbour do precisely as she wishes. But at the moment I'm still groping in the dark trying to unearth something unsavoury about a person who appears to have led a totally unblemished existence.'

'From what I've learned of your sister from various sources in recent months, her character leaves much to be desired, but is she so loathsome as to stoop to blackmail?'

Elizabeth didn't even take a moment to consider the question. 'Oh yes. Short of cold-blooded murder, I think her capable of anything.' Her smile was a trifle rueful. 'Never take anything she says or does at face value. Just look at what she did to us when we were in Devon!'

Again he studied her closely, and she held his gaze levelly, without so much as a single blink. 'When did you discover that she had planned your incarceration in the cellar? You certainly didn't suspect anything at the time—I do realise that, now.'

'No, foolishly it never occurred to me that it was anything more than an innocent mistake. But I should have realised, knowing Evadne's character so well. My only excuse for being so foolishly obtuse is that I assumed she had outgrown her childish acts of malicious spite.'

Now that she had begun to confide in him, he wasn't prepared to let this golden opportunity to discover as much as he could slip away. 'How and when did you discover the truth?'

'From Caroline on the morning she left for Hampshire.'

Had he foolishly retained any lingering doubts about Elizabeth's possible involvement they would have been irrevocably quashed by this intelligence. 'But how on earth did Caroline uncover the truth?'

'After we had left the Chilthams' house that morning, she overheard Evadne berating the butler again. Something my sister said made Caroline suspicious. She went down to the drawing-room and retrieved those pieces of paper on which our names were supposed to have been written. We all saw Evadne go over to the table and pick up the quill...but the slips of paper were blank, Richard.'

He shook his head. 'It quite amazes me how anyone can be so despicably underhanded.'

Elizabeth smiled rather enigmatically. 'It must be something in the blood.'

'If that is so, you've certainly escaped the malicious taint.'

'Very true. Thankfully, I am not similarly afflicted.'

She hovered for a moment, debating whether to tell him something rather astonishing about Evadne, but then decided against it. She fully intended to confide in him eventually, but now was certainly not the time. What she knew about her sister was so astounding that there was the very real possibility that she might not be believed without that all-too-important written proof. So, for the time being, at least, it must wait.

'I'm tired of talking of my sister. I shall see all I wish of her and more, I expect, on Saturday night at the ball.' She rose to her feet and moved towards their mounts. 'Whilst we're returning to the Hall you may tell me what you have been doing with yourself this morning.'

After helping her back into the saddle, Richard smiled up at her with all the indulgence of some doting uncle. 'Had you done me the courtesy of awaiting my return, you would have been able to put the rather pretty dapple-grey mare I acquired for you earlier through her paces.'

'You've purchased a mare for me?'

'Don't sound so surprised, my dear. You are my wife, after all, and I believe it's expected of a husband to bestow pledges of affection on his spouse from time to time.'

He saw at once by the sudden guarded look which took possession of her features that she was suspicious of his motives; that his gesture had been misconstrued. Their relationship had improved immeasurably during the past couple of weeks, but she still wasn't ready to place herself entirely in his hands. What would it take to win her back completely?

The following afternoon Elizabeth journeyed to Melcham in the carriage. The equipage was being tooled by one of the estate workers because Hodge was busy moving his belongings out of the room above the stables and into a cottage on the edge of the estate, where it was to be hoped that young Jem might quickly grow accustomed to his new-found freedom and not prove quite so disruptive.

When she and Richard had returned to the Hall the previous morning to view the new mare, Jem, armed with a substantial shovel, had foolishly chosen that precise moment to declare war on a large rat which had found its way into the long stable. His frantic battle cries as he had given chase had startled the mare, who had been interestedly inspecting her new surroundings, and several of the other horses, too, and Richard had decided there and then that Jem just could not be allowed to roam free near such highly prized and sensitive creatures. If Hodge wished to continue caring for the boy then he must move into one of the estate cottages. Elizabeth had not remained to hear what else Richard had had to say, but he had informed her later that Hodge had been quite happy to take full responsibility for Jem and, furthermore, had been quite content to retire once a replacement head groom had been found.

She smiled to herself as she glanced absently out of the carriage window. Yes, she mused, yesterday had certainly been a day full of incident. Firstly, there had been Caroline's rather revealing visit, and then later that relaxed conversation with Richard, followed by his rather unexpected gift of a dapple-grey mare. It had been a very kind gesture on his part to purchase a mount for her alone to ride. She couldn't deny, though, that it had briefly crossed her mind to wonder whether he would expect something in return, but she had wronged him—he had not attempted to come to her room last night. She wasn't perfectly certain whether this fact pleased her or not, and a heavy sigh escaped her as the carriage pulled up outside the haberdasher's in the main street. Her mind might advise a continuation of aloof caution, but her body was beginning to demand something else entirely.

After making several necessary purchases in the various shops and depositing them inside the carriage, she asked the rector's wife, who happened to be passing by, the whereabouts of the new doctor's house. Mrs Archer was a pleasant, kindly soul, an ideal wife for a man of the cloth, but her tongue did tend to run on wheels, so it was quite some time before Elizabeth finally discovered what she wanted to know.

Very well aware that Richard owned the smart red-brick house in the centre of Melcham, Elizabeth was rather surprised that he hadn't taken the trouble to inform her that his new tenant was none other than the new and muchneeded doctor, especially as she had mentioned that very morning that she had every intention of making the physician's acquaintance and asking him to take a look at Jem.

A young boy was busily polishing the new brass plaque on the front wall, thereby obscuring the name engraved in the shining metal, as Elizabeth walked up the short path to the front door. So it wasn't until her summons was answered and she looked down in delighted surprise at the small, plump woman with kindly grey eyes, whom she knew so well, that she had her first intimation of who the new doctor might be.

'Middie!' she exclaimed, using the pet name she had always used when addressing her grandmother's housekeeper. 'What in the world... Tom? Is the new doctor Tom?'

'Well, of course it is! Surely that handsome husband of

yours told you that,' Mrs Middleton responded after giving her old mistress's granddaughter a fond hug, and then leading the way down the narrow passageway where two workmen were busily engaged in fitting a second front door.

Still somewhat bemused, Elizabeth followed the housekeeper, whom she had firmly believed had every intention of retiring once the house in Bristol had been sold, into the small, cosy back parlour, where she wasted no time in echoing her thoughts aloud.

'And so I did, Miss Elizabeth…I mean, my lady. The new owner is taking up residence at the end of the month, and I had every intention of going to live with my sister, but then I got to thinking. I've a few good years left in me yet, and I didn't like the idea of sitting around all day with nothing to do. So when Master Tom came round to see me a few weeks ago, and told me that he was leaving Bristol and coming here to work, and that he would be needing a cook-housekeeper…well, I didn't take a moment to consider.'

'I did offer you the opportunity of coming with me to the Hall,' Elizabeth reminded her.

'And very kind it was of you, too. But I don't think I would have fitted in there, Miss Elizabeth, not with all those gentry folk and their fancy ways. Not that I don't consider Sir Richard a charming gentleman, because he most certainly is. But I'm a plainspoken woman, miss, as you well know, and I'm better suited in a situation like this. Besides—' she gave a loud sniff of disapproval '—Master Tom needs someone to look after him. He's lost a deal of weight since leaving your dear grandmother's house last autumn. He needs me around to make sure he eats proper!'

Elizabeth couldn't prevent a smile at this. Mrs Middleton wasn't above scolding Tom for rushing out and leaving his meals, just as though he were some unruly schoolboy, instead of a full-grown and very intelligent man. He would accept such reprimands from her, whereas he wouldn't, perhaps, from anyone else.

'I'm very glad that he has you to look after him, Middie. But what quite astonishes me is that he left Bristol at all! I thought nothing would ever induce him to try to better himself.'

'I can't deny I was surprised myself. I rather think your husband might have had something to do with it,' she disclosed, amazing her listener even more. 'Doctor Carrington thinks very highly of Sir Richard.'

'Oh, those dratted workmen!' she exclaimed as a further bout of hammering reverberated down the passageway. 'It's been like this since we arrived. What with the large front parlour being fitted out and turned into an apothecary's shop, and now this second front door... Still, I suppose I oughtn't to complain, really. This new door is for my benefit. The first entrance will be for those wanting to purchase things in the shop, and will be left open during the day, so I'll only need to concern myself with those people wishing to see the doctor.'

'Is Tom here now?' Elizabeth put in as the housekeeper looked as though she was about to stigmatise the workmen further.

'Yes, but he has someone with him... No, it sounds as though the patient's leaving,' she added, hearing Tom's deep voice in the hall. 'I'll inform him you're here.'

'But please don't tell him who I am...just say there's a lady wishful to see him.'

Mrs Middleton had known Elizabeth for too many years not to have a pretty shrewd notion by the extra sparkle in her lovely eyes that her former mistress's granddaughter was about to play some mischievous prank. And she wasn't wrong. Although Elizabeth was overjoyed to have Tom living so close by, she was feeling slightly nettled because he hadn't taken the trouble to write to her informing her of his pending move.

After being told that her surrogate brother would see her now, Elizabeth whisked herself silently into the first room on the left of the passageway and quietly closed the door. Tom was seated behind his desk and glanced briefly up from the notes he was writing, but Elizabeth was fairly confident that he hadn't a clue to her identity. The large poke on her very fashionable bonnet hid much of her face when her head was lowered, and the handkerchief she had had the forethought to press to her lips hid the rest.

'Please take a seat, madam. What seems to be the trouble?'

'It's my nerves, doctor,' Elizabeth managed in a high-pitched, beautifully disguised voice which shook slightly, but certainly not from any nervous disorder. She was very well aware that if there was one category of persons for whom Tom had scant regard, it was those females whom he irreverently called 'twittie' women.

'Such palpitations!' She dared not peer across the desk at him, but instinctively knew by the sudden low growling sound in his throat that his heavy scowl had descended. 'Such fluttering in my bosom!'

'And when, precisely, do you suffer from these attacks, madam?'

'W-whenever in the c-company of men.'

'Are you married?'

'Y-yes.' She could almost hear him saying, 'I pity the poor fellow'. 'But my husband is quite old. It is only young, handsome men who seem to affect me so, you see.'

A long silence, then, 'Tell me, ma'am, would that be all young men or, perhaps, just one in particular?'

The oozing sarcasm was just too much for her, and she gave way to uncontrollable mirth.

'Elizabeth, you little baggage! I'll give you palpitations if you try any more of these tricks!'

After dabbing at her streaming eyes, she looked across the desk at him properly for the fist time, and knew that he wasn't really angry, just pretending to be. 'Well, you deserved it, Tom. It was downright shabby not to let me know you were moving into the district!'

His brows rose. 'Didn't Richard tell you? It was he who put the notion into my head in the first place. I wrote to him several weeks ago, accepting his kind offer.'

'No, he never mentioned it at all,' Elizabeth admitted, wondering why not.

'Ha! A man of sound good sense, then. Probably knew the first thing you'd do would be to try to badger me into letting you come with me on my calls, just as you did when we lived in Bristol.'

'You make me sound like some stray pup that was forever following you about. I used to accompany you out occasionally.'

'Well, you'll not do so again!' he informed her in his brusque, no-nonsense manner. 'You're a married lady and have a position to uphold.'

'I have no intention of offering you my help,' she countered, looking and sounding decidedly miffed. 'I have better things to do with my time than bear you company, Dr Thomas Carrington! And if it wasn't for the fact that I require your professional services, I tell you plainly I wouldn't be sitting here bandying words with you now!'

Smiling at her all-too-evident pique, he rose to his feet and moved round the desk. 'Here, let me take a look at you.'

'It isn't I who require your services,' she informed him when he placed his hands on her neck, and was told in no uncertain terms to sit still and do as she was told.

'Yes, you've fully recovered,' he announced after completing his brief examination. 'So, who is it you want me to see?'

Elizabeth dropped her affronted pose and told him all about the climbing-boy she and Richard had rescued from a life of sheer misery. 'I don't think there is anything seriously wrong with him that a continued substantial diet won't put right, but I'd just like to be certain.'

'Any sign of a persistent cough?'

'No, not that I've heard.'

'I'll check him over, none the less. I'll call on you tomorrow morning and you can take me over to the cottage. It will give us the opportunity to catch up on each other's news.'

Friendly relations having been restored, she allowed him to accompany her outside as far as the gate. 'You needn't walk with me to the carriage. It's only a short step away.' She smiled glowingly up at him, all the deep sisterly affection she bore him mirrored in her eyes. 'It is good having you close by, Tom,' she admitted at last. 'I missed you, you know.'

'Strangely enough, I missed you, too, you infuriating little minx,' and then, as he had done so many times in the past, he placed his arms about her and gave her a smacking kiss on one cheek, before holding her away, a rather rueful expression taking possession of his features. 'Dear me, I must stop doing that. Here you are, a respectable married lady and flirting shamelessly with the doctor. What will people think!'

The lady who had just passed by in a very elegant travelling carriage was certainly doing plenty of thinking after witnessing the affectionate little scene. A rather calculating gleam sprang into her cornflower-blue eyes as she leaned back against the plush velvet squabs. 'Well, well, well! And what goes on here? I was in two minds whether to make this trip or not. Now, I'm very glad I did. Unless I'm very

much mistaken it will offer me some very good sport...
Who would have thought it? And so soon after her marriage, too! My sweet little goody-goody sister really is full
of surprises.'

The inside of the carriage echoed with a trill of feminine
laughter. 'First thing tomorrow, Quimper, you are to return
to this misbegotten place and discover precisely who lives
in that red-brick house we've just passed.'

Chapter Eleven

As Richard turned his head to stare through the carriage window at the passing countryside bathed in the pleasant glow of fading evening light, Elizabeth took the opportunity to study him closely, wondering yet again what manner of man she had married.

That erstwhile nonpareil of her childhood imaginings had been remoulded through the passage of time into something a little more human; but even on the day they had married she had, perhaps, credited him with rather more than his rightful share of the gentlemanly virtues. His expeditious descent into the stinking pit of debauched humanity had turned out, surprisingly, to be only a temporary fall from grace. Even in those early weeks of her illness, some detached part of her fevered brain had registered that he was far from the hardened roué her battered heart had proclaimed him. Now, she looked upon him as neither saint nor monster, merely as a man, a man who, for the most part, was touchingly thoughtful to the needs of others…but a man who continued to remain, frustratingly, something of an enigma.

Having looked his fill of the familiar countryside, Richard turned to catch a pair of puzzled eyes studying his physiognomy with apparent rapt interest. 'By your far-from-smiling countenance, I can only deduce that either you're not looking forward with any degree of enthusiasm to the evening ahead, or my appearance doesn't meet with your approval.'

'You're wrong on both counts,' she didn't hesitate to assure him, with a sudden lightening of her brow. 'Although, if I'm truthful, I rather think riding gear is more flattering to a man of your excellent stature and rugged good looks.'

The latter remark came so easily to her lips that it was out before she realised what she was saying. Heavens above! Whatever had come over her? She was flirting—yes, unashamedly flirting with him! Was it normal for wives to flirt with their husbands? By his spontaneous smile it was quite evident that he appreciated it, at any rate.

'I was considering you, though, Richard,' she admitted, spurred on by his appreciative reaction to her honesty, 'but not your attire. Amongst other things, I was wondering why you should have chosen not to inform me of Tom's arrival in the district. I cannot perceive what motive there could have been for keeping such a thing secret from me.' If the admission surprised him he certainly betrayed no outward sign of its having done so.

'When I first put the idea to him you were still most unwell. Later, when he had made up his mind, I fully expected him to write to you personally, seeing how the two of you are so very close.' He remarked upon this fact without experiencing the least pang of annoyance or jealousy. 'When he didn't, I naturally thought that he wanted to surprise you, as his being in Melcham evidently did.'

He didn't add that he had feared at one time she might well suspect him of trying to curry favour by making it possible for the man she looked upon as a brother to live nearby.

It was quite evident, though, by her warm smile that she suspected him of nothing so base, even before she said, 'You are to be congratulated, Richard. I doubt there are many who could influence Tom in such a way. I certainly have never been able to do so. I tried to persuade him to accept Caroline's invitation to her party tonight, when he called to take a look at Jem the other day, but as usual the stubborn wretch flatly refused to commit himself.'

'It certainly wouldn't do his practice any harm to attend,' he responded, somehow managing to suppress a smile at her obvious lack of patience with the young doctor. 'There are very few occasions when most of the gentry hereabouts are gathered together in one place. It's an ideal opportunity for him to make himself known.'

'Ha! I doubt even that consideration would prove sufficient inducement for him to bestir himself and socialise for an evening.'

But in this Elizabeth had wronged him, as she discovered not many moments after she had entered Caroline's large ground-floor salon, charmingly decorated for the special occasion with numerous vases of beautifully arranged summer flowers and several cool green potted-palms.

Tom, amidst a group of gentlemen, was standing at the far end of the room. Catching sight of Elizabeth within moments of her entering the room, he raised his glass in silent greeting. Her immediate response was a glowing smile of approval at his attendance, which was noted by several persons present, including Lady Chiltham who had been keeping half an eye on the doorway since the arrival of the man who, only days before, had been so warmly embracing Lady Knightley in the front garden of that smart red-brick house in the local town.

Whenever attending an occasion such as this, where most people present were completely unknown to her, Lady Chiltham could always somehow manage, within a very short space of time, to attach herself to some garrulous person who was not averse to indulging in a little malicious gossip. The lady seated beside her, dressed in a fussily adorned gown of purple silk and a rather ugly turban of the same hue, didn't disappoint her.

'It would seem that your sister is already on remarkably friendly terms with our new practitioner,' Lady Pentecost remarked, levelling her lorgnette in the doctor's direction. 'An excellent young man, I do not doubt, but I prefer a physician a little more advanced in years. Any young matron seeking his services with any degree of frequency will simply be begging the gossip-mongers' tongues to start a-wagging.'

Evadne did not even attempt to respond to this. After excusing herself, she merely rose to her feet and made her way across the crowded room in the direction of the door. Lady Pentecost, without that affected use of the lorgnette, studied the younger woman's progress. Like her sister's, Lady Chiltham's carriage was undoubtedly graceful, the white spider gauze alternately swishing about and clinging to the wonderfully proportioned slender figure as she moved. Lady Pentecost approved wholeheartedly of the warm embrace Evadne bestowed upon her sister, but the sentiment most certainly wasn't experienced by the recipient, nor by the man who stood close by, watching the performance with a cynicism engendered by recently acquired knowledge.

Although he had tactfully refrained from alluding with any degree of frequency to his wife's early life, Richard had by this time gained a fair understanding of what Elizabeth had endured at her sister's hands during childhood. His lip curled at the nauseatingly false display of affection, and it took a monumental effort on his part to remain silent at Evadne's spurious expressions of relief and gratitude at seeing her sister looking so well. Caroline, however, for once was unable to exert such firm control.

'If the letters both Richard and I wrote were insufficient to assure you of Elizabeth's continued progress after her illness, you could quite easily have journeyed here and discovered the truth of the matter for yourself.'

'I wished to do just that,' Evadne responded, but the promptly spoken assurance fooled no one. 'You must remember, though, that I had my family to consider. Deeply concerned though I was, I couldn't risk taking the infection myself and passing it on to my husband or children.'

'Very understandable, Evadne,' Caroline agreed fair-mindedly, 'but it would have been a simple matter to assure yourself of your sister's progress by writing a letter. I wrote to you on more than one occasion, but I certainly never received a reply throughout your sister's illness.'

The sweetly serene smile remained, but there was a menacingly calculating look in Evadne's blue eyes as she turned them in their hostess's direction. 'You should know by now, my dear Caroline, that I've never been much of a scribbler. Besides, one needs to be so very careful when putting pen to paper. Letters can occasionally go astray, or even fall into the wrong hands entirely, can they not?'

Just for one moment, before she turned to greet some new arrivals, Caroline's complexion seemed to grow ashen. Evidently Evadne's observations had not been so innocent as they had sounded, but Elizabeth wasn't given the opportunity to dwell on the possible sinister connotations, for the eldest son of one of their close neighbours approached to claim her for a partner in the next set of country dances.

During her years in Bristol she had attended numerous parties where country dances were preferred to the waltz, a dance which was her particular favourite, but which many members of the older generation continued to view with disfavour. It took very little effort on her part, therefore, to perform the intricate steps while keeping an eye on certain other persons present. Richard, she noticed, had wasted no time in excusing himself, and was now conversing with Tom and several other gentlemen. Evadne had returned to her seat beside Lady Pentecost, who was following the set with apparent rapt interest, no doubt hoping to catch some poor unfortunate miss a step, and Caroline, still stationed by the door, was looking quite animated as she greeted yet more guests. Elizabeth couldn't help wondering, though, how much of that light-hearted manner was merely for show.

The set came to an end, and the musicians hired for the occasion immediately struck up a waltz, Caroline not being amongst those who disapproved of the dance. Elizabeth would have been quite content to leave the floor and refresh herself with a glass of champagne, but the gentleman swiftly approaching to claim her hand was someone she could never find it within her heart to refuse.

'My, my! You are turning over a new leaf,' she teased as a shapely, long-fingered hand was placed lightly on her waist. 'Indulging in such frivolous pastimes as dancing, Dr Carrington? Whatever next! And looking as fine as five-pence, too? Who loaned you the evening garb, by the way? Was it Richard?'

'No, it wasn't, you impertinent little baggage!' he returned good-humouredly. 'Anyone listening to you might suppose I didn't have a decent shirt to my name.'

She refrained from responding that she suspected he hadn't that many and asked, instead, what had prompted him to accept Caroline's invitation.

'Oh, I just thought I'd cast an eye over the local populace to see what ailments I'm likely to be called upon to treat. Not surprisingly, many here suffer from too much, rather than too little. Besides, I rather like Mrs Westbridge. Struck me as a kind-hearted, sensible sort. Which is more than can be said for that dragon-faced harridan seated beside your sister.'

'Ah! So you've been introduced to the formidable Lady Pentecost and the oh, so charming Lady Chiltham, have you?'

'Yes. And didn't care for either of them,' he responded in his usual forthright fashion. 'A right pair of vicious tabbies, if I'm any judge.'

'Remind me to loan you a book on etiquette, some time.' She twinkled up at him. 'I see that you still lack a number of the social graces, Dr Carrington. Might I remind you that it is my sister of whom you speak.'

'Don't hide my teeth when I'm with you, Elizabeth. You should know that.'

'No, and I'm very glad you do not. But it might be wise to choose your words carefully when conversing with Lady Pentecost,' she warned him.

'It would be wiser for her to consider carefully anything she says to me,' he countered, that all too familiar hard-edged note of determination in his deep voice. 'I cannot abide people of that ilk, Elizabeth, as you very well know, and have no intention of kowtowing to them.'

Although still in his twenties, Tom was already quite set in his ways, with definite and immovable views on certain subjects. Elizabeth knew him well enough to be sure that nothing she said would induce him to tread warily with certain members of the gentry hereabouts and, truth to tell, she had no wish to change him, even if she could. He wouldn't be her darling irascible Thomas if he were to become a grovelling toad-eater in order to make his way in the world. So, she prudently changed the subject and, when the dance was over, remained at his side to drink a glass of ice-cool champagne.

It was while Tom was speaking to the local squire and his wife, who also came across to refresh themselves, that

Elizabeth happened to turn her head and noticed Caroline slip out through one of the long French windows, which had been left wide open to allow some much-needed fresh air into the crowded salon. At first she gave little thought to their hostess's sudden departure and continued to watch the dancers, all decked out in their finery, swirling about the room, but after some minutes, when Caroline hadn't returned, she began to feel a little uneasy and decided to investigate her new friend's continued absence.

There were several couples enjoying the cooler air on the terrace, but, surprisingly, Caroline was not amongst them. Several lanterns adorned those trees closest to the fine Tudor manor house, and Elizabeth had little difficulty in picking her way along one of the many paths which criss-crossed that part of the garden closest to the building. After walking some little distance, without catching sight of their hostess, she was about to retrace her steps, when she noticed a shadowy movement near one of the ornamental trees.

'Ah! So there you are!' Uninvited, she seated herself on the wooden seat beside her friend. 'I was beginning to think I would need to return for reinforcements in order to track you down.'

'Oh, dear! Have I been missed already?' She sounded genuinely perturbed, as though she had been found lacking in her duties as hostess. 'I didn't realise I'd been out here for so long.'

'Rest easy, you haven't,' Elizabeth assured her, but added, having by this time detected the telltale signs of an unsuccessfully suppressed bout of weeping, 'You haven't remained out here nearly long enough for your eyes to recover from tears recently wept.'

Caroline made a half-hearted attempt at denial, but then abandoned the rather pointless exercise. 'Yes, very foolish after nearly six years of widowhood, but it's at times like these when I miss Giles dreadfully.'

Elizabeth didn't doubt the sincerity of this, but felt certain that this fact alone wasn't wholly responsible for her friend's present distress. She had no wish to pry, but at the same time couldn't sit idly by while someone she cared for very much was suffering deeply when she might be in a position to help.

'Very understandable,' she responded softly, staring sightlessly across the darkened garden, 'but that doesn't account for your moment's disquiet earlier this evening. Has my sister said or done something to upset you since her arrival here?' There was no response, but, undaunted, Elizabeth added, 'Or has she, perhaps, some hold over you?'

Caroline's audible gasp of dismay was confirmation enough. 'You know, don't you!' It sounded more accusation than question. 'She's told you, hasn't she?'

'No one has told me anything…yet.' Elizabeth turned her head and gazed at her neighbour's distraught features steadily, knowing that if she was to get to the truth, she mustn't be reticent herself. 'You hold my sister in scant regard. You've admitted as much. The darker side of my sister's nature is not unknown to me, so it didn't take a great deal of intelligence to puzzle out the possible reason for your strange behaviour.

'I shall not attempt to intercede on your behalf unless you wish me to do so, Caroline,' she went on gently, 'but if you do wish me to help, then I must know precisely why you find yourself in my sister's coils.'

'Oh, if only you could help me!' Tears barely held in check began to well again. 'I have carried this burden of guilt for such a long time, and yet I don't deserve such torment, but for my son's sake I've been forced to endure your sister's malice, pander to her every whim. You see,

Elizabeth, my husband's death was not an accident…it was suicide.'

If she had hoped the pronouncement would be met with astonished disbelief, she was destined to experience disappointment. 'You don't appear in the least surprised, and yet you couldn't possibly have known.'

'No, I didn't know, but I cannot deny that that distinct possibility hadn't occurred to me,' Elizabeth acknowledged with brutal candour. 'And this is the hold my sister has over you, is it?'

'Not entirely, no,' Caroline admitted without the least hesitation. Now that she had begun to unburden herself she experienced no reluctance in revealing the whole truth to this young woman whom she instinctively knew could be trusted implicitly.

'Giles was a wonderful husband and father,' she began, a distinct catch in her voice, 'but he wasn't without his faults. I'm sorry to say that his ruling passion was gambling. I never attempted to curb this weakness in him, and am honest enough to admit that I believe I would have been unsuccessful if I had tried. Lady Luck had been kind to him over the years, but I suppose it was only to be expected that *she* would transfer her loyalties eventually.

'Some months before he died he invested a deal of money in a friend's venture in South Africa. He ought, of course, to have compensated for this by exercising economy.' She sighed. 'Sadly, though, that wasn't Giles's way. He continued to gamble and lost heavily at the tables. I didn't know it at the time, but we were seriously in debt. Giles, then, committed the unforgivable sin of cheating at cards. Faced with ruin, the young man whose fortune Giles had stolen—and it can be termed nothing less than that—took his own life soon afterwards. The final irony was that Giles's investment in South Africa then began to show a return, but he couldn't live with what he had done.

'I discovered the terrible truth only after Giles had died,' Caroline divulged, having taken a moment to regain her composure. 'He left a letter for me confessing all. The Chilthams happened to be staying with us at the time. Foolishly, I left that damning letter lying about in my room, and your sister apprised herself of its contents, and has retained it to this day.'

Elizabeth reached out a hand to grasp trembling fingers. 'It was hard, I know, for you to tell me all this, but you shan't regret it.'

'Could you succeed where I have failed and persuade her to return Giles's letter?' Hope sprang into Caroline's dark eyes. 'Could you appeal to her better nature?'

'I wasn't aware that my sister possessed a better side to her nature,' Elizabeth returned with gentle irony. 'Oh, no. I must adopt methods of persuasion that Evadne would certainly not appreciate, but couldn't fail to understand. Fight fire with fire, as one might say.'

She smiled at Caroline's look of bewilderment. 'How long does Evadne intend remaining here with you?'

'I'm not sure. A few days, certainly.'

'That's good, because there is something I must do before I confront her.' The smile she bestowed could not have been more reassuring. 'You had better return to the house now, otherwise your absence will be noted. It would not serve our cause if Evadne suspected that you had confided in me. Continue as best you can to behave quite naturally whenever in her presence. But be assured you shall not long remain in her clutches.'

Mindful of the warning, Caroline took the precaution of returning to the salon with two of her female guests who had been amongst those enjoying a breath of fresh air on the terrace. As she resumed her role as hostess she found the smile coming quite effortlessly to her lips, a genuine smile of combined relief and renewed hope for the future.

Confiding in someone at long last had considerably lessened the heavy burden of guilt which she had been carrying
round with her during these past years. Elizabeth, blessed
girl, had betrayed not the least feeling of condemnation or
disgust after learning the appalling events leading up to
Giles's tragic death, and although Caroline still retained
grave doubts about ever regaining her husband's damning
letter, she was now determined never again to submit to
what had been nothing short of emotional blackmail.

Darling Elizabeth's reactions had given her every reason
to hope that other friends would behave with the same kind-
hearted generosity when they learned the truth. But first,
she must confide in her son. He had been twelve years old
when his father had died. Now, he was no longer a boy,
but almost eighteen: old enough to be told the sad truth.
As soon as he returned from Scotland with his friends, she
would confide all, but in the meantime she would do as
Elizabeth had asked, she decided, fixing her gaze momentarily on the woman who had caused her untold anxiety
during the past five years.

'Caroline looks sublimely pleased with herself,' Evadne
remarked, catching their hostess's swift scrutiny. 'I wonder
what has occurred to lift her spirits?'

'The success of this evening, I shouldn't wonder,'
Richard responded without much interest.

He had long since become faintly bored with his sister-
in-law's company. While Elizabeth had been dancing with
Tom, Evadne had positioned herself at his side, and he had
considered many of the remarks she had passed highly provocative and faintly distasteful. She had almost insisted that
he dance with her, and although it would have afforded
him immense pleasure to refuse, he had decided that as
relations between his wife and her sister were, to say the
least, precarious, it would be wrong of him to place a further wedge between them.

Successfully suppressing a sigh of relief as the dance came to an end, Richard was on the point of returning his partner to the vacant chair beside Lady Pentecost, when Evadne thwarted his intentions of being rid of her by requesting him to accompany her outside for a breath of air. He managed to check the blunt refusal that rose in his throat at his lips, as he tried in vain to catch a glimpse of Elizabeth in the crowded room, but when Evadne made her way down the terrace steps into the garden, he momentarily hindered her progress by announcing quite bluntly, 'I cannot remain with you for long. My wife has promised me the supper dance, which will be taking place very shortly.'

'How very unfashionable to dance with one's wife!' she exclaimed, possessively entwining her arm through his and steering him ever further away from those people on the terrace. 'Still, I suppose it's expected of a recently married couple to make, at least, a pretence of a joyful union.'

Disengaging his arm with ruthless efficiency, Richard came to an abrupt halt just beyond the wooden seat where his wife and Caroline had been sitting a little earlier, and looked down at Evadne with a disdainful curl to his lips.

'Be assured, madam, there is no pretence on my part.'

For a moment Evadne was taken aback by the vehemence of the assertion, but then she smiled, a sickly sweet smile which he found nauseating.

'Come now, Richard. There is no need for these blatantly false protestations. I am fully aware of the reason why you married my sister, and I did try to tell you that there was absolutely no need for such a sacrifice on your part.'

He stared down at her in silence, his features as coolly expressionless now as those of a marble statue; but she refused to admit defeat on this romantic night when the balmy air was heavy with the fragrance of roses and sweetly scented stocks. He didn't care for Elizabeth. She was firmly convinced that a marriage between them would never have taken place if it hadn't been for her butler's stupid blunder on the night of the dinner-party. He had always preferred her; had wished to marry her once, she reminded herself with a deep feeling of satisfaction. And she was still a very desirable woman.

'Remain stubbornly silent if you will,' she husked, running her hands up the muscular arms to entwine them at the nape of his neck, 'but I know the truth. Reports of your amorous exploits in London during the early part of the Season even reached us in Devonshire. You quickly grew tired of my sister, but you won't so easily tire of me.'

Without waiting for a response this time, she pulled his head down and placed her invitingly parted lips on his, but the reaction to her advances could hardly be described by even the most optimistic as encouraging. His mouth remained firmly closed and coldly unresponsive during those few brief moments before he raised his hands and placed them round her wrists in a bone-crushing grip that almost brought tears to her eyes.

Retaining his far-from-gentle grasp, he held her at arm's length, that disdainful smirk she had seen earlier returning to twist one corner of his unreceptive mouth.

'If you are in need of further confirmation of my feelings for your sister then I shall tell you this. I married Elizabeth because I had fallen in love with her. She is the only woman I have ever truly loved. She is the only woman I shall ever love, and as long as I have her I shall neither require nor covet the charms of any other female.'

It was like being dealt a punishing slap in the face. Evadne could only stare up at him in astonished disbelief, unable to draw her eyes from the humiliating depths of disdain in his own.

'I trust I do not intrude?' a soft voice unexpectedly enquired. 'But I think you should know, Richard, that the supper dance is about to begin.'

Releasing his hold abruptly, he swung round to find Elizabeth, with an unreadable expression on her lovely face, standing a little way down the path. In three giant strides he was beside her and, without knowing or caring whether his sister-in-law followed, escorted his wife back towards the house.

Evadne remained perfectly still, disbelief having been replaced by ice-cold anger at the humiliating rejection she had just received. Even after all Richard's assurances, there was still some doubt in her mind that her sister had won the heart of the man whom she herself would quite happily have married years ago if his position on the social ladder had been higher. She had never made any secret of the fact that wealth and status had always been of paramount importance to her and marriage to George Chiltham had given her both, even if it had provided her with precious little else. She had always found the physical side of their union abhorrent, and even though she had indulged in the occasional, if discreetly conducted, extramarital affair, intense satisfaction had come from the slavish adoration she had evoked in her various lovers rather than from any activities between the sheets. An interlude with Richard might have been different, might have proved more physically satisfying, for there was no denying he was an intensely attractive member of the male sex, but she was destined, now, never to find out. Richard, she felt certain, would never add his name to her list of devoted admirers.

Having her amorous overtures so blatantly spurned was a new and vastly unpleasant experience which had left her with an insatiable desire for revenge. She would make him pay dearly for his insulting behaviour, she vowed silently, vengeful determination adding an extra sparkle to her eyes. And if she could also manage to bring about her precious sister's downfall, all well and good. But she must plan carefully, for Richard was no fool, and neither was Elizabeth.

How that girl had changed during these past years, and not just physically, either! Her revenge on them both must be sweetly merciless, and that, she was very well aware, would take considerable thought and very careful planning.

Chapter Twelve

Debauched! An abhorrent scrap of humanity too loathsome to be touched was how Elizabeth must surely view him now, even if she hadn't before that sickening interlude with her sister had taken place earlier, Richard decided, his spirits plummeting to an all-time low. And who could blame her? How would he himself have felt if he had come upon his wife in a starlit garden, wrapped in another man's arms? The mere thought was enough to engulf him in a positive tidal wave of rage, so he could hardly upbraid Elizabeth for having jumped to the totally wrong conclusion when she had witnessed such a nauseating spectacle with her own eyes.

Suddenly ceasing his brooding pacing, he stared sightlessly across the bedchamber. The trouble was, though, she had given him no positive indication of just how she felt. There had been no tearful recriminations, no words of reproach. Had she turned on him, and lashed out with sharpened claws, he would have understood, but her impeccable behaviour throughout the remainder of the evening had been faintly unnerving.

When they had danced that one and only dance together she had disarmed him by indulging in polite small-talk.

When they had gone in to supper later to join Tom and
several others at one of the large tables, she had been both
witty and animated, entertaining all with her amusing conversation. Only in the carriage during the journey home had
he been given an inkling of how she had been feeling.
Disinclined to talk, she had sat staring through the window
into the darkness, deeply immersed in her own private
thoughts.

Dear Lord! And what darkly depressing thoughts those
must have been! He ran impatient fingers through his hair,
sending his recently combed locks into disorder. Catching
her husband in a compromising situation with her sister of
all people! Why, it smacked of little short of incest!

It was so damnably unfair, too! Slumping down on the
chair before his dressing-table, he suddenly felt bitterly resentful. No one could have tried harder than he had to prove
how deeply he cared. He had been patient and understanding, which was nothing less than Elizabeth deserved after
the heartlessly cruel way he had behaved towards her; but
all his good intentions, all those weeks of trying to rebuild
their relationship, had been destroyed in a few short
minutes, simply because he had felt obliged to be polite to
someone he didn't even like. And therein, he decided, his
temper returning with a vengeance, was the reason he found
himself in this unfortunate predicament now.

He didn't resent one single act of kind consideration
which he had bestowed on Elizabeth during the weeks since
her illness, but he was forced to admit that his behaviour
could hardly be described as natural. The fault might have
been his in foolishly accompanying Evadne into the garden,
but he had certainly not instigated or desired what had
taken place between them. So why the devil should he be
held responsible for that scheming harridan's unwelcome
attentions?

Patience and understanding had proved excellent weapons in the past, but they would not serve his purpose now. No, only a direct approach would serve. Much better to thrash things out tonight than allow her to continue to suppose that he was some monstrous cad who harboured unwholesome designs on her sister.

Some detached part of his brain had registered that Aggie had left the adjoining room some minutes ago. The chances were that Elizabeth would now be tucked up in bed, but it was unlikely that she would have succumbed to sleep so quickly, he decided, striding purposefully across to the connecting door and throwing it open so forcefully that it banged against the chest of drawers, startling Elizabeth who was not, in fact, in bed, but sitting at the gilt-legged table in the corner of the room, busily composing a letter.

'Elizabeth, we must talk! And it will not wait until morning.'

She found his moderately domineering tone as deeply attractive as the man himself. Dressed, she suspected, with nothing beneath the crimson brocade robe and with his bare feet planted slightly apart in the thick pile of the patterned carpet, he reminded her of some proud eastern potentate considering the fate of an erring subject.

'It just so happens that I wished to speak to you, Richard,' she momentarily startled him by announcing. 'This letter I'm composing is to my late grandmother's man of business. He retains in his safekeeping a small chest containing several personal letters and important documents. I need it brought here urgently, and was wondering if you'd allow me to despatch Jenkins, the footman, to collect it first thing in the morning?'

'Yes. Yes, of course,' he responded, taken aback slightly by the unexpected request and the impassive, enquiring way she was regarding him. How on earth could she remain so calmly self-possessed after what she had witnessed tonight? The dreadful fear that she might not actually care whether or not he was contemplating an affair with her sister momentarily crossed his mind, but he swiftly suppressed the soul-destroying notion. She wasn't so coldly indifferent to him. No, he was firmly convinced she was not.

'I—er—wanted to talk about tonight,' he began cautiously, not quite knowing now how to broach the somewhat delicate subject.

'Oh, yes. A lovely party, wasn't it?'

'Yes. Yes, it was.' He cleared his throat noisily. 'But I was—er—referring specifically to that unfortunate interlude involving your sister.' She unnerved him further by remaining silent, one finely arched brow raised in half-mocking enquiry. 'I don't know what you must have thought—what you believed was going on between—'

'Oh, I know what was going on, right enough, Richard,' she interrupted, turning her attention once again to the half-finished letter. 'You were making love to Evadne.'

'No, I was not!' he countered staunchly, and in his rapidly growing irritation didn't notice the wickedly teasing smile playing about her mouth.

'Very well,' she compromised. 'You were merely kissing her, then.'

'That's precisely it—I wasn't. She was kissing me!'

'Is there a difference?'

'Of course there is, damn it!' he snapped, forgetting to put a guard on his tongue in his determination to win back at least a modicum of her regard. 'I didn't know the confounded woman was planning a seduction scene when she asked me to escort her outside for a breath of air.'

'You must have offered some encouragement, Richard,' she suggested, sounding so matter of fact about the whole business that he experienced the strong urge to take her by the shoulders and shake her until her teeth rattled. 'I cannot imagine that even Evadne would demean herself by offering her charms to a man she knew to be completely indifferent to her.'

'I don't give a damn what that designing harpy would or would not do,' he responded sharply, fast coming to the end of his tether. 'I have never ever given her any reason to suppose that I have designs on her person.'

'Now that, Richard,' Elizabeth countered, turning her head and waving her quill at him like some irate schoolma'm, 'is a downright untruth. And well you know it! I recall quite clearly hearing you say that you wished Evadne was the one your father had wished you to marry… And you kissed her then, too!'

He couldn't have been more stunned if she had announced that she was secretly married to Bonaparte himself. 'What nonsense is this?' he demanded, making it abundantly obvious that he retained no recollection of the incident whatsoever. 'I've never said any such thing!'

'Oh, but you did, Richard,' she argued, certain of her facts. 'You would have been about nineteen, twenty at most. You were taking a stroll with Evadne in my parents' garden at the time, in the shrubbery to be precise, and I overheard you. And that,' she added before he could give voice to further denials, 'is precisely why I sought refuge with my grandmother within a year of my father's demise.'

Ignoring his astounded expression, she began to brush the feathers of the quill back and forth across her chin. 'Although my father desired the match, I do not believe he would have forced it upon me in view of the fact that you preferred my sister to me. But my mother most certainly would have done so. It is quite a lowering experience discovering that the man one has been groomed to marry infinitely prefers someone else. And that, of course, is in essence the reason why I wrote to you when you were out in the Peninsula. I didn't refuse to marry you because you had no title then, as you seemed to suppose. I merely refused to marry someone who infinitely preferred my sister to me.'

It was wicked of her, she knew, but she simply couldn't help feeling a deal of satisfaction from his bewildered discomfiture. He gaped across the room at her as though she had just sprouted a second head, and then clapped a hand over his eyes as if to dispel the hideous vision.

'I don't believe I'm hearing this,' he muttered, removing the hand from his face. He took a hesitant step towards her, about to reiterate that Evadne meant less than nothing to him, when he stepped on something sharp and ended by uttering a loud and rather rude expletive.

'What on earth have you done?' Elizabeth flew across to the bed where he had seated himself in order to examine his injured foot. 'Here, let me. My nails are longer than yours.'

'You can thank your niece for this,' she told him after extracting the small, sharp object from the flesh. 'She was in here this afternoon and had scattered my box of bits and pieces over the carpet before I could stop her. She is getting quite naughty, Richard. You really must take a firmer hand with her.'

'She isn't the only one,' he muttered, and this time he didn't miss the wickedly provocative smile before she went across the room to collect a towel.

Kneeling in front of him, Elizabeth began to dab the small cut, which was bleeding slightly, with the towel. Richard gazed down at her bent head, thinking as he always did how lovely she looked with those glossy russet locks cascading about her shoulders, while at the same time trying desperately to ignore the gentle touch of warm fingers on his ankle.

'You truly don't believe I care tuppence for your sister, do you?' he asked, his voice suddenly husky and throbbing with emotion.

'Not now, I don't.'

'I never went out into the garden with her in the hope of seducing her. Believe me, that would never enter my head.'

'No, I know it wouldn't.'

'You do?' His triumphant smile was instantly erased by a suspicious frown. 'How long were you out there before you made your presence known?'

'I had been in the garden for a little while. I saw you and Evadne walking down the path, and hid in the shadows,' she admitted at last. 'There was a reason why I didn't want Evadne to know I had been outside. You stopped only a few yards away from where I was standing, and I overheard everything that was said. One should, I suppose, consider eavesdropping a reprehensible habit, but I'm not in the least sorry that for once I gave way to temptation.'

She raised her head and what he saw mirrored in her eyes made his spirits soar to record heights. 'If I hadn't remained to listen to your conversation I would have missed hearing something that I've been longing to hear for such a very long time.'

'And what was that, Elizabeth?' he asked, his voice a gentle caress.

'That you loved me.'

The towel slipped from her fingers as he took a hold of her upper arms and drew her unresistingly against him. 'But you knew that...surely you must have known? I have been in love with you, Elizabeth, almost from the moment I walked into that small parlour at Dartwood Manor and saw you sitting there.'

She didn't reply, couldn't reply, for Richard's lips had fastened over hers with a possessive hunger, and her immediate response was wonderful confirmation, had he needed any, that the breach between them had finally been healed.

He did sense a moment's restraint, a fleeting disquiet, after he had laid her gently into the bed and had peeled away her clothing, but his exploring fingers soon had the reserve melting away and he extricated those soft moans of pleasure he had waited so long to hear again. His many weeks of self-imposed abstinence was not without its penalty, however, and the exquisite pleasure was over all too quickly, but he consoled himself with the knowledge that next time it would be more rewarding for them both, and that the next time would not be long in taking place.

For her part Elizabeth was blissfully happy, but then she would have been so even if he had not come to her room and the inevitable outcome of two people very much in love hadn't taken place. His lovemaking had been a wonderful confirmation of those precious words he had spoken in the garden earlier, adding a further layer to the cloak of blessed contentment which had shrouded her during these past few hours.

History, however, had an unfortunate habit of repeating itself as she discovered moments later when he didn't attempt to gather her into his arms. Suddenly thrusting the bed covers aside, he swung his feet to the floor, and unpleasant memories returned with a vengeance and began to strip away the layers of exultation, threatening to leave her naked and vulnerable as she had been on that never-to-be-forgotten occasion before.

'What is it, Richard?' she forced herself to ask while at the same time dreading the answer. 'What's wrong?'

His flashing smile acted like an emollient, instantly soothing away all distraught thoughts. Without bothering to retrieve his discarded dressing-gown he padded, naked, across to the connecting door, offering her the unfettered view of his wonderfully proportioned muscular frame before he disappeared for a few moments into his room.

'I am taking the very necessary precautions of ensuring

that we shall not be disturbed,' he answered on his return, repeating the procedure of moments before by locking her bedchamber door and then blowing out the various candles, leaving just the one on the bedside table alight. 'I give you fair warning now, madam wife, that it is unlikely I shall allow you to rise early in the morning, if I permit you to rise at all.'

By the contented smile she cast him as he slipped into bed beside her again, and propped himself up on one elbow, it was quite evident that she had no fault to find with these arrangements. 'But first we must talk, Elizabeth,' he told her, suddenly serious. 'I never again want hurt... misunderstandings between us.'

He paused for a moment to run one finger along the outline of her jaw, his dark eyes betraying clearly enough the anguish of bitter regrets, even before he said, 'My behaviour towards you in the past has been, to say the least, less than just. I overreacted when I discovered that you— that I was not the first man you had—'

'Richard, there is something you should know,' she interrupted gently, but he was determined to have his say, and placed his exploring finger over her lips.

'No, my darling, there's no need for you to explain. The fault was mine. I behaved like a damnable fool!' he rasped in violent self-reproach. 'I loved you so much that when I discovered another man had known you, I felt bitterly hurt and resentful. My liaison with that woman in London meant nothing.' The shadow of pain flitting over her features brought a further stab of self-disgust, but he forced himself to go on. 'It was a cruel and heartless way of taking my revenge, I know. My only excuse is that I was consumed with rage and jealousy, and was still, even then, labouring under a heavy burden of guilt.'

He saw a moment's puzzlement replace the sadness in her eyes, and knew he must explain everything if his callous behaviour towards her in the spring was ever to be truly forgiven and forgotten.

'You know that I was injured at Waterloo. The most frightening legacy of that terrible battle was my temporary blindness. I was nursed back to health by a young woman called Mary Smith. I truly don't believe I would have survived if it hadn't been for that blessed girl.'

So wrapped was he in bittersweet memories that he failed to notice lips curled in a sweetly knowing smile. 'One night I selfishly took her innocence. I was prepared to do the honourable thing and marry her, but Mary, ever giving, expected nothing in return, and started back for England the following day.' He released his breath in a heartfelt sigh. 'She must have suspected that my feelings for her were only deep affection, not love.'

Elizabeth regarded him in silence for a moment, her expression unreadable. 'Did you never attempt to find her?' she asked, rampant curiosity momentarily holding back her long-overdue confession.

'I fully intended to do so. She left me a letter, which I still retain to this day, but it contained no forwarding address. It was while I was awaiting the return of the owner of the house which she had hired in Brussels that I learned of her death.'

'Death?' Elizabeth echoed, not attempting to hide her astonishment. 'What on earth makes you suppose that she died? I mean,' she amended when he regarded her searchingly, 'if you didn't know her whereabouts in England, how could you possibly have known that she had died?'

'She never reached England,' he astounded her by responding. 'A Mrs and Miss Mary Smith were amongst those who took passage on *The Albatross*. It capsized in mid-Channel on its return to Southampton last summer.'

Lowering her eyes, she absently regarded the dark hairs at the base of his throat as memory flooded back. *The*

Albatross had not departed when she had arrived at the port. There had been no earthly chance of her attaining passage back to England on that particular vessel, however, for not only was it fully booked, but her grandmother's health had deteriorated during the journey from Brussels to such an extent that they had been forced to put up at an inn for a few days before embarking on the sea voyage home. Naturally, she had learned of the terrible tragedy, but she had never seen a list of casualties. Not for an instant had she believed that he had tried to find her, for it would not have been an impossible task. When the weeks had passed without seeing him on her grandmother's doorstep in Bristol, or without receiving a letter from him, she had believed that her decision to leave him in total ignorance of her true identity had been justified. But he had tried to find her, and all this time he had believed that she, his Mary, had lost her life in that terrible tragedy at sea.

'Oh, God! If only I'd known,' she murmured, and didn't realise she had spoken aloud until he responded with, 'How could you have known? I've never spoken of it before. Besides, I should never have allowed my feelings of guilt to interfere with our relationship. I wasn't in love with Mary, but I did fall in love with you. And never again will I risk losing you because of stupid pride, or thoughtless actions.'

'Richard, you do not perfectly understand.' She simply must tell him the truth now! 'Richard, I have a confession to make. It concerns that man—that first time I—'

'No, Elizabeth!' he ground out. 'I never wish to know his name!' Then, more gently, 'I don't want to know who it was. It doesn't matter. Our marriage starts now. What has gone before is best forgotten. Let's away with recriminations and regrets. Let us, now, lay the past quietly to rest, and think only of the future.'

'Yes, Richard, I know, but—'

She got no further, for he was determined to have his way, and the methods he adopted to achieve his aim were so sweetly pleasurable that she couldn't summon up further resistance. Some deep recess of her brain suggested that an opportunity would arise for her to broach the subject again, but now was hardly the most appropriate time, when it seemed that the only concern of the man she loved was to demonstrate the depth of his feelings in a peerless display of masculine passion.

After returning his pen to its position on the standish, Richard rose from his desk and stretched contentedly. He looked a man thoroughly satisfied with life, and his appearance was not deceptive. Since the evening of Caroline's eventful party he had experienced nothing short of perfect contentment: the fulfilling pleasures of his wife's lovely body lying beside him at nights; and long periods of her unrivalled company during the days. It had brought a whole new meaning to his life to know beyond a shadow of doubt that he was cherished in return by such a wonderfully caring young woman as Elizabeth: unique, unequalled; fulfilling the smallest requirement of a wife.

He turned as the door opened, hoping to see his perfect companion enter the room, and experienced more than just a twinge of disappointment when his butler walked into the library.

'There is a gentleman called to see you, sir, by name of Collingworth—a Captain Simon Collingworth to be precise.'

'Good Lord!' Richard was surprised and didn't attempt to hide the fact. He hadn't set eyes on that young rogue since Waterloo. 'Yes, Finch, show him in,' he said, while moving over to the decanters in readiness for the entry of the man who had been affectionately christened 'The Scourge of the Regiment'.

'Simon, this is an unexpected pleasure!' he remarked, genuinely delighted to see the tall, loose-limbed young man who strode with a swaggering gait into the room moments later. 'What on earth brings you to this neck of the woods?'

'I'm paying a necessary visit to a favourite aunt of mine. Don't intend she should pop off and forget me in her will,' he divulged with raffish honesty. 'It's no joy being an officer on half-pay in peace time, I can tell you.'

Richard accepted this with a knowing half-smile. The Collingworth family was a wealthy one and Simon, being the likeable rogue that he was, wouldn't think twice about approaching his elder brother to bail him out if he did find himself under the hatches.

'Trying times, indeed,' he responded wryly, handing his incorrigible young guest a glass of Madeira before seating himself in the chair opposite. 'Your unfortunate situation apart,' he went on, serious for a moment, 'it quite grieves me to see the plight of so many of those brave soldiers who fought with us. Unable to find work they are treated with less sympathy and compassion than lepers!'

'Very true. And that, Ricky, old boy, is precisely why I took the trouble of looking you up.' Tossing the contents of his glass down his throat, the young captain took a moment or two to savour the taste. 'Excellent wine! Nothing less than I would expect from your cellar... Now, where was I?'

'You haven't reached anywhere as yet, Simon. I'm still waiting to hear the reason why you chose to honour me with your company.'

The younger man's eyes began to dance. Had the reason behind his visit not been so serious, his ever-lively sense of fun would certainly have prompted him to indulge in some harmless bantering with this gallant, one-time commanding officer.

'It's poor old Hawk that brings me here,' he surprised

Richard by announcing. 'Came upon him quite by chance a few days ago when I was taking m'brother's new turnout for an airing in the park. Some silly clunch lost control of the high-spirited gelding he was riding, and who should come to the fop's aid but old Sergeant Hawker.'

He shook his head sadly. 'Didn't recognise him at first out of uniform. His clothes were tatty, little better than rags. He hasn't lost his knack with horses, though. Never known a man who has such a way with beasts as old Hawk. Had that gelding quietened down within seconds.'

Richard stared down into the contents of his glass wondering what his old sergeant was doing in the capital. Tobias Hawker had been born and raised in the country and hated large towns. He wouldn't have been in London unless he had no option but to be there.

'Did you get a chance to talk with him? Why didn't he return to his home in Nottinghamshire after the war?'

'He did, old chap. Apparently, though, his old master died last summer. The old man's eldest son turned Hawker's wife out of the cottage as soon as he had inherited the property, and told Hawk his services were no longer required on the estate when he eventually arrived back there. Mrs Hawker had come to live with her sister in London, and poor old Tobias followed as soon as he had discovered where she had gone. But London's like everywhere else. Times are hard. Hawk gets work when he can to earn a crust, but he's having a rough time of it—anyone can see that.'

Richard's feelings of sympathy were swept aside by a sudden surge of annoyance. 'Why the devil didn't the silly clunch get in touch with me? He knows where my house is in London. A message would have been sent on to me here.'

Captain Collingworth shrugged. 'Pride, I suppose. It

would go against the grain for a man of Hawk's stamp to beg.'

'Stubborn fool!' Richard muttered. 'Do you know where he's residing at present?'

'That I don't… Well, at least not precisely. We chatted for a bit. The poor chap looked all in after traipsing round the capital for hours looking for work, so I offered him a ride home. As soon as we were south of the river he didn't want me to take him any further, but I did manage to persuade him to join me in a tankard of ale.'

'And where is this tavern to be found?'

'Green Street. It's called the Three Bells. You can't miss it. It's on the corner. Not one of the finest inns I've entered, I have to say. The landlord recognised Hawker, so I should imagine he can't live too far away from the place.'

After a quick glance at the mantel-clock, Simon rose to his feet. 'I'd better be making tracks if I'm to reach my relative's house in good time for dinner. I've still a fair way to travel,' he announced, looking down at Richard's troubled face. 'I would have helped old Hawk myself if I had been in a position to. I'll spread the word when I return to Horse Guards. Someone may be able to offer the poor devil employment. But I know you had a deal of respect for him, so I couldn't pass so close by without putting you in the picture.'

'Yes, thank you. I'm glad you took the trouble.' Richard rose to his feet and, with a promise to look his visitor up in London in the autumn, he escorted him to the door.

His thoughts were still very much on the plight of his sergeant when Elizabeth joined him a short time later. She had some concerns of her own, but couldn't mistake the look of disquiet on her husband's face, even though he did his best to conceal the fact behind a warm smile and a loving greeting.

Placing her hands on his upper arms, she held him away in order to study his features more closely. 'What's wrong, Richard? Has something occurred to upset you whilst I've been out?'

'No—yes… Well, I'm not upset, precisely, just concerned over someone,' he admitted, and then went on to relate the conversation he had had with his unexpected visitor earlier.

'There are old soldiers, unable to find work, begging on street corners in every town and city in the land,' he went on bitterly. 'It would be foolish to imagine that one could aid them all. But this particular man I would definitely help if he'd let me. He has a natural gift, Elizabeth. He can handle horseflesh better than any other person I know.'

'You think there's a good chance he'd refuse your help, Richard?' she asked with her innate perspicacity, after seeing his brows snap together in an angry frown.

'Yes, stubborn fool!' Moving away, he began to pace the room in irritation. 'I doubt he'd accept charity, especially from me.'

'But it wouldn't be charity, now, would it, Richard?' she pointed out with a quizzical smile, as the most obvious solution to the problem had already occurred to her, even if it hadn't occurred to her very worried husband as yet. 'It seems to me that he would be the ideal person to take charge of the stables here at Knightley Hall.'

He stared across the few feet that separated them in blank amazement for several seconds, just as though she had suggested something so outlandishly foolish that she must have taken leave of her senses, then he uttered a triumphant shout of laughter.

'Elizabeth, my darling, you're a marvel!' Bridging the short distance between them in three giant strides, he took her in his arms again. 'Now, why the deuce didn't that obvious solution occur to me at once?'

She didn't for a moment suspect that he required a response, but the fun-loving side of her nature decided to answer him nevertheless. 'You've evidently a deal on your mind, Richard, and your wits have become addled somewhat under the pressure. You'll recover your natural thought processes given time, I dare say.'

'I'll take leave to inform you, madam wife, that both mind and body have been under considerable pressure for quite some weeks, and the sole culprit for my continued disorderly state is right here next to my heart.'

'In that case it is up to the wrongdoer to put matters right.' The smile she cast him before taking the precaution of slipping out of his arms was a study in roguishness. 'And you'll be forced to admit, Richard, that I have been doing my level best to effect a cure during these past few days.'

A husky growl of well-remembered pleasure was sufficient to warn her, and she neatly avoided his outstretched hand as he made to pull her back into his arms. 'Behave, Richard! This is neither the time nor the place to indulge in such conduct. Instead, channel your thoughts on how best to go about finding this old army acquaintance of yours.'

'I have one small lead,' he announced, reluctantly doing as she asked. 'Collingworth took him to a certain tavern. I'll begin my search there.'

'When will you leave for London?'

'Tomorrow morning, if you think you can be ready by then.' He watched a frown replace the smile. 'What's wrong, Elizabeth? Don't you wish to accompany me?'

'I'd like to very much, Richard, but I feel I must forgo the pleasure this time. There is something I've promised to do for Caroline which concerns my sister.'

She hadn't mentioned anything about that very enlightening conversation she had had with their neighbour on the evening of the ball. It wasn't that she wished to keep him in ignorance over her sister's behaviour. He was under no illusions, now, about Evadne's true character, so it would come as no surprise to him to learn of her appalling behaviour towards Caroline. But the issue was a sensitive one and the means by which she intended rescuing her neighbour from Evadne's clutches was equally so. Her sister deserved no consideration, she knew, but she refused to lower herself to Evadne's level and, therefore, would do her the undeserved courtesy of speaking to her in private.

'I must have a talk with my sister before she returns to Devonshire. That is why I went out this morning, as it happens. Unfortunately, Evadne had gone out somewhere and Caroline wasn't certain when she would return.' Her frown grew more pronounced. 'Caroline tells me my darling sister's been out and about a good deal during her visit. Apparently she's struck up a friendship with Lady Pentecost.'

'Ha! That doesn't surprise me in the least. A well-matched pair!'

She couldn't prevent a chuckle at the scathing tone, but sobered almost at once. 'Be that as it may, I still need to see her, and I'm not sure just how long she intends to inflict her company on poor Caroline, so I think in the circumstances I must stay here. Added to which, I'm rather concerned that Jenkins hasn't returned from Bristol with that small chest. He should have been back by now. If he hasn't returned by tomorrow evening I think I shall need to make a flying visit to Bristol.'

'Well, you're not going by yourself!' he told her roundly, every inch the possessive, domineering husband. 'I'll leave for London within the hour. I'll visit that tavern, but if I'm unsuccessful, then I'll pay a visit to an acquaintance of mine at Bow Street. I shall be back here tomorrow evening at the latest, and if Jenkins hasn't returned by then we can leave for Bristol the following day.'

'How very kind you are to me, Richard.' She went smilingly up to him and slid her arms about his waist with wifely familiarity, which seemed to please him immensely. 'I shan't delay your departure by explaining things now, because it would take too long, but when you return I'll tell you precisely why the contents of that chest are so very important. In the meantime, I shall be counting the minutes until your return, and shall be on the doorstep, waiting to greet you with open arms, unless of course something, or someone, prevents my doing so.'

Innocent enough words, but words that would return to torment him in the not-too-distant future.

Chapter Thirteen

Richard left Knightley Hall early in the afternoon. Driving himself in his racing curricle, he made excellent time. He kept several pairs of horses, all in prime condition, stabled at various inns along the main road to London. Changes were effected smoothly and he arrived at his town house in good time to begin his search for his old comrade early that evening.

After tooling the curricle round to the mews, he carried his small portmanteau to the front entrance of the house. His servants, not expecting their master's return, had put into effect the customary practices of protecting the delicate furnishings in holland covers, and removing the brass knocker from the door to indicate to any would-be caller that the master of the house was not in residence. It took Richard several minutes to attract someone's attention, but eventually Medway, busily working away in the butler's pantry, heard the pounding and came up from the nether regions to investigate the imperious hammering on the front door.

'Why, Sir Richard!' he exclaimed, not attempting to hide his surprise at his master's unexpected return. 'If I had known of your intention to come up to town, I would have put the house in order.'

'Don't concern yourself, Medway,' Richard responded, handing over the portmanteau as he stepped into the hall. 'It's a flying visit. I intend staying for only one night. Just have my bedchamber made ready. There's no need to concern yourself with the other rooms, and I shall be dining at my club later, so inform Cook not to concern herself, either. Although we shall need a good breakfast in the morning before we leave.'

Medway's ears pricked up at this as he followed his master up the stairs. 'We, sir? Shall I be going somewhere with you.'

'Yes. You'll be returning with me to Knightley Hall,' his master explained, leading the way into his bedchamber. 'I intended to send for you a couple of weeks ago, but, like so many other things of late, it slipped my mind. Finch is retiring and I should like you to take his place and accept full responsibility for both residences.'

Medway's dearest wish had been granted, and it took several moments before he regained enough control of himself to stutter out his grateful thanks at being offered the opportunity to prove his worthiness. He had not, as yet, attained the age of thirty, and being offered such an exalted position at his young age in a respected peer of the realm's household was no mean achievement.

'There's absolutely no need for all this gratitude, Medway. You've worked hard and loyally for my family for many years, and have earned the promotion. Finch will be no easy act to follow, but I do not doubt you'll prove yourself a worthy successor. Now,' he went on, collecting a clean shirt from the wardrobe, 'do you consider young Frederick competent enough to look after this place in your absence?'

'He's conscientious, sir, and there's little enough to do

here when you're not in residence. I think he deserves the chance.'

'Very well. You can tell him he'll be starting his new duties from tomorrow.' Richard shrugged himself out of his slightly travel-creased jacket and tossed it over a chair. 'Whilst I'm changing I'd like you to go down into the street and hail me a hackney carriage. Find me one whose driver knows the area around the Three Bells on the corner of Green Street, which is situated somewhere south of the Thames.'

By the time Richard had finished changing, Medway returned to say that a hackney awaited him at the door. The coachman knew the tavern's whereabouts, and the surrounding area like the back of his hand, or so he said, and Richard didn't delay in making use of the jarvey's knowledge.

As the rather musty smelling equipage headed in a southerly direction, Richard stared out of the window at the people going about their business. The Season had been over for several weeks and most of the *ton* had either followed the Regent to fashionable Brighton, or retired to their country estates to recuperate for a while before they returned to the capital and the next hectic round of social engagements. Life in London didn't stop, however, just because those most privileged persons in the land had left the heat and smells behind for the fresher country or sea air. The city was still bustling with life, though it was quite noticeable that there were far fewer fashionable carriages thronging the busy streets, and very few members of the *haut monde* wishing to parade in their finery for the edification of the populace.

As they crossed the river, the distinction between rich and poor became more marked. No fine mansions here, only streets and streets of tightly packed houses built in sentinel-like rows. There were no crossing boys to keep the streets clean and fit to stroll along and, apart from the occasional dilapidated private carriage, the only vehicles to be seen were lumbering carts, pulled by ill-nourished, work-weary horses.

It was rare for Richard to venture into this part of the city; after all, he had little reason ever to do so. He was not, however, completely ignorant of the misery of hardship. During his years in the army he had known what it was like to do without the basics of life; but his periods of privation had been short, whereas to the poor devils living here it was simply a way of life with little or no hope for improvement.

When the carriage drew to a halt, Richard alighted and, after requesting the jarvey to await his return, went striding towards the tavern. The instant he walked through the door, the smattering of patrons ceased their chattering abruptly, and he could not forbear a smile as all eyes, betraying blank astonishment, followed his progress to the counter.

It was safe to assume that a person of his evident means was a rare sight in this particular establishment. Which was in no way surprising, for Richard couldn't imagine any gentleman of his acquaintance, no matter how purse-pinched, demeaning himself by entering such a lowly place, where each worm-eaten table boasted a thick film of dust and all the walls were besmirched with large patches of black mould.

In fact, he was in two minds whether to chance a tankard of ale, but then decided it might be worthwhile taking the risk, as it was likely to make the landlord, who was eyeing him measuringly from his side of the counter, a little more forthcoming.

The ale, surprisingly, turned out to be very palatable, and Richard, ever polite, complimented mine host on the brew before asking outright if he was acquainted with Tobias Hawker.

'All depends on who be a-wanting 'im whether I be or no,' was the surly response from the near-toothless and far from personable owner of the tavern.

'Perhaps this will help make up your mind.' Richard drew out a shiny gold sovereign, holding it temptingly just out of reach of the landlord's eager fingers. 'It has always been my policy to pay for goods after they have been delivered.'

'I knows 'im right enough,' the innkeeper growled, not taking his eyes off the glinting largesse.

'Does he reside nearby?'

'Ee may do.'

Richard's smile was not pleasant. 'My patience is not limitless, my friend. Either you tell me where he lives or—' he cast a brief glance at the several interested onlookers '—perhaps one of these other gentlemen might be more eager than yourself to earn some easy money.'

The threat lost nothing for all that it was softly spoken, and the reaction to it was not slow in coming. 'Ee lives in Brenner Street wi' 'is wife's sister and family. Don't know which 'ouse, though, but you'll find it no bother.'

'Thank you, my good man.' He tossed the sovereign high into the air and had reached the door before it had been caught in the landlord's greasy palm.

'Brenner Street,' he called up to the carriage driver. 'Do you know where that is?'

The jarvey stared down at Sir Richard in amazement, wondering what a man of his undoubted quality could be wanting in such a run-down slum, but decided it might not be in his own best interests to enquire, and merely nodded. A few minutes later he drew the vehicle to a halt again at the entrance to one of the more noisome streets in the area, where the sun rarely managed to filter between the tightly packed buildings and the air was heavy and always foulsmelling.

'I don't know how long I shall be,' Richard remarked, stepping down from the carriage and neatly avoiding a pile of filth in the road, 'but I shall reward you handsomely if you do me the courtesy of once again awaiting my return.'

'I wouldn't leave a dog alone round 'ere, sir,' the jarvey announced, gazing about him in distaste. 'I'll wait for you, don't you worry. And should you—er—be needing my services in any other way, then just you holler and I'll come a-running.'

Richard cast a shrewd, assessing glance up at the small but sturdy individual perched on the box. 'Yes, you look as though you'd give a good account of yourself if you were called upon to do so.'

The jarvey didn't pretend to misunderstand and tapped the side of his broken nose in a meaningful way. 'That I would, guv'nor. Not that I'm one to go looking for trouble, you understand, but there again I ain't never been known to turn tail and run, neiver.'

He paid Richard the silent compliment of deciding that, for all he resembled some swaggering Bond Street beau, the body beneath the immaculate attire belonged to a man in fine physical condition, muscular and strong.

'I mind you'd handle yourself well enough if it came to a bout of fisticuffs, sir.'

'I've been known to spar from time to time,' Richard admitted with a ghost of a smile before turning and picking his way carefully along the narrow garbage-ridden street.

When he drew level with the group of children, who had all simultaneously abandoned their game in order to gape at the spectacle in their midst, he beckoned to one of the boys. Rampant curiosity quickly overcame the street urchin's innate mistrust of strangers, and a well-to-do stranger at that, an uncommon sight, indeed, in this rat-infested slum! He disengaged himself from his companions, his wide eyes and gaping mouth ample testament to his continued awe-struck state.

'A shilling for you, boy, if you can point out the home of Mr Tobias Hawker,' Richard offered temptingly, and then took the precaution of moving back a pace when the boy lifted his hand to his matted hair, and an alarming memory of an unwashed climbing-boy flashed before his mind's eye.

'I reckon ee be the one living wiv the Joneses, guv'nor. They lives there.'

Richard glanced in the direction of the grimy pointing finger, tossed the boy the promised largesse and then went over to the house on the opposite end of the street. From the outside, at least, it looked as if the occupants had made some attempt to improve their lot. Brightly coloured curtains hung at the windows, and the area outside the front door had been recently swept.

The woman who came in answer to his summons was like a refreshing breath of fresh air in this less-than-wholesome place. Her mousy-brown hair was closely confined in a bun at the back of her head, and the apron that covered the front of her faded grey gown was as clean and well starched as any of those worn by the female servants in his own employ. For all that she was plainly attired in worn clothes and shoes, she was as much out of place in this locale as he was himself, and he had a suspicion of who she might be even before he introduced himself and she betrayed instant recognition of his name.

'Oh, sir! Do step inside, won't you? It isn't fitting for a gentleman like yourself to be standing outside in the street.'

Mrs Hawker moved to one side to enable Richard to enter the small front parlour which, though shabbily furnished, was both clean and tidy, without so much as a speck of dust to be seen anywhere. Hawker had frequently remarked on the fact that, although his estate cottage might

ot be grand, one would need to travel a long way to find
a cleaner abode.

'As you may have gathered, Mrs Hawker, I am here to
see your husband. What time do you expect him home?'

Surprised that he should have known who she was, for
hey had never met before, as her husband hadn't approved
of soldiers bringing their wives with them to Portugal and
Spain, she silently gave herself a scold for forgetting her
manners and not introducing herself to the man her husband
had admired above any other during his years in the army.
Determined not to be found lacking again, she politely invited the distinguished visitor to seat himself in the most
comfortable chair, before offering him some refreshments.

'I have a bottle of brandy put by for medicinal purposes,
sir, but you're most welcome to a glass while you're wait-
ng for Toby. He shouldn't be too long now. Unlike my
brother-in-law, he rarely goes to the tavern after he's fin-
shed work.'

Richard was in two minds. He didn't wish to hurt this
polite woman's feelings by refusing, but at the same time
felt guilty at depriving her of something she could ill afford
to replace, so he decided on a compromise. 'That is most
kind of you, madam, but just a small one, thank you.'

Delving in a cupboard, she drew out a bottle and a clean
glass and allowed him to help himself. 'You say Hawker
has found work?' he remarked, pouring himself a very
small measure of the amber liquid.

'Until the end of the week, sir, yes.' She betrayed her
concern with a deep sigh. 'It's difficult finding anything
round here. Work is offered to the locals first, which I suppose is only fair. Coming from the country, Toby and me
are considered outsiders, you see, although I did manage to
find a few weeks' work during the spring, making gowns
in one of the fashion houses in Bond Street.'

Richard was only too well aware that that particular trade

was nothing short of slave labour, with the poor women working up to sixteen hours a day in the cellars beneath the fashionable shops in poor light and airless conditions. 'And you're not working now, I take it.'

'I did manage to find work in one of the big houses for a while, but the owners returned to the country. Perhaps I'll have more luck in the autumn when some folks return to the capital. I'm looking after my sister's baby at the moment. He's upstairs, sound asleep in his cot. My sister married a Londoner, you see, sir, so she's considered a local and has no trouble in earning a few days' pay now and then. This is their house. It was very good of them to take us in like they did,' she finished, trying desperately to sound contented with her lot, but she didn't fool Richard for a moment.

She was a woman accustomed to better things and a woman, unless he was very much mistaken, who would be prepared to work all the hours God sent in order to have a home she could call her own again.

'I understand that you were evicted from the estate cottage you'd lived in for many years when the estate came into the hands of your old master's heir.'

She looked faintly surprised that he should have known this, but nodded in confirmation. 'I suppose in a way it was Toby's fault. He took a riding crop to young Master Roland several years ago, when he caught him one day whipping a horse. When the old master learned what had occurred he didn't dismiss Toby, as Master Roland had hoped, but carried on from where Toby had left off and beat his son. The young master never forgave us for that. As soon as his father died, he turned me out of the cottage. I wrote a letter to Tobias to tell him what had happened, but it must have gone astray. He returned to the estate after Waterloo to find strangers in our old home, but one of the estate workers told him where I had gone and he came to London to find me.'

'Why, then, did he not come and find me, too? It is not, after all, such a distance to travel to my London residence from here.'

She looked faintly discomposed by this direct attack, but before she could offer an explanation the door opened and the subject of the discussion strode into the room, his expression suddenly changing to one of blank astonishment as his eyes fell upon the gentleman sprawled at his ease in the chair.

'Major, sir! You…here? But…' His words faded and he slanted a decidedly disapproving look in his wife's direction. 'Is this your doing, Edith? I thought I told you—'

'No, it was not,' Richard announced, coming to Mrs Hawker's defence, 'but it ought to have been yours.'

He rose to his feet and stared at his old sergeant in angry silence. They were both of a similar height and stature, and suddenly seemed to fill the small room, dwarfing everything else in it, including Mrs Hawker who, just for one dreadful moment, thought that blows might be exchanged, so belligerent did both men appear. Then, thankfully, her husband seemed to collect himself, and turned away, running impatient fingers through his short, curly black hair.

'You know why I couldn't do that, Major, sir,' he said, almost brokenly, the unexpected sight of the man at whose side he had fought for so many years bringing him to the verge of tears. 'I've too much regard for you, that's why. You'd have found work for me—I know that. Then word would have got round that you were a soft touch, and you'd 'ave 'ad every raggedy ars—every poor devil in the regiment who hadn't been able to find work banging on your door looking for a hand-out.'

'You damned fool!' Richard returned mildly, touched by the depth of his old sergeant's regard.

'Aye, that I may be,' Hawker countered, a spark of the old defiance returning, 'but I've kept my self-respect. I've worked when I could find it, and when not I've gone without. Me and Edith will go on that way. We'll not accept charity.'

'Who said I was offering you any, may I ask?' Richard responded suavely as he resumed his seat. 'I am here to offer you employment. No, kindly allow me to finish,' he went on when Hawker threatened to interrupt. 'I have semi-retired my old head groom for reasons I shall not go in to now, and as yet have been unable to find a suitable replacement. Now, if you would like to be considered for the position, then kindly say so. If not, then I shall not take up any more of your time.'

Hawker regarded him in silence for several moments, not knowing whether to believe him or not, and then echoed his thoughts aloud, but his wife experienced no such doubts.

'Sir Richard's in earnest, Toby. Anyone can see that. He ain't spinning no yarn. It's a real job, and one you were born to do.'

'It would appear that your wife has far more wit than you have, Hawker. And, as further inducement, I should add that the position is at Knightley Hall, for the most part, and not here in town.' He glanced from eyes betraying dawning wonder to those glowing with deep gratitude. 'When can I expect you to take up your duties?'

'God damn you, sir!' Hawker cursed, but with all too evident gratitude seeping into his voice. 'My life wouldn't be worth living if I refuse now.' He cast tear-filled eyes in his wife's direction. 'The country, Edith... We're going back where we belong, old girl.'

'Excellent!' Richard announced with an approving half-smile, before tossing the meagre contents of his glass down his throat. 'We'll take it as settled. Now, when can I expect your arrival at the Hall?'

'My brother-in-law managed to get me work in the docks until the end of the week, sir. It would show 'im in a pretty poor light with the folks round 'ere if I didn't turn up. So, if you've no objections, I'd like to do right by 'im, and then travel into Hampshire early next week. That'll give us time to collect our bits and pieces together, and settle everything nicely at this end.'

'That's fine. I fully intend to return to my estates tomorrow. So, you'd better take this to tide you over.' He tossed a leather purse in his ex-sergeant's direction. 'And don't argue, Hawker,' he added, checking the recipient's intention of doing just that. 'I know precisely the amount contained in that purse and fully intend to deduct a little at a time from your wages for the next few weeks.'

Richard then turned his attention to Mrs Hawker, who had sat silently regarding him as though he were some kind of saint. He swiftly disabused her. 'I am not, sadly, in a position to offer you work, madam. There may be work in the house, but that is my wife's department and I have no intention of interfering in what is strictly her domain.'

'There's no need to concern yourself on my account, sir. I'm quite capable of finding myself— Oh, heaven's above!' she broke off to exclaim. 'Tobias, where are our manners? We haven't even congratulated Sir Richard on his marriage. We did read about it eventually, sir,' she explained. 'The announcement was placed in one of the newspapers that came our way.'

'Taken to reading journals now, have we, Hawk?' His smile was full of gentle humour. 'My, my! I have acquired an educated man as a head groom!'

Tobias took the gentle teasing in the spirit it had been intended. 'As you know, sir, it were Edith, here, who first started to teach me to read and write. She having been a tire-woman, she were taught by her mistress. You were kind enough to spare me a little time when you were able when we was in Spain. But it were Miss Mary that really made me see 'ow important it were to be able to read and write. Hours she spent with me, sir. Brought me on a treat, she did. God bless the darling girl!' He glanced across at Richard. 'Do you ever think about her, sir?'

'Not so much now, no,' he admitted softly, 'but I shall never forget her. I kept the letter she wrote to me, but…but I just wish I had something else to remember her by.'

Hawker exchanged a meaningful glance with his wife. 'Do you know where it is, Edith? Go fetch it. Miss Mary would have liked the Major to have it, I know. She were right fond of him.'

'Have what, Hawker?' Richard enquired.

'She loaned me a book of poems, sir, belonging to her old lady, and what with one thing and another I never got round to giving it back. I never could bring myself to sell it, even though it would have brought us a shilling or two.'

He laughed suddenly, the first unforced rumble of laughter he had managed in many a long, unhappy month. 'Snipped off a lock of her hair once, sir, so I did, when Miss Mary weren't looking. Mad as fire she were, but I wouldn't give it back. Placed it in the book for safe keeping. Pretty reddish hair it were too.'

'Red?' Richard echoed. 'But I thought her hair was blonde.'

'Bless you no, sir! Why on earth did—? Oh, begging your pardon. I were forgetting your condition. You never saw her, did you, sir?'

'No, Hawk, I was denied that pleasure.'

He turned his head as Mrs Hawker came back into the room holding a thin, leather-bound volume which she instantly placed in his outstretched hand. He raised the cover to see a very familiar shade of red-brown hair curled in an almost perfect circle. He gazed at the silken russet strands for several long and thoughtful moments before transferring his gaze to the faded writing on the inside front cover. The sentiment was too indistinct to read, but the names Mary and Smith were discernible enough. He studied the faded lettering more closely, turning the cover to the light, and the letters 's.o.n.' tacked onto the surname were just legible. The surname was not Smith, but Smithson.

He looked across at his latest employee keenly, but managed to hide quite beautifully the deep-rooted suspicion which had firmly embedded itself in his brain and which was rapidly growing into an ever-increasing astounding conviction. 'Mary's relative, Hawker—you always referred to her as "the old lady". I had assumed by this that she was Mary's mother. Might I have been incorrect in that assumption?'

'I only ever clapped eyes on her once, sir, but she looked more like Miss Mary's grandmother to me.'

Richard, his eyes narrowing to slits, focused on the beautiful russet-coloured strands again. Blonde hair and blue eyes, indeed! he fumed inwardly, remembering clearly Mary's own description of her colouring. And that West Country accent she had perfected so well... After living in Bristol for so many years that had, evidently, been easy to imitate.

Experiencing a strange mixture of exultation, because there wasn't a doubt in his mind of who had taken his wife's innocence, and seething anger because she had kept the wonderful truth to herself for so long, he looked at his ex-sergeant again.

'And Miss Mary herself...? What was she like?' He didn't wait for a response, but, of course, there was absolutely no need to. 'Were her eyes greenish-grey, one colour more prominent than the other depending on her mood? And did her mouth curl up slightly at the corners even when she was not actually smiling? And did she move with all the elegant ease of a thoroughbred filly, a floating, graceful motion?'

'Bless you, sir! Anyone would think you'd seen her yourself.'

'Oh, but I have,' he responded with a smile that would have frozen a desert oasis. 'I most definitely have.' He rose to his feet, clasping the book tightly in one hand. 'I think it only fair to warn you, Hawker, that you are going to experience a rather severe shock when you reach Knightley Hall... But it is as nothing to what my darling wife shall experience when I reach my ancestral home!'

Chapter Fourteen

Elizabeth stared for several thoughtful moments at the small chest the young footman had just placed in front of her, before delving into the top drawer of her husband's desk and drawing out the small key which she had had the forethought to place there in readiness for just this auspicious moment.

'I'm sorry I were so long in returning,' Jenkins apologised, watching his young mistress turn the key in the lock and open the lid. 'I found the offices without no trouble, but Mr Ainsworthy weren't there and his clerk wouldn't hand over the box without Mr Ainsworthy's say-so. So I thought it best to await his return from Bath.'

'You were right to do so,' Elizabeth assured him, not in the least annoyed over the delay. 'It would have been pointless your returning here. You would have needed to set out for Bristol again almost immediately. Did I give you sufficient funds for the extra nights' lodgings?'

'Yes, my lady,' he answered delving into his pocket and drawing out a purse that was now woefully slim, 'but I'm afraid there ain't much left.'

'No. You keep that,' Elizabeth ordered when he made to hand over the remaining few coins. 'You did very well,

Jenkins, and deserve some recompense. It's the Melcham Fair in two weeks' time. I'm sure you'll be pleased to have a little extra money to spend on fairings.'

After taking out a pile of letters, neatly tied together with a thin strip of black ribbon, Elizabeth closed the lid of the box. 'Carry that up to my room. Aggie will know where to put it. Then take yourself down to the kitchen for some refreshments. You must be tired after the journey, so inform Finch that I have excused you your duties for the remainder of the day.'

Elizabeth waited until the touchingly grateful young footman had left the room before turning her attention to the pile of letters. As she untied the ribbon she couldn't help wondering just why her grandmother had retained the evidence of her wrongdoing. Perhaps she did so as a kind of self-enforced punishment, to bring out and read from time to time and torment herself with the only thing she had ever done in her life of which she had been ashamed.

'My disgrace,' she had said to Elizabeth, handing over the yellowing bundle just a few days before she had died. 'Keep them or throw them away as you will, my dear, for you shall learn here and now what they contain from my own lips.'

Elizabeth recalled vividly that particular hour she had spent with her grandmother. When Mary Smithson had divulged the contents of the letters, Elizabeth had experienced no disgust or shame over her grandmother's actions, for she could not help wondering whether she would have acted any differently in a similar situation. After all, her grandmother had been prompted by motherly love only, and not out of any considerations for herself.

But Mrs Smithson had not been seeking forgiveness for actions she had been forced to take many years before, and had responded to her granddaughter's sympathetic utterances with, 'Nothing anyone could say would ever ease my conscience, Elizabeth. It was all my fault that it happened in the first place. I'm only too well aware of that. When your grandfather died I transferred all my love on to your mother. I spoilt her, Elizabeth. Anything she craved, she was given, except that one thing. In preventing her from making such a foolish mistake, I unwittingly ruined her life. She never forgave me for forcing her into a loveless union with your father, and for that I cannot blame her.'

'Does Evadne know the truth?' Elizabeth had asked.

'Your father would never have told her, of that I am certain. Your mother, however, was less considerate of her daughter's feelings. Yes, she told her. Perhaps she had hoped that it would increase the bond between them. From your own lips I have learned that your mother preferred your sister to you... But, then, my daughter never was very wise.'

'And neither is Evadne, because her reprehensible behaviour has now forced my hand,' Elizabeth murmured, returning to the present.

She turned her attention to the bundle of letters, and for the next hour meticulously studied the contents of each one in turn before tying them neatly together with the black ribbon once again and placing them in the top drawer of her husband's desk. She experienced no qualms over Richard's knowing the truth. He was a gentleman of honour, and she trusted him implicitly. He would never betray her family's secrets to any other living soul, unless she bid him do so.

It took some little time before Elizabeth could put the sad written confirmation of what her grandmother had told her to the back of her mind, but eventually she was able to channel her thoughts in a new direction. It was while she was engaged in the agreeable task of responding to a letter recently received from her dear friend Lady Dartwood that Aggie unexpectedly entered the library.

'Have you put that small chest away for safekeeping?' she asked, casting a brief glance at the person who would always be much more than just a trusted servant.

'Yes, Miss Elizabeth,' she responded in the familiar way she always addressed her mistress when they were alone together. 'But I really came to see you on a different matter. Miss Juliet is still troubled with that niggling cough. I'm not really worried, as I mentioned this morning, but the linctus I've been giving her is having no effect, and I was wondering whether you'd ask Tom to take a look at her?'

Elizabeth glanced at the mantel-clock. It was only a few minutes after three: time enough to ride over to Melcham to visit Tom and return to the Hall before Richard arrived home, surely?

'Lay out my habit, Aggie. I'll ride over myself. I could do with a bit of fresh air after being cooped up indoors all day.'

Agatha turned, about to do as bidden, when the door opened and Finch came into the room. Before the butler had time to inform his mistress that Lady Chiltham had called, the lady herself, without waiting to be granted admittance, swept into the library, just as though she had been mistress of the house. Elizabeth, not in the least incensed by the imperious action, silently awarded her sister ten out of ten for sheer brass-faced impertinence; but Agatha betrayed her intense disapproval by a very unladylike snort.

'Something troubling you?' Evadne snapped out, more than matching the maid's far-from-kindly regard with her own look of avid dislike. She had never cared for the woman and was very well aware that the enmity was entirely mutual.

'I'll lay out your habit, *my lady*,' Agatha said, and the deliberate emphasis on the polite form of address was not wasted on Evadne.

'Both my sister and I have earned the right to that particular title,' she reminded the maid with honeyed sweetness.

'But there's only one lady in this room from where I'm standing,' Agatha retorted, earning herself a dagger-look as she swept from the room, the wickedly grinning butler in her wake.

'That woman is excessively impertinent! I don't know why you put up with her, Elizabeth, really I don't.'

'No, I don't suppose you do, and as I'm tolerably certain you would be completely uninterested in listening to the very long, long list of Aggie's many fine qualities, I suggest we don't waste each other's time, and that you come straight to the point of your visit.'

My, my! Her dear little sister had changed over the years. Quite the self-assured lady of quality now! Evadne mused while thinking how infinitely satisfying it was going to be bringing about her downfall.

'I cannot stay. I'm in something of a hurry,' she announced, completely ignoring her sister's polite request to take a seat. She moved nonchalantly to the side of the desk and, totally unobserved by her sister who, at that precise moment, happened to be delving into the drawer for a knife to sharpen her pen, dropped a folded sheet of paper into the wastepaper-basket. 'I'm here merely to take my leave of you. I'm returning to Devon in the morning.'

And what have I done to deserve such a courtesy? Elizabeth wondered, more than just a little surprised, but said in a tone that gave nothing away, 'In that case, Evadne, you may expect a visit from me this evening. I have something rather important I wish to discuss with you.'

Hiding a self-satisfied smirk, Evadne moved over to the door, but suddenly turned back to say, 'Oh, by the by, Elizabeth. Whilst I was travelling back from Lady Pentecost's earlier, I came upon an accident just this side of... Oh, dear, what is the name of that wretched little hamlet a matter of only half a mile from dear Lady Pentecost's home?' She raised her shoulder in a negligent shrug. 'Not that it matters. But the person who was being carried to that tumble-down old tavern there looked very like that young doctor friend of yours whose name for the moment escapes me. I can only assume he took a tumble from his horse. I certainly noticed someone leading a saddled mount towards that inn.'

Elizabeth was suddenly alert. 'Tom? Are you certain?'

'Not one hundred per cent, no. I should have stopped the carriage to offer assistance, I suppose, but I have had such a lot of errands to run today,' she responded with such a complete lack of concern that Elizabeth for the first time in her life felt the strong compulsion to box her sister's ears soundly.

'Anyway, I mustn't stay. I'll see you later,' and with that she was gone, leaving Elizabeth with a positive vortex of emotions spiralling through her, not least of which was deep concern over the injured man who might possibly turn out to be Tom.

Leaving the half-finished letter on the top of the desk, she went straight up to her room to find Aggie there, placing some freshly laundered dresses in the wardrobe.

'Has that viper slithered away yet?'

Elizabeth frowned dourly at this rudely worded enquiry, but could not find it within herself to reproach her maid. Aggie had always had scant regard for Evadne, and she wasn't likely to change her very low opinion of her now. So she merely said, 'Yes, she's gone, but not before she had imparted some rather disturbing news.'

Agatha paused in her task, and looked searchingly at her young mistress's worried face. 'What bad news, my lamb?'

'She came upon an accident on the outskirts of Eastlynch. She seems to think the injured man might well have been Tom. Needless to say, she didn't stop to offer assistance. If it was Tom, he has no doubt been taken back to his house by now, but I fully intend to make certain.'

Knowing how concerned her young mistress must be, no matter how hard she tried not to show it, Agatha didn't waste a moment in helping Elizabeth to change into her habit, and then watched from the bedchamber window as her young mistress, a few minutes later, rode up the driveway out of sight.

She was not the only person to witness the departure. In an area of the park densely covered by trees, Evadne had ordered her coachman to pull off the driveway. From the vantage point she was able to watch, unobserved, Elizabeth ride out of the estate and take the road to Melcham.

'So far so good, Quimper,' she remarked with feline satisfaction.

'But will she go to that inn, mistress?'

'Oh, yes, she'll go sure enough. I've learned from several sources just how very fond she is of young Dr Carrington. Her disposition is such that she could never rest easy until she had discovered what had befallen him. And if you have performed your tasks thoroughly, by six this evening, or thereabouts, the trap will be beautifully sprung.'

'But supposing Sir Richard goes searching for his wife?'

'I learned from Mrs Westbridge that he's due to arrive home this evening. I doubt very much that he'll be in time to discover his wife's whereabouts before Lady Pentecost has looked her fill on the oh, so charming scene. Believe me, I've got that middle-aged tabby's measure. I chose her with particular care. She would never miss the chance of spreading such a monumental piece of scandal.'

Quimper was not so certain of success. The plan was far from foolproof—too much left to chance for his liking. 'What if Sir Richard arrives home earlier than expected and discovers that forged letter you wrote? Do you think he's likely to believe such a thing about his wife?'

'That, I'll admit, remains in the balance,' she responded after several moments' intense thought. 'If Elizabeth repeated what I had told her to anyone, then it would have been to that obnoxious maid of hers. Agatha Stigwell is devoted to Elizabeth, and Sir Richard must surely know this. Therefore, he might suppose that Agatha wouldn't hesitate to lie in order to protect her mistress.'

Evadne paused to remove a speck of fluff from her primrose-coloured carriage dress. 'Although he has professed deep love for Elizabeth, after further consideration, I still remain not wholly convinced of the depth of his affection. After all, Quimper, what man in love with his wife indulges in a sordid affair within a few short weeks of his marriage taking place? That apart, a person of Sir Richard's stamp could never withstand being branded a cuckold. And we can rely on dear Lady Pentecost to start labelling him just that. Oh, no, Quimper. No matter whether he personally believes his wife guilty of adultery or not, in the eyes of the world he will be made a laughing stock. Knightley's a proud man. The humiliation would be too much for him to bear. Believe me, the marriage will be over before the end of this day.'

Elizabeth arrived at Tom's house just as the church clock in the centre of the small market town chimed four. After looping the reins over the black painted railings, she hurried up the path, but, worried though she was, she still took the trouble to exchange a greeting with the boy Tom had engaged to do odd jobs about the place, as he busily worked in the front garden.

Mrs Middleton was prompt in answering the door, but not so speedy when it came to disclosing where her master had gone. 'To tell you the truth, my lady, I can't rightly remember whether he said exactly where he was bound or no. But he has been gone a fair time, so I shouldn't imagine he will be too much longer, if you would care to wait inside?'

'What time did he go out?' she asked, ignoring the request.

'Oh, it would have been about two hours ago.'

Elizabeth was trying not to be pessimistic, but she couldn't help silently acknowledging that this would tie in with what Evadne had told her.

'Dr Carrington answered the door himself, as I was busy at the time in the kitchen when the caller arrived. Before he left the house he did say that he'd learned of a lady taken rather poorly, and that he would be out for some little time. So, I can only assume that whoever he was going to see doesn't live nearby.'

'Was the name Eastlynch mentioned, do you recall?'

Elizabeth could see by the widening of the housekeeper's dark eyes that the name had struck a chord of memory even before she said, 'Yes. Now you put me in mind of it, I do believe that was the name of the place where he was bound.'

With a hurried farewell, Elizabeth sped down the path, leaving Mrs Middleton to watch the abrupt departure with surprised interest, before closing the door again and returning to her tasks in the kitchen.

Although the tiny village of Eastlynch was only a matter of three miles from Melcham, it was only accessible by a series of narrow and twisting high-hedged lanes. Once the market town was left behind, Elizabeth, riding her mare at a brisk trot, didn't catch sight of a single soul to enquire if a gentleman had met with an accident earlier that afternoon. Although Evadne had been rather sparing with details, her sister had surmised that the unfortunate man had taken a fall from his horse. Accidents happened to the best of riders. Tom was certainly not in Richard's class when it came to equestrian skills, but he was still a very competent horseman, and would certainly not risk proceeding at a gallop along winding lanes like these, where any obstacle blocking the road might be concealed round the next bend.

By the time she had arrived at the village inn, which was ill kept and uninviting, Elizabeth was still experiencing grave concern, and a deal of puzzlement too. Surely if the injured man had been Tom, someone would have sent word to his home long before now? She knew for a fact that Tom always carried an identity card on his person, so it would have been a simple matter to discover who he was.

Leaving her mare tied to a rough wooden stake, Elizabeth approached the front entrance. The cracked and decaying outside walls gave her a shrewd idea of what the interior would be like, and she wasn't in the least surprised to discover the deserted tap had been left in disorder, with several used tankards dotted about on the unpolished, ale-stained tables, and a liberal amount of dirt smeared over the unswept flagstone floor.

'What can I be doing for you?'

Startled, Elizabeth swung round to see a sparse, middle-aged woman step out from a shadowy corner of the tap. As there was no doorway in that area of the room, she could only surmise that the woman had been standing there all the time, her black, birdlike eyes watching her visitor's every move.

'I understand that a gentleman met with an accident not far from here earlier today.' Suppressing the strong desire to back away as the woman slowly approached and the stench of an unwashed body hit her like a kick from a horse, Elizabeth took in every detail of the woman's unkempt appearance, from the filthy cap doing little to confine the matted, greying hair to the rough workman's boots on her feet. 'I was informed he was carried to this inn. Is he still here now?'

'That ee be,' the woman responded, peering at

Elizabeth's features closely, before giving a near-toothless half-smile. 'I put 'im in my own bedchamber, so I did, and he still be there now, sleeping like a babe.'

'May I see him? It's just possible that I might be acquainted with the gentleman, and can arrange for his removal from this house so that you won't be inconvenienced further.'

''Cause you can, m'deary. Just you come wi' me.'

Keeping a discreet distance, Elizabeth followed the woman up a narrow, creaking staircase and into a low ceilinged bedchamber. Tom, lying in the large bed, had had his clothes removed and was sleeping soundly, a little too soundly for Elizabeth's peace of mind.

'What are the extent of his injuries?'

'He received a bit of a blow to 'is 'ead, as yer might say.'

'And he hasn't regained consciousness at all?' Elizabeth frowned suspiciously as she studied the rhythmic rise and fall of Tom's bared chest. 'Have you administered a potion of any kind?'

'That I did, m'deary. Just to keep 'im quiet, like…until you arrived.'

Elizabeth swung round to find the grinning woman flanked by two burly men, one of whom held a small glass in one grimy hand. The resemblance was too marked for them not to be related. Mother and sons, she guessed, trying to control the rising panic at the men's lascivious expressions and the evil smile of triumph twisting the woman's thin-lipped mouth.

'And you're going to take a drop of the same,' she added, taking the glass out of her younger offspring's massive hand.

Instinctively, Elizabeth backed away, but she realised there was no possible hope of escape even before the filthy old crone advised, 'Now, deary, you be sensible and do as

I say, and I'll see no 'arm comes to you, but if you tries anything foolish I'll be forced to let me boys at yer. And they'd like dealing with a pretty wench like you.'

'Ain't you going to let us undress 'er fust?' the elder son asked hopefully and earned himself a resounding box round the ear from his mother. Although she was a dwarf by comparison, it was quite obvious she was more than equal to the task of keeping her progeny in order if she wished.

'No, I ain't, unless…' she looked back at Elizabeth in a meaningful way '…the little lady doesn't do as she's told.'

What choice had she? It was in her own best interests to offer no resistance at the present time. The mere thought of those two filthy oafs laying hands on her brought a sudden surge of nausea to rise in her throat. 'I shan't give you any trouble.'

'There's a sensible girl!' The woman shooed her sons from the room, just as though they were two erring infants and, ordering them to see to the stabling of the lady's mount, closed the door firmly behind them before turning back to Elizabeth once more. 'Take your clothes off, and get into bed!' she ordered. 'And hurry up about it, I ain't got all day.'

Elizabeth began to peel off her habit and placed it with Tom's apparel on the chair. When she had removed the last of her garments, she didn't delay in slipping between the far-from-clean sheets beside her friend. He didn't stir; he remained completely oblivious to what was happening. He was in no state to help himself, let alone aid her, and yet she found the warmth of his strong body strangely comforting.

'Now you drink this down,' the woman ordered in a sickeningly coaxing way, handing over the glass. 'I ain't giving you nearly as much as I gave 'im. Don't want you completely knocked out, just a trifle woozy, as yer might say.' She tut-tutted as she glanced at Tom. 'Gave 'im too strong a dose, I reckon, but then I ain't never done anything like this afore. So 'ow was I to know?'

Elizabeth, her mind working rapidly, placed the vessel to her mouth and allowed the milky-coloured liquid to seep between her slightly parted lips. Then, without being told, she laid her head on the pillow and after a few moments, during which the old woman continued to watch her closely, she lowered her eyelids. The bedchamber door opened and then closed again before she heard the grating sound of the key being turned in the lock, and the thud of retreating footsteps.

Sitting up abruptly, she quickly spat the liquid she had been holding in her mouth on to the floor, and then tiptoed across to the washstand, where she made good use of what remained of the contents of the pewter jug. After swilling her mouth out several times with the cold water, and spitting it out on to the floor, she was confident that she would suffer no ill effects, even if a drop of the nostrum had managed to find its way down her throat. This conviction was thankfully substantiated when she experienced no dizziness whatsoever as she tiptoed over to the chair.

How very fortunate it was that that dreadful woman hadn't considered it necessary to take their clothes away with her when she had left, Elizabeth mused, wasting no time in dressing again, and trying as she did so not to step about too much in case her movements could be detected below.

What on earth was going on? She stared down at Tom's pale face in some concern as she fastened the last tie on her skirt. Why, if Richard had walked in and had caught the pair of them naked in bed, heaven only knew what he would have thought... No, she amended silently. It was quite obvious what he would have thought—that she and Tom were having an affair...

Of course, that was it! She almost gasped as realisation

hit her with lightning clarity. That was why this little charade had been planned! Tom had been merely the bait, lured here and no doubt attacked by those two ruffians in a wicked attempt to draw her to this out-of-the-way inn. And wasn't it obvious who was behind the despicable plot to ruin her reputation and destroy her marriage? Evadne!

The whole contemptible plot smacked of her sister's particular kind of malice. It wouldn't matter a whit to Evadne if Tom had to be hurt during the execution of the plan so long as she achieved her aim. Well, this time, Elizabeth decided, experiencing for the first time in her life a desire for revenge, Evadne had gone too far and would pay dearly for her evil-minded machinations. But before she could sample the sweet taste of justifiable retribution, she would need to get herself and Tom—for she had no intention of leaving him to the tender mercies of that trio below—well away from this place. Although it had to be faced that Tom, poor wretch, looked as if he would be of precious little assistance for some considerable time.

She began to examine him more closely and quickly detected a large lump on the back of his head, no doubt inflicted before the drug had been forced down his throat. She pulled back the sheet and saw to her horror that his hands and feet were bound so tightly that the cord was biting into his flesh. That, at least, she could remedy immediately, she thought, reaching for his bag which their obliging captors had evidently overlooked and had conveniently left beside the chair.

As she had suspected, the bag contained his small box of surgical instruments. Extracting the razor-sharp knife, she quickly had his hands and feet freed, but there was little else she could do for him until the effects of the drug had begun to wear off. Before that happened, though, she felt certain that someone would return to the room to ensure that they were both sleeping soundly in readiness for…what? Richard's arrival? She shook her head. No, that seemed most unlikely. Although he was due back at Knightley Hall today, there was always the possibility that he might be delayed. Besides which, Richard was no fool, and to alert him to his wife's presence in this inn would very likely have the opposite effect and merely make him suspicious, but not of his wife's possible infidelity. No, it was someone else who was supposed to catch Tom and herself *in flagrante delicto*, as one might say…but who? she wondered, going across to inspect the window.

This offered no means of escape. Not only had it been securely nailed shut, but from what she could see, even if she did manage to prise it open, there was nothing for her to climb down, not even a conveniently placed tree, and she certainly wouldn't trust those worn, threadbare sheets on the bed to bear her weight if she were to make the attempt and climb out. She turned and tiptoed across to the door but, as she had suspected, it had been securely locked.

Things were looking decidedly bleak for the pair of them, but she refused to give in without a fight, and went about the room picking up various objects which might prove useful weapons to add to the knife she had slipped into the pocket of her skirt. Whether she could bring herself to wield it with violent intent remained to be seen, and she was offered plenty of time to ponder over this rather morally disturbing issue before she became aware of a commotion below: low growls, a series of thuds and what sounded suspiciously like a table being overturned. Dear God! Surely those oafish sons weren't engaged in a drunken brawl?

Moments later she heard the sound of hurried footsteps mounting the stairs. Just one person, she felt certain. Quickly taking up a position behind the door, the heavy pewter water jug raised high above her head in readiness to strike the unsuspecting visitor, she waited, heart pounding beneath her ribcage, as the key turned in the lock and the door swung open.

Chapter Fifteen

Richard's elegant long-striding gait had not infrequently been admired by both men and women alike, but there seemed an extra spring in his step as he walked from the stables to the front entrance of Knightley Hall. After being informed that his wife had left the house a short while earlier, he took himself off to his library where he poured out a good measure of burgundy. Raising the glass to his lips, he sipped the rich red liquid and took a moment or two to savour its excellent taste, just as he fully intended to savour those delicious moments when he told that wickedly deceiving and adorable wife of his that he had discovered her outrageous deception during her time in Brussels the year before.

Taking his glass of wine across the room with him, he drew the thin, leather-bound volume, given to him by Sergeant Hawker, from his pocket and placed it for safekeeping in the top drawer of his oak desk. He noticed the pile of letters in there at once, but it was the half-finished missive on top of his desk which captured his attention, and he shook his head in disbelief.

Why on earth hadn't he realised long since? The clues had all been there right from the start, loads of them, but he had been too foolishly blind to recognise them for what they were and solve them. Elizabeth's reticence to discuss her time in Brussels had been the first, and the way she had neatly avoided discussing the subject for very long when he had happened to raise it. That distinctive smell of lavender-and-rose water he had detected in her hair on numerous occasions had been a complete giveaway and yet, fool that he was, he still hadn't realised. And then there was this, he mused, holding up the letter written in Elizabeth's beautiful flowing hand. He had seen numerous samples of his wife's handwriting during these past weeks, and yet not once had it dawned on him that it was the same hand that had penned that letter of farewell to him in Brussels.

Again he shook his head, marvelling at his own stupidity. His only excuse, he supposed, was that Mary had intruded in his thoughts only rarely during these past weeks, his mind having been totally focused on the lady he had married. He gave a sudden shout of laughter. Even now that he had been given irrefutable proof, he still looked upon Elizabeth and Mary as two separate people.

Having had nearly twenty-four hours to get over the initial shock, he found that he could no longer be angry with her for the diabolical way she had deceived him. He didn't doubt for a moment that she had had a very good reason for trying to keep her identity secret when she was in Brussels, although her motive for having done so still eluded him. She could, of course, have been trying to safeguard her reputation. After all, it was hardly deemed acceptable practice for a gently bred, unmarried young woman to take on the role of nurse to six British soldiers. He couldn't imagine Elizabeth worrying herself too much over any possible gossip arising from her actions, though. No, there had to have been some other reason, but just what continued to elude him, and it was fruitless, he knew, trying to speculate. He would no doubt get to the bottom of the enigma when she returned.

And where the deuce had she gone? he wondered, glancing at the mantel-clock whose hands told him it was half past four. The little wretch had promised faithfully to be here to greet him when he arrived home, and yet she had gone gallivanting off somewhere, forcing him to wait a while longer before extracting a suitable penance.

After taking a further fortifying mouthful of wine, he placed his glass down, and his eyes fell upon the neatly folded sheet of paper in the basket beside his desk. Was that supposed to be there? It wasn't, after all, screwed up. Had the letter been accidentally knocked off the edge of the desk? he wondered, bending to retrieve it.

Had anyone else been standing in the room he would have been unable to tell what was going through Richard's mind as he ran his eyes over the few boldly written lines, for his expression gave nothing away. He merely placed the missive down on his desk before going across to the door.

'Finch,' he called, interrupting the conversation the ageing butler was having with his replacement in the hall, 'do you happen to know precisely where your mistress has gone and what time she left the house?'

'Lady Knightley went out about an hour ago, sir, but where she was bound I couldn't say. Perhaps Miss Agatha might know. Would you like me to fetch her?'

'Yes. Request her to come to the library.'

She entered the room a few minutes later, her thin-lipped mouth curled into a rare smile at her master's return. 'You wished to see me, sir?'

'Yes, Aggie. Come in and close the door.' He waited until she had approached the desk before asking if she knew where her mistress had gone.

'To Melcham, sir, to see Dr Carrington. She was a little concerned about him.'

Richard handed her the note and watched her closely as she read,

My darling Elizabeth, I must see you today. Richard is not likely to be home until the evening, which will give us several precious hours alone together. Meet me at the usual rendezvous. I beg of you, don't fail me, my love. Tom.

'Would you say that that was Dr Carrington's handwriting?' he asked when she raised puzzled eyes to his.

'It certainly looks like it, sir, yes. But—but Tom would never write Miss Elizabeth a letter like this. Why, it's—it's like a love letter!'

'Isn't it just!' he quipped and Agatha looked up at him, aghast.

'Sir! You don't imagine for a moment that there's anything improper going on between—'

'No, Aggie, I don't,' he interrupted reassuringly. 'But that, I should imagine, is what I was supposed to think.' He moved across to the window and stared out at the sunlit park. 'Even if I did suspect that my wife's feelings for Tom went somewhat deeper than mere sisterly affection, which I don't, I certainly credit her with more sense than to leave damning evidence of an affair between them lying about for me to find. No, Aggie, I doubt your mistress has even read this letter. Someone planted it here.'

'Evadne!' the loyal maid spat, hard-eyed and disdainful. 'Up to her old tricks again, I don't doubt. She was always trying to get my lamb into trouble when they were younger. She was here, sir. Here, in this very room, earlier this afternoon!'

'Was she now?' His voice betrayed nothing more than mild enquiry, but the look which sprang into his eyes was anything but gentle.

'Yes, sir, and it was shortly after her visit that Miss

Elizabeth went out. She suspected that Master Tom had been involved in some kind of accident.'

Richard turned to look at the very concerned maid once again. 'I want you to tell me exactly what your mistress said to you, Aggie, before she left this house.'

Once he had learned all, Richard was galvanised into action, issuing orders to his servants which were obeyed with lightning speed. Within a relatively short space of time, he, Medway and the estate worker who had temporarily taken on the duties as coachman were riding at the gallop towards Melcham.

Mrs Middleton betrayed a moment's surprise at seeing Sir Richard on the doorstep at this hour of the day, but didn't waste any time in relating the puzzling events of the afternoon, for she too, now, was rather concerned that Dr Carrington hadn't returned.

'And you, yourself, didn't see the person who came to the house requesting his assistance for the lady at Eastlynch.'

'No, sir, I didn't.'

'But I saw 'im,' a voice from behind announced, and Richard turned to see Tom's odd-job boy, who had been tidying the front garden for most of the day, staring up at him.

'What was he like? Can you describe him?' Richard asked, and wondered why it was that every boy he happened to speak to these days had the rather alarming habit of raising a hand to scratch his head.

'He were small and thin and was wearing a black coat. Looked like a servant to me. Don't live in Melcham, sir. I never seen 'im round 'ere afore. Ee gets out of a carriage stopped further down the street. Ee spoke to Dr Carrington. Didn't 'ear what ee said, though, 'cause they goes inside.'

'Did you see anyone else in the carriage?'

'No, sir. It were too far away. But it were a fine carriage, pulled by a right 'andsome team of 'orses, like the sort o' turnout you'd ride in, m'lord.'

Worried though he was, Richard couldn't help smiling at this rather artless remark and tossed the boy a coin before remounting his horse. 'I want you to return to the Hall to collect the carriage,' he said, addressing his estate worker. 'Bring Lady Knightley's maid and one of the footmen— Jenkins will do—to the inn at Eastlynch.'

'Lord bless you, sir! You don't think anything's 'appened to the mistress, do you?' he asked, his tanned forehead furrowed by deep lines of concern. Like all the other servants, he had swiftly grown very fond of his young mistress.

'I sincerely hope not, Ben, but it's as well to make provisions for every eventuality. Be as quick as you can,' and with that Richard turned his mount in the direction of Eastlynch, leaving an equally troubled Medway to follow in his wake.

Sir Richard uttered not a word during the time it took them to reach the small village, but the taut set of his mouth told its own tale. No matter how strange his master's behaviour had been in London during the spring, there was nothing puzzling in his conduct now: he was a man deeply worried, and it showed in every contour of his face.

Leaving their mounts tethered at the rear of the inn, Richard had a quick look inside the rundown old stable, and it told him much of what he needed to know. He delved into the left-hand pocket of his jacket and drew out a handsome silver-handled duelling pistol, one of a pair which he had had the forethought to collect from his gun room before leaving the house, and promptly handed it over to his new butler.

'I sincerely trust, Medway, that you are not completely ignorant in the use of firearms?'

'My experience isn't great, sir,' he admitted, 'but I believe nine times out of ten I could manage to hit what I was aiming at, providing my target wasn't moving too quickly.'

'I hope you're not called upon to substantiate that statement, Medway, but it's as well to be prepared, for it's my belief that my wife is somewhere within that building, and I don't suppose for a moment that she is there of her own free will.'

Medway grimaced as he entered the foul-smelling interior of the inn, but his master's face betrayed no emotion whatsoever as he made good use of a used tankard by hammering it down on the counter while setting up a shout for attention. It took some little time, but eventually the slatternly owner of the tavern, accompanied by an equally unkempt individual of the opposite sex, came in answer to the summons. A moment's surprise flickered in the woman's eyes as she surveyed the amazing sight of a top-of-the-trees Corinthian standing in her inn, but her hope that money would be coming her way was quickly dashed when he said,

'My wife is here. Kindly take me to her at once!'

It was abundantly obvious by the sudden panic that replaced the avaricious gleam in her eyes that Sir Richard was the last person she had been expecting to see.

'Don't waste my time, woman!' he ordered, cutting across her pathetic attempt to deny all knowledge of his wife's existence. 'Either you take me to her at once, or I send my man, here, for the constable and magistrate, and have these premises searched from cellar to attic.'

It was no idle threat. Richard, watching her closely, saw her eyes betraying the conflicting thoughts passing through her mercenary little brain before they suddenly focused on a spot somewhere behind him, and he swung round to see the third member of the obnoxious family moving stealthily towards him

Both sons dived at him simultaneously, but Richard was more than equal to the combined attack. Within seconds he had the younger son writhing on his knees in agony, having received a well-aimed kick in the region of his groin, and he felled the elder brother with just one punishing blow to the jaw, the force of which sent him crashing against a table before crumpling, momentarily stunned, to the floor.

He then took the precaution of drawing the second pistol from his jacket pocket in case either man should foolishly attempt a further assault upon him. Medway, too, had drawn his weapon and had it levelled at the woman behind the counter, just in case she should foolishly make some sudden move.

'Well, madam, which is it to be—the magistrate, or an answer to my question?'

She cast a far-from-sympathetic glance at her incapacitated offspring, which boded ill for them later. 'The lady be upstairs,' she capitulated, drawing the key from the pocket of her grimy apron and tossing it to him. 'First door along the passageway.'

After handing his pistol to Medway, and urging him not to hesitate in using them both if necessary, Richard wasted no time in reaching the floor above. He turned the key in the lock and the first thing he saw after the door had swung open was Tom lying perfectly still in the bed. He took a step into the room, caught a sudden movement out of the corner of his eye and instinctively raised his right arm to ward off the blow aimed at his head. His elbow made accidental contact with a high cheekbone, sending his would-be assailant stumbling backwards on to the floor.

'God in heaven, Elizabeth! Are you all right?' He was kneeling down beside her in an instant, and could see clearly the livid red mark he had unintentionally inflicted just below her left eye.

'I think so,' she answered weakly, still slightly stunned,

but too deliriously happy to see him to worry too much over her hurts. 'I never expected to see you,' she admitted, allowing him to raise her gently to her feet. 'I thought it was one of those brutish sons coming back into the room, and I had every intention of rendering him senseless.'

The look he cast her betrayed his unholy amusement, but a deal of admiration, too.

'Oh, Richard, they were planning to ruin me. They've drugged poor Tom, but I managed to fool that odious woman and spat out what she had forced me to take the instant she had left the room.'

'What charming habits you have acquired, my darling,' he remarked lightly, going over to the bed to take a closer look at his friend.

'It's as well I did have my wits about me,' she announced, slightly nettled by his frivolous attitude. 'What would you have thought if you'd walked in here to discover Tom and myself stark naked in bed together, because that is what they had planned. At least,' she amended, 'I suspect someone was supposed to catch us that way.'

'No doubt you're right,' he agreed. 'There's little we can do for our doctor friend, though, until the carriage arrives, so I suggest we return downstairs and see what we can discover from your oh, so charming captors. Our new butler is guarding them,' he added, leading the way out of the room, 'but I don't think it would be advisable to leave Medway alone with them for very much longer.'

Elizabeth derived a deal of wicked satisfaction when she entered the tap and saw the two men nursing their hurts, and their mother paying not the least interest in either of them as she sat broodingly on one of the stools, no doubt cursing fickle fate for guiding Sir Richard Knightley to her hostelry. Elizabeth then transferred her gaze to the man who had successfully guarded the trio.

'How very brave it was of you, Medway, to come to my

rescue! I shall be forever in your debt,' she told him with such a glowing smile that he became her devoted slave from that moment in time.

After relieving his new butler of one of the pistols, Richard perched himself on the edge of a table and began to swing one booted leg to and fro as he surveyed the highly disgruntled woman. 'It would be in your own best interests, madam,' he advised her, 'to explain precisely what has been going on this day. And you can begin by telling me the name of the woman who, no doubt, paid you handsomely to hold my wife and Dr Carrington hostage here.'

'It weren't that much,' she mumbled, 'and it weren't a woman, neiver.'

'Would the person who approached you offering financial rewards for the perpetration of this outrage be small and sparse and dressed in a coat of black cloth?' he asked, repeating the odd-job boy's description.

'Yes, that ud be 'im. Shifty-eyed little rodent! Comes in 'ere a few days back asking if we'd be interested in earning a few guineas.' She cast a sorrowful look up at him in an attempt to gain his sympathy. 'Well, I puts it to you, m'lord—what poor, 'ardworking woman wouldn't be willing to earn a bit extra?'

Richard's lip curled at this. 'By the condition of this place, I'm given every reason to suppose that you haven't done a hard day's work in your life, but we'll let that pass for the moment. Did you gain the impression that this man was negotiating on behalf of someone else?' She looked totally bewildered at this, just as though he were speaking in some foreign language. 'I'll rephrase the question,' he continued with praiseworthy forbearance. 'Did you think this man worked for someone who was willing to pay for your services?'

She nodded. 'When I told 'im I'd want more, he said as

'ow the person ee worked for wouldn't pay n' more. It were a case of take it or leave it, as yer might say...so I took it.'

'I think we both know who was behind this fiasco, Richard, don't we?' Elizabeth announced, coming to stand beside him. 'The description of the go-between sounds suspiciously like a certain butler we saw in Devonshire. But what I should like to know,' she went on, fixing her gaze on the landlady, 'is how long you intended keeping Dr Carrington and myself locked in that room?'

'Only until a certain person arrived. And I don't know who, neiver, so it ain't no good you asking me,' she added when Elizabeth opened her mouth to do just that. 'All I knows is that someone was supposed to come 'ere, and I was to take 'em upstairs. And I was supposed to tell 'em that it weren't the first time you and the gentleman 'ad made use of my bedchamber.'

As if on cue the sound of a carriage could be heard pulling up at the door. After handing Medway the second pistol again, Richard wasted no time in going outside to investigate, and successfully thwarted the sole occupant of the elegant, but rather antiquated, vehicle from alighting, simply by positioning himself in front of the carriage doorway.

'Why, Lady Pentecost! What in the world brings you to this far-from-comfortable establishment?' Elizabeth distinctly heard him say, and raised her eyes ceilingwards. Of course, Lady Pentecost! She might have known!

'I could ask you the same question, Sir Richard,' the formidable matron responded, but he had been expecting that.

'We met with a slight accident and were forced to seek sanctuary here while waiting for the carriage to be repaired. I hope it won't take too much longer. I shouldn't like it to become common knowledge that I patronised such a place as this,' he remarked with a look of distaste as he cast a glance over his shoulder at the dilapidated building.

He could not have said anything more likely to appeal to a person of Lady Pentecost's snobbish disposition. 'Quite! I trust no one was hurt?'

'Lady Knightley suffered a slight facial bruise, but apart from that we came through unscathed.'

Frowning slightly, Lady Pentecost tried to peer past him into the inn's rather gloomy interior. 'Is there no one else here?'

'Only my new butler, ma'am. Why? What makes you ask? Were you expecting to see someone here? If so, I cannot say that I applaud your choice of a meeting place.'

She hesitated for a moment before drawing out a letter from her reticule and handing it over to him. He cast his eyes over the brief note and looked back at her with raised brows.

'What on earth could you find intriguing in this place, I wonder? I can only assume that someone has been playing a practical joke on you, ma'am, for I cannot imagine that our slight misfortune with the carriage is of very much interest to you. When did you receive the letter?'

'My butler found it pushed under the door an hour ago, though just how long it had been there is anyone's guess. And I was forced to put back dinner an hour in order to be here,' she finished, sounding decidedly nettled over the inconvenience of having to wait for her meal.

He tut-tutted sympathetically. 'It never ceases to amaze me what some people find amusing. Dragging you here for no purpose is unpardonable. Ha! My carriage at last!' he announced, not without a certain amount of relief. The last thing he wanted was for her to insist on alighting and see the landlady and her progeny being held at gunpoint.

'Are you sure I cannot be of assistance, Sir Richard?'

'Thank you, ma'am, but we'll do very nicely now that

our transport has arrived. I think what we all need is to get home to enjoy a good dinner,' and with that he took up the steps and closed the carriage door, thereby giving her no reason to delay her departure further.

He remained outside until his own carriage had drawn up; after issuing instructions to Agatha and the footman to go upstairs and tend to Tom so that he could be carried out to the carriage, he rejoined his wife in the taproom, handing her the letter which had been sent to Lady Pentecost and which he had quite artfully retained.

'Recognise the handwriting?' he asked after she had cast her eyes over the unsigned brief note which merely said, *If you wish to learn something of immense interest then go to the inn at Eastlynch at six o'clock this evening.* She shook her head, and he delved into his pocket. 'What about this one?'

'Why, this is Tom's handwriting. At least,' she amended, studying the bold scrawl more closely, 'very like. But he never sent this to me. I've never seen it before. Where did you find it?'

'In the wastepaper basket in the library.'

'Evadne must have dropped it in there!' Elizabeth responded, unable to keep her annoyance from creeping into her voice. Her eyes narrowed. 'When Evadne was a child she used to practise forging other people's handwriting— she was very good at it, too. I don't for a moment doubt that this is her work. She must have got her hands on a sample of Tom's handwriting from somewhere. And, I suppose, she must have learnt during her stay here how very fond of Tom I am, and viewed him as the ideal candidate to carry out her despicable scheme to try to ruin me in the eyes of the world. She might have succeeded, too, if Lady Pentecost had discovered us together in that bedchamber.'

'Even if that had occurred, you don't suppose for a moment that I would have believed you guilty of adultery, do you? If I hadn't seen for myself that poor Tom is incapable of opening his eyes, let alone making a cuckold of me, I still wouldn't have suspected you two of being lovers,' he assured her gently. 'Evadne is incapable of comprehending that a man and a woman can love each other without any physical desires. She also very much underestimated my own depth of feeling. I may be a proud man, Elizabeth, but my love for you far outweighs my pride. I should have quashed any rumours very swiftly, believe me.'

She didn't doubt him for a moment, and smiled lovingly up at him before transferring her gaze to her erstwhile captors. 'My sister has a great deal to answer for, Richard. But what do you intend to do about these three?'

'You have only to say the word and I shall summon the magistrate.'

'No, I don't want that,' she answered, experiencing no desire whatsoever to see any one of them end up in prison. 'Their only real crime is wishing to earn some easy money. I truly don't believe they intended any lasting physical harm to either Tom or me. A few choice words from you and I don't think they'll get involved in anything like this again.'

'Very well. It shall be as you wish. But I must confess that it grieves me to think that that sister of yours will get away, scot-free, with what she tried to do to you.'

'Oh, she won't, Richard,' Elizabeth assured him, her voice hard-edged and determined. 'You can safely leave Evadne's punishment to me... It is long overdue.'

Chapter Sixteen

Caroline Westbridge checked in the act of pouring her most unwelcome guest a cup of tea as the door opened, and her butler unexpectedly announced the arrival of Sir Richard and Lady Knightley. She didn't notice Evadne blanch slightly, nor did she see the sudden guarded look in her eyes, for it was as much as she could do to keep a firm grasp of the teapot's handle when she saw her friend's dishevelled state as she swept majestically into the room ahead of her husband.

'Heavens above! Elizabeth! Whatever has happened to you, my dear?' she demanded, aghast, when she noticed the purplish hue beneath the left eye. 'Have you taken a tumble from your horse?'

'No, Caroline, nothing so dramatic, I assure you. I have merely been held against my will in one of the most disgusting taverns it has ever been my misfortune to enter.'

'Whatever do you mean?'

The surprised enquiry was uttered by her sister, and Elizabeth fixed her eyes on Evadne with such a look of revulsion in their grey-green depths that Caroline could hardly believe that it was her young, kind-hearted friend whom she looked upon.

'Do sit down, my dear,' she urged her, but Elizabeth

declined the invitation. Richard, however, was not feeling quite so unsociable and accepted their very amiable neighbour's suggestion and seated himself beside her on the sofa, a rather odd smile playing about his mouth.

Although Elizabeth had hardly spoken more than a dozen words during the time it took them to ride here, he had the feeling that her taciturn frame of mind was rapidly coming to an end, and that he was about to witness a side to his wife's character he had never glimpsed before. On the surface she appeared perfectly composed; a little dishevelled after what she had been through, it was true, but that was only to be expected. Yet, beneath that calm exterior, he suspected her blood was flowing through her veins in a white-hot craving for revenge. And he wasn't wrong.

Moving towards her sister's chair, Elizabeth stared down at her, the look of disgust not diminishing from her eyes one iota. 'You know very well what I mean, Evadne, so do not nauseate me further with any sickening protestations of ignorance or innocence. But for Caroline's benefit I shall explain what has taken place this day.'

She turned her head to look at her friend and her expression softened at once. 'My darling sister paid me a visit this afternoon and casually informed me that she believed Dr Carrington had been involved in an accident. She knew what my reaction would be, of course, and I must confess that in that one instance her judgement was not at fault. I do love Tom,' she freely admitted, 'but the love I bear him is purely platonic, like that of a sister. Which is something Evadne could never comprehend. Richard, however, understands perfectly and wasn't fooled for an instant by that forged letter which you foolishly left for him to find,' she went on, turning to look at her sister once again.

Evadne rose from the chair with panic-engendered swiftness. 'I don't intend to sit here listening to this farrago of lies a moment longer!' she announced, but before she had taken more than a step towards the door, Elizabeth was in front of her, her slender, tapering fingers clenched in tight, angry fists.

'Sit down, Evadne, or so help me I shall knock you down,' she warned in a voice that seemed all the more threatening because of its even timbre. 'Believe me, it would afford me the utmost pleasure to do so.'

Caroline, for one, didn't doubt for a moment the truth of this statement. She cast a fleeting glance in Richard's direction and suspected, by the hopeful gleam in his dark eyes, that he wished his wife would carry out her threat, but Evadne denied him the pleasure of seeing her receive a well-deserved slap in the face by doing precisely what her sister had ordered.

'I shan't bore you with all the details of my ordeal now, Caroline. I shall save that for another time,' Elizabeth continued, turning her head to glance briefly at the two occupants of the sofa once again. 'Suffice it to say that my sister's intention was to have me discovered in a compromising situation with Dr Thomas Carrington. Fortunately, Richard discovered my whereabouts and my sister's foolish scheming was foiled. Had it not been for the fact that Evadne had involved Tom in her childish act of spite, I might well have attained satisfaction enough from the fact that she had not succeeded in her intention of ruining me in the eyes of the world. But she did involve Tom, without caring whether or not he might be harmed and, equally contemptible, without experiencing the least concern that his reputation might be irreparably damaged hereabouts if her vile plan had succeeded.

'Which brings me quite nicely to the point of my visit,' she went on, keeping her eyes firmly glued on her sister's far-from-serene expression. 'Dr Carrington isn't the only friend of mine to suffer from your pernicious activities, is he, Evadne?'

'I haven't the slightest idea what you're talking about,' she countered, determined to brazen it out, even though she

had a strong suspicion to whom Elizabeth referred. She cast
a fleeting glance in Caroline's direction and couldn't imagine that she had divulged her heartbreaking secret to anyone, but Elizabeth swiftly disabused her by announcing
quite calmly that she was very well aware that Giles
Westbridge had committed suicide and, furthermore, that
she knew precisely why he had done so.

'And you, Evadne, shall return the letter he wrote to
Caroline before he died, which you quite heartlessly, and
with malicious intent, purloined from this house.'

For several moments no one spoke. Richard, pausing in
the act of raising a pinch of snuff to one thin nostril, cast
a disdainful glance in Evadne's direction; Caroline, looking
remarkably composed in the circumstances, did the same;
and Elizabeth, hard-eyed and resolute, waited silently for a
response.

'Oh, very well,' Evadne capitulated, before a trill of nervous laughter escaped her. 'To be perfectly honest with
you, I had forgotten that I still retained the wretched thing.'

The blatantly false admission fooled no one, least of all
Richard who didn't attempt to suppress the deprecating
sound that rose in his throat from passing his lips. Without
waiting to be offered, he reached for the teapot and helped
himself to a cup, which drew a genuine gurgle of amusement from his wife.

'Need to wash down a surfeit of bile, Richard?'

'Something of the sort, my love.' Leaning back against
the sofa, he peered up at Elizabeth above the rim of his
cup. 'Loath though I am to mention this, my darling, but
are you perfectly certain you can trust Lady Chiltham to
keep her word and return Caroline's property?'

'How well you have come to know her, Richard!
Naturally, I cannot. She isn't in the least like me, as you
and Caroline have remarked upon on more than one occasion.' She looked from one to the other with an enquiring
lift to one finely arched brow. 'Has it never occurred to

either of you to wonder why we should be so dissimilar, not the least alike, not even in looks?'

In truth, before that moment it had certainly never crossed Richard's mind to wonder, but now the reason positively screamed at him. 'She is, perhaps, only your half-sister?'

She did not need to respond, for Evadne, after a horrified gasp and a feeble attempt at denial, buried her face in her hands and indulged in a bout of bitter weeping.

'I fully intended to speak to her in private this evening, Caroline,' Elizabeth announced, deliberatcly raising her voice so that she could be heard above what had become hysterical sobbing. 'But after her evil machinations of this day, she deserved no such consideration, and shall receive none from me from this day forward.' As though to add credence to her words, she rounded on her sister with a merciless lack of pity. 'Stop that infernal racket at once! You always could manage to burst into tears at the drop of a hat, and you're fooling no one, least of all me!'

'I—I don't know how you can be so—so cruel,' Evadne responded in a pathetic whisper, having rapidly controlled what had threatened to be an inexhaustible flow.

'That's rich, coming from you!' was Elizabeth's forthright rejoinder. She felt tired after the events of the day, and discovered that the sympathy she had experienced for her sister when reading that pile of letters several hours earlier had long since ebbed away.

'Now, you listen to me, Evadne, and listen well. I have a number of letters in my possession which state clearly enough that you are the bastard daughter of a feckless and mercenary individual who was once in our grandmother's employ. No one will learn of this from me, unless you give me cause to reveal your unfortunate parentage. You *shall* leave this house first thing in the morning, and you shall *not* return here unless invited. When you reach Devonshire you *shall* return Caroline's property without delay. And you shall *never* divulge to another living soul what you know about Giles Westbridge's death.

'Should you be foolish enough to go against my expressed wishes, then I will not hesitate in making the contents of those letters widely known. I cannot imagine that Lord Chiltham, complacent though he is, could withstand the humiliation of being married to a bastard. You would be ruined in the eyes of the world, and could expect no help from me. I shall disown you entirely.'

Richard waited until Evadne, earnestly sobbing this time, had fled the room before turning eyes, filled with admiration, up to his wife. 'I think, my dear, we are likely to see a great change in Lady Chiltham in the future, thanks to you.'

'You may be sure that I shall not repeat what I have just learned,' Caroline assured them, still somewhat bemused by the startling revelations. 'I cannot thank you enough, Elizabeth, for forcing her to return Giles's letter. You did, however, make me realise on the night of the ball how foolish I have been all these years in allowing Evadne to retain such a hold over me. I fully intend to disclose the sad truth about his father's death to my son when he returns next week. I had also decided to confide in my close friends, too, at least, those whom I knew I could trust. Which, of course, included you, Richard. But I shan't attempt to do so now. Elizabeth, poor girl, looks worn out, and your only desire at this moment must be to take her home.'

It was true—Richard was most concerned about her, and had been doubly so since their departure from the inn. The events of the day had taken their toll, and the confrontation with Evadne seemed to have sapped the last of Elizabeth's strength. She had handled herself superbly and had come out the clear victor, but it was quite evident to any one with a modicum of sensitivity that the annihilation of her sister had brought her no pleasure whatsoever—quite the opposite, in fact.

Caroline, always so very considerate, offered to put her light carriage at their disposal, but Elizabeth, surprising them both, politely turned down the kind offer, declaring that she would much prefer to ride home in the fresh air. She surprised Richard further on their arrival back at the Hall by announcing her intention of joining him for supper, once she had rid her person of the unpleasant odour acquired at that obnoxious inn.

He awaited her in his library, occupying his time by reading the pile of letters she had left for his perusal in the top drawer of his desk. They made interesting, if rather sad, reading, for the events which had taken place thirty years before had had an adverse effect on several lives, not least of which had been Elizabeth's, whose childhood had been far from happy.

By placing the yellowing sheets in strict chronological order he was able to piece together what must have taken place. Louisa Smithson, at the tender age of seventeen, had come under the spell of a certain John Taverner, second in command on one of Mary Smithson's trading vessels. A devil-may-care, handsome rogue, he had seduced Mrs Smithson's daughter and then, in return for a generous remunerative consideration, and a captaincy on one of the sailing ships, he had agreed to have nothing further to do with his employer's daughter; but the damage, Mrs Smithson was to discover shortly after acquiescing to the demands, had already been done.

Louisa was with child, and Mrs Smithson had looked about in haste for a suitable husband for her daughter. Henry Beresford had been in Bristol at the time, staying with friends, and Mrs Smithson's eyes had fallen upon this younger son of an earl. The wedding, naturally, had had to be arranged swiftly, but it was only to be expected that the Honourable Henry Beresford would have become suspicious when his young bride had presented him with a perfectly formed child within seven months of their marriage taking place, even if he had never suspected anything before.

After reading the bitterly resentful letter Henry had written to his mother-in-law after Evadne's birth, Richard deduced that Elizabeth's father had considered the marriage at an end. Evidently, though, Mrs Smithson had somehow managed to change his mind, no doubt by digging deep into her purse once again, for he had not sought an annulment and, of course, seven years later Louisa had presented him with a second daughter, definitely his child this time. At some point after Elizabeth's birth Henry must have forgiven his mother-in-law totally, for he had visited her from time to time, occasionally taking his baby daughter with him.

From her letters it was quite obvious that Louisa had never forgiven her mother for forcing her into a loveless union. Learning of John Taverner's death at sea within a few short weeks of her marriage to Henry Beresford taking place certainly wouldn't have improved her attitude towards her mother, and Richard supposed that it had been only natural for Louisa to display such affection for her love-child, but her coolness towards her legitimate daughter had been unpardonable. After all, it had hardly been Elizabeth's fault that her mother had been denied the man she loved, but then, he reminded himself, it had hardly been Evadne's, either. No wonder Elizabeth had gained such little pleasure from their confrontation earlier. It was all so very, very sad for all concerned.

He had just placed the letters back in the drawer when Elizabeth, restored to her normally well-groomed self, came storming into the room, looking not in the least desirous of his sympathy. 'Richard, I could quite cheerfully murder you!' she astonished him by announcing, and sounded as if she meant it, too. 'What in the world do you mean by letting me go to Caroline's looking like a besom broom in a fit? And with a black eye, too! I was mortified when I caught sight of my reflection in my dressing-table mirror.'

'My dear, you were determined to go,' he reminded her soothingly, 'and I am rather glad that I didn't attempt to dissuade you. I wouldn't have missed that performance for a king's ransom. You were magnificent!' he assured her, going across to the decanters and filling two glasses.

She accepted the Madeira with scant grace, but her resentment didn't last very long and she swiftly channelled her thoughts to more mundane matters. 'I hope supper isn't too long. I'm absolutely famished. I've arranged for trays to be brought in here. I hope you don't mind.'

'Not in the least, my darling. I can think of nothing I would enjoy more than a private supper with you, and then bed, I think, for both of us. I can only guess how you must be feeling after the events of this day, but I certainly feel exhausted. What with the journey from London, and all the excitement since, I feel I could quite happily sleep for a week.'

Elizabeth was suddenly contrite. 'Oh, Richard, I am sorry! It completely slipped my mind to ask before, but did you manage to locate your old army friend?'

At this artless enquiry the hand raising the glass to his lips checked for a moment. He had not intended broaching the subject of her reprehensible deception after what she had been through that day, but now the opening was there, was he gentlemanly enough to let it pass...? No, most assuredly not!

'Yes, I discovered his whereabouts, my sweet,' he responded with such a wickedly smug grin that she ought instantly to have been suspicious, but she wasn't.

She asked eagerly, 'And did you manage to persuade him to accept the position, here, as head groom?'

'Yes, my darling, I did. He'll be arriving here with his wife early next week.' He paused to toss the Madeira down his throat and place the empty glass down by the side of his chair before adding, 'Mrs Hawker is a very likeable woman. I'm certain you'll get along well with her. Perhaps you might find her work in the house?'

'Hawker, did you say?' Elizabeth frowned. The name struck a chord of memory, but where she had heard it before eluded her for the present.

'Yes. Sergeant Tobias Hawker's wife.' He noted with immense satisfaction that she nearly choked on her Madeira before she placed the glass, with a hand that was far from steady, down on the table for safety. 'He was my batman for many years. And—would you believe it!—we were both injured at Waterloo, and convalesced together in the same house. Now, isn't that a coincidence?' he finished, nailing down the final screw in her coffin.

She cast him a half-penitent, half-amused look. 'You know, don't you?'

'Yes, you little baggage, I do now!' and before she could utter more than a startled gasp he had hauled her out of her chair and had her firmly imprisoned on his lap. 'Why, if you had been there when Hawker handed me the book of poems you had loaned him in Brussels, and I saw that lock of your hair... Blonde, indeed! Now, what the deuce do you mean by keeping the truth from me all this time?'

'Were you very angry?' she asked, suddenly finding the folds of his cravat of immense interest.

'Yes, I was. And still am, for that matter!' he retorted, but a fleeting glance at his eyes was sufficient to inform her this was far from the truth.

'You would have married me, Richard, after what had taken place between us. I realised that at the time, but I also knew that you didn't love me. You've admitted as much, haven't you?'

'I would swiftly have come to love you,' he responded without a moment's hesitation. 'After all, that is precisely what did happen when we met in Devon, remember?'

'Yes, I remember,' she said, laying her head against his broad shoulder. 'But if I had stayed in Brussels I would always have carried the nagging doubt in the back of my mind that you had married me because I was Elizabeth Beresford and you had taken my innocence away.'

He could understand this, but was still far from satisfied. 'But why didn't you tell me shortly after I was brought to the house after the battle?' he asked, not unreasonably.

'Because, my darling, I didn't want there to be any awkwardness between us. You wouldn't have felt comfortable being nursed back to health by a gently bred young woman whom you had known since she was a girl, now, would you?'

Recalling clearly the many tasks she had performed for him whilst he had been too weak to help himself, he couldn't help but agree wholeheartedly with this, but felt entirely justified for remarking, 'But you ought to have told me on the day we were married.'

'Yes, I know. And I hold myself entirely to blame for what happened between us shortly afterwards,' she announced with a complete turnabout of her former opinion, and with a generosity of spirit that he considered did her great credit. 'It is little wonder you reacted as you did. And yet when I did try to explain on the night of our—er—reconciliation, you wouldn't let me, my darling,' she reminded him with the most deliciously wicked feminine smile he had ever witnessed, but he couldn't find it within himself to be even remotely annoyed now, and betrayed the fact by kissing her in a way that left her in no doubt that he wasn't as tired as he had professed to be.

'Richard, it isn't the done thing, you know, to be discovered making love to your wife in the library!' she told him roundly, managing eventually to extricate herself from his embrace and return to her own chair. 'What would poor Medway have thought if he had walked in with our supper and caught us?'

'Can't really say I give a damn what he might have thought!' he returned bluntly, and consoled himself by pouring a second glass of his excellent Madeira.

'You might not, but I most certainly do. Why, he must have a very odd opinion of me already!' she announced, growing quite pink with shame. 'The poor man hadn't been here above an hour before he was called upon to rescue me. And what he must have thought when he learned that his mistress had been lying naked in a bed beside the local practitioner is anyone's guess!'

'More to the point, what did Tom think about it?' Richard countered, his shoulders shaking with suppressed laughter. 'I take it you have been in to check on him already?'

'Yes, though why I concern myself with such an ungrateful wretch, I'll never know! I hadn't been in the room above five seconds before he had the sheer effrontery to scold me for having had him brought here for Aggie to look after, instead of taking him to his own house. He's still a little woozy, but had certainly recovered sufficiently to notice my black eye. The callous monster seemed to find it highly amusing that you had done it! And not satisfied with that, he had the unmitigated gall to wonder why it had taken you so long to inflict such an injury on my person!'

Ignoring her highly amused husband's deep rumble of laughter, Elizabeth shook her head, genuinely troubled. 'He worries me sometimes, Richard, really he does. When I explained to him what had been happening, and then mentioned that, for all of two minutes, we had been naked in a bed together, he didn't so much as bat an eyelid! No, truly he didn't even blink,' she reiterated, decidedly piqued. 'There is something wrong with him, so there is. I'm certain he looks upon the entire female race as nothing more than skin and bone and put together slightly differently than males.'

Richard tactfully refrained from informing her that Dr

Carrington had been seen on more than one occasion visiting the cottage of the delightful young widow whose son did odd jobs for him, and merely said, 'I don't think you need concern yourself unduly on Tom's behalf. There's not much wrong with him.'

'I wish I were as certain. I have never seen him look at any female twice, unless she happened to be one of his patients and then, of course, it was only from a medical standpoint. But I shan't give up hope!' she announced, brightening perceptibly. 'What he needs is a good wife to humanise him. I'm positive that somewhere in the length and breadth of this land of ours there must be a girl just waiting to capture his attention. It's just a simple case of finding her, and bringing them together.'

'You can let Tom do his own finding, madam wife. I forbid you to interfere,' he told her, his tone brooking no argument. 'Besides which, he isn't nearly ready for matrimony yet.'

'I am forced to agree with you on that point, at least,' she conceded, conveniently forgetting propriety by sitting herself on his lap once more, and casting him one of her most captivating smiles. 'But if, in the future, he did happen to cross the path of a certain someone, you'd help me to give him a little push in the right direction, as it were, wouldn't you, Richard?'

'Most assuredly not!'

Elizabeth, her hopes not in the least dampened, smiled to herself as she laid her head upon his shoulder. It was not unheard of, after all, for a gentleman to change his mind.

And he did...

* * * * *

*Travel to the British Isles
and behold the romance and
adventure within the pages of these
Harlequin Historicals® novels*

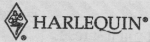

If you enjoyed what you just read,
then we've got an offer you can't resist!

Take 2
bestselling novels FREE!
Plus get a FREE surprise gift!